I0665315

White Water Passion

A Montana Mountain Romance

Dawn Luedecke

LYRICAL PRESS
Kensington Publishing Corp.
www.kensingtonbooks.com

Lyrical Press books are published by
Kensington Publishing Corp. 119 West 40th Street New York, NY 10018

Special Sales Manager:
Kensington Publishing Corp.
119 West 40th Street
New York, NY 10018
Attn. Special Sales Department. Phone: 1-800-221-2647.

First Electronic Edition: November 2017
eISBN-13: 978-1-5161-0343-0
eISBN-10: 1-5161-0343-2

First Print Edition: November 2017
ISBN-13: 978-1-5161-0346-1
ISBN-10: 1-5161-0346-7

Printed in the United States of America

To my agent, Jessica Watterson, for believing in me, and helping to make White Water Passion *what it is now. I am forever grateful.*

Glossary

Backcut-One of the cuts needed to fell a tree. Located on the opposite side of the trunk from the face.

Bateau-A flat-bottomed boat used to assist the rivermen. Often the men would loosen a log 'nest' and then fling themselves into the bateau to avoid being sucked down into the dangerous white water beneath the logs.

Beat the Devil Around the Stump-To evade responsibility or a difficult task.

Big Bug-An important or official person. The boss.

Bosh-Nonsense.

Bucker-A logger who cuts the tree into smaller, more manageable pieces; as well as de-limbs the trunk.

Bulldoze-To threaten or bully. Coerce.

Chisler-A cheater.

Chute-A makeshift sloping channel constructed of special treated wood to get the logs from the forest to the lake.

Chute Monkey-Logger responsible for greasing the chute and pulling the logs across The Deck with a team of horses.

Crosscut saw-A saw with a handle at both ends, used by two loggers to cut across the wood grain.

Deadbeat-A lazy person.

Fall-The act of bringing down a standing tree. Note: Fall/faller/falling used interchangeably with fell/feller/felling.

Faller-The logger actively chopping/sawing down the tree.

Flannel Mouth-Smooth talker.

Got the Bulge-Have the advantage over.

Half Turn-A partial supply of logs.

Homeboy-Loggers from the local community.

Lady of the First Water-Elegant woman.

Log Nest-A logjam.

Misery Whip-A slang term for a crosscut saw that doesn't cut well.

Mudsill-A lowlife.

Peavey-A logging tool consisting of a handle (30-50 inches long) with a cant hook and metal spike at the end. Used by rivermen to keep the logs moving down the rivers.

River Drive-The movement of the logs from the lumber camp, down the rivers and lakes, and to the mill.

Riverman-A logger who rides the logs down the rivers and lakes to bring them to the mill.

River Rat-A riverman who drifts from lumber camp, to lumber camp, working only as long as they want to stay in the area.

Scallywag-A person who behaves badly. Scamp. Reprobate.

Shave Tail-An unexperienced person. A greenhorn.

The Bull-The boss of the loggers working The Grove.

The Deck-The area between The Grove and the chute.

The Grove-The area where active logging is taking place.

Timber beast-A logger who works the timber.

Wannigan-A cook raft constructed with a crude building on top. Often the building would contain bunks for the rivermen to sleep if needed.

Widowmaker-A dead branch balancing precariously high in a tree, which could fall and kill a man without notice.

Chapter 1

Missoula Montana, 1888

Elizabeth Sanders could vanish right now, and no one would notice. She blended in with every other woman by wearing her matching pinstriped walking skirt and blouse. Each store clerk and patron in Missoula, focused on their affairs without a care to their neighbor, would fail to notice if she walked through Higgins Street naked, let alone disappeared into thin air. They certainly wouldn't look twice when she came back this way a different person.

Hundreds of people bustled in the heat of the Montana sun doing the same old things, the same old ways, with nothing to show for their trouble but dirty shoes. If Elizabeth was going to get her shoes dirty, she preferred to have fun doing it…the Devil May Care way.

Navigating the pedestrian-riddled streets was treacherous at best. Times like this made her wish she'd taken her grandmother's buggy. At least then she wouldn't be jostled around like a dirty shirt in a churning wash bin. A deep exhale boosted her determination enough to risk a step to the side to duck around a particularly slow matriarch. The small triumph lasted only a moment before she slammed into a hard chest.

The soft fabric of a well-tailored suit skimmed her cheek a split second before warm hands reached out to steady her. The touch—firm, yet gentle—made her feel like she now balanced on the back of a high-strung and wild mustang as it fled down a hill with uncontrolled freedom. She hadn't needed the extra hand. Wasn't in danger of falling over. What sort of dullard rescues a woman in no need of liberation? She pulled away and adjusted her skirts as he let go. Her mind focused once more.

"Pardon me." She glanced up to a familiar face. One she'd seen many times in her dreams. Her breath failed as her brother's friend, Garrett Jones, peered down at her with silver-clouded eyes. Oh, how he made the world spin whenever he drew near. His handsome, yet rugged, face made her fingers ache to touch the severe lines of his jaw. The rich scent of tobacco infused with lavender and some sort of citrus drifted on the breeze. Eau de Cologne. A fragrance only the wealthiest of men in Montana could afford. A scent belying the canvas pants, spiked boots, and sturdy cotton shirt he sported every time she'd seen him on the train platform.

"Elizabeth." Did he say her name, or did she dream the word? Oh to be noticed by a man like Garrett Jones. The only man who could make butterflies flit around in her stomach and fear slide through her chest in the same confusing moment.

The hem of her dress hovered mere inches from his feet. Her face heated and heart began to pound. Try as she might, she couldn't keep her eyes off the man who led the Devil May Care boys. The man who held her future in his hands if she succeeded in becoming part of his crew at the logging camp. If things went the way she planned, she'd be staring into his amber and steel speckled eyes for the rest of the season. Did he truly recognize her after all these years of no more than a passing glance?

"Terribly sorry, sir." She shifted her bag to the other hand. "I didn't see you."

He shook his head, but remained silent. The gray in his eyes shone in a color she couldn't quite name, but it softened his jagged expression enough to make her blush once more. A slight movement in his right hand caught her attention as he tapped his leg with his index finger and shuffled his feet, but his chest remained still. After a brief, uncomfortable silence with Garrett offering no more than a fleeting glance, she chewed on her lower lip.

"I suppose I should get going." She took a half step around him, and stopped.

He nodded and gave a bow with an air so refined she paused in surprise. Throughout her years in Montana, she'd grown used to the hard and less-than-mannered ruffians who usually passed her on the street. Even those on the social circuit rarely bowed in such a stiff and crisp manner. He'd certainly never shown such niceties where she was concerned. With one last look at his emotionless face, she nodded and stepped around his broad frame. She locked eyes with him, and felt his gaze follow her while she walked by. Beth forced herself to keep a steady breath as she left.

She hugged her satchel and skirted the shadows until she rounded the corner of a residential street, and all but ran the remaining distance to her friend Carrie's house. She rapped on the large pine door, and took a quick step back as it swung wide open. Finally, she was here. Now she had to force herself to follow the plan.

"It took you long enough, Beth." Carrie grabbed her arm and yanked her into the foyer.

As the huge front door closed behind her, Carrie shoved her forward, causing her to trip quite improperly into the adjoining parlor. Swinging around, Beth flinched as Carrie peeked down the hallway and slammed the parlor door. Carrie pivoted, and shifted her weight onto one leg. "Well?"

"Well, what?" Beth dropped her satchel next to the cold fireplace, trying not to smile at her friend's trepidation, letting the emotion bring her focus back to the issue at hand. She faced Carrie as if nothing out of the ordinary were about to happen.

"Well, what did he say?"

"He?" The image of Garrett on the street took over her thoughts. His strong shoulders, the stiff way he'd bowed, and the whisper of her name on his lips. There was no way Carrie could have seen the awkward exchange, was there? Beth peeked out of the large bay windows across the room, but as she already knew, the view to where she'd bumped into Garrett was blocked by several houses and streets.

Carrie rolled her eyes. "You darned well know who I'm talking about. Your brother."

"Yes, of course." Gracious be, where was her head? Stuck back on Higgins Street and Garrett's disarming gaze. "Simon said yes." Beth raised her chin, and silently dared her friend to argue. She couldn't be swayed. "Tomorrow, I will become a logger."

Carrie dropped her shoulders in defeat, but she folded her arms and glared in a blatant show of disapproval. "Please tell me you are going to help with the cooking, or at least cut the trees like your brother."

"Nope." Beth felt the lack of air plaguing her lungs. Carrie was like a sister, and perhaps a voice of reason, so it was hugely important to get her approval for this adventure—a blessing of sorts.

Carrie frowned and the disapproving look in her eyes deepened. "Don't tell me—"

"Yep, a riverman." Her heart shouldn't run away at such a statement, but it did. To be a riverman and experience the sheer sensation of total control over Mother Nature would be the boon she needed. And in her plight, she'd save not only her brother's job, but an entire town from certain destruction by a saboteur. If she could control those logs down the river, she could easily squash a snake in the grass...or rather trees. It didn't hurt that Garrett would be there. With him at the helm—the man her brother had talked about so often over the last few years—she knew she could accomplish anything.

"Didn't you see the journal last month? They did an exposé on the Missoula rivermen. They said they're ruffians…vagabonds. The men who ride the river have a devil-may-care attitude toward life, and the social skills of a spring hog."

"My brother hasn't said such things, and I'm inclined to believe him over some two-bit reporter. I am going to be a Devil May Care boy."

"I honestly don't know why you want to do this. It is pure madness, not to mention dangerous. I can't believe Simon agreed to your foolish scheme."

"Simon's word isn't law. Please don't tell me you still have that silly schoolgirl crush on my brother."

Carrie's cheeks dusted in a pink hue. "No, but he's a voice of reason."

Beth pursed her lips to stop all the dirty secrets on how she tricked her brother from spilling out like a waterfall. The secret buggy rides where he insisted he needed to go alone to clear his mind. The midnight voices in the garden beneath her bedroom window. All of which allowed Beth this small handful of leverage over her beloved brother. "I don't want to risk making him a target for the saboteur, or losing his job if I end up being wrong. I know it's dangerous, but I have to do this. You don't know how important it is I go."

"I figured you'd say that, and when you get an idea in your head, not even a blizzard in July can stop you. Just promise you'll be careful. Perhaps you should take along someone else to help you, or let me write my godmother. She is a cook somewhere up there. You can see if there are any other positions at camp, one more suitable for a woman. You cannot traipse around like a wild woman in the mountains. It isn't proper." Carrie mimicked the look of a concerned mother.

Beth shook her head and waved off her friend's trepidation. "I want to be a riverman, not a cook. I need to have complete access to the camp, including the dangerous areas. From what Simon has told me in the past, cooks aren't always allowed up there. I can't get close enough to the action while working as a cook. I'll be fine, trust me. Simon wasn't happy about letting me tag along, but after I convinced him—quite forcefully, might I add—he had no choice." She plopped down on a chair. "He or one of his friends will watch me every second of the day. As per his direction, I'm to try to stay away from trouble."

"Everything you've ever dreamed of, a man to watch over you every second of the day." Carrie's mouth twitched in an unsuccessful attempt to hold back her 'you got what you deserved' grin.

Beth wrinkled her nose and sat back in her chair. She wasn't fool enough to think this summer would be easy, but Carrie was right. She didn't want someone watching her every move, especially when she was investigating. There were ways to get around a guard. "A little imagination could serve me well I should think."

"Are you really going down the river?"

"If I can manage it, I will. The log drive is the target, and that's where I need to be."

"You do realize the men who do that particular job are considered wild and touched in the head. Most aren't allowed in polite society."

"I can't go into the upcoming season without helping to secure a future for my brother. I'm to be presented to every eligible bachelor this year." She took a deep breath, and shook her head. "We've always been close, and I don't want to see him suffer while I go off to a life of marital bliss. He needs this job, and I need to know he's happy."

"Why would Simon need you to help? He's done fine at the lumber camp without you so far." Carrie rolled her eyes. "Really, Beth. You must think these things through."

"I have." Beth dropped her shoulders and wiggled to the edge of the seat. "There was a man. On the platform a week ago."

Carrie scooted to the edge of her own chair, and furrowed her brows. "What man? A handsome one? Are you in love already? Oh, I knew it. Just the other day I..."

Carrie's words were lost on her as the memories of the man on the platform flooded back to her.

The early spring chill had penetrated her wrap, and she'd snuggled deep into the fabric as she waited for her brother to return from his pre-season meeting at the mill. Off in the distance the train bellowed and made her sit up tall to look for the engine.

That's when she heard the man with the drawl. A voice she'd never forget. "And they are willing to pay one thousand dollars if the drive never gets to the mill. Destroy the drive, destroy Big Mountain Lumber Mill. The mill will have to pay severance, and they won't be able to recover."

The deep mumble of another man's voice sounded, but he spoke so low she couldn't make out his words. Was that a hint of a Spanish accent? She couldn't be certain.

After the man with the possible Spanish accent finished speaking, the first man continued, "I suppose the families of Bonner will be forced to find a home elsewhere?"

There was a hint of sadness in the man's words—or was it cold-hearted malice? Who were these men?

Beth's breath grew shallow. Whoever they were, they planned to destroy the mill without a care to anyone else involved. What would Simon do for work? What would the families who lived in Bonner do once the mill closed and their livelihood was torn from them? *Dear Lord, she had to do something.*

"Well, is it?" Carrie's voice penetrated Beth's thoughts, but the question was lost on her.

Is it what? Blast. What was the best response when faced with a question you didn't hear? "Yes."

"So the man from the platform is the man you danced with from the Mayfield's ball?"

Oh good Lord. Beth waved her had across her face. "No, no, no. I overheard two men plotting on the train platform the other day. After they finished their vile conversation, the man with the cane hobbled around the corner with a smug smile. As if he hadn't been plotting Great Mountain's downfall. A place my brother loves dearly. Not that he knew Simon works there, but that's beside the point. Someone wants to destroy the Big Mountain Lumber Mill. Imagine what would happen to all of the families if the mill were shut down. The babies would starve. The fathers would have to leave their homes and families behind to find new work, and who's to say they will? There's an evil plot afoot, and I'm the only one who can identify the culprit."

"Oh my God!" Carrie's eyes flashed in concern. "You need to tell Simon."

Beth nodded. "I will. Eventually. After I've found the man in question, I'll let Simon know. As I said before, I don't want to risk his life, or job, if I'm wrong. I'll go up and identify the culprit, and then tell him once I'm certain. My brother has done so much for me since our parents' deaths. I need to do something for him in return. If I tell him now he'll only leave me behind, and they may never find the saboteur."

Carrie slouched in a show of defeat. "Promise me you'll take care to not get into trouble. If you see the man from the platform, tell Simon. Don't go getting yourself killed."

"Of course. I'm not a fool. I have no intention of getting myself into trouble."

"But how will you pass as a man? With your curves and long hair, you're the perfect example of a woman." Carrie waved toward Beth's hair, piled high on top of her head in the latest fashion.

With a secretive smile, Beth reached into the satchel and searched through the clothing within to pull out her mother's old silver-handled scissors. She reached up to her perfect coif, a style she often worked hours on perfecting. How would she feel without the familiar weight of her hair?

Carrie eyed the sharp tool. "Please tell me you brought those to cut paper."

"Not paper." Beth forced a smile. If she was going to do this, she would do it right. Although set in her decision, she reached up to touch the silky tendrils she'd grown to love. Her best feature. She forced back the tears burning behind her eyes. The sacrifice of her hair was worth saving her brother and his job. She firmed her lips, and held the scissors out to Carrie.

"What will your nana say?" Carrie asked.

"She has taken to her bed as of late, and only leaves to visit her matron friends for tea on Tuesdays. Her maid is there with her every second of the day, so I'm of little help. I asked her if I could accompany you to visit your sister for the spring, and she agreed. I'll come home after the drive, and she'll be none the wiser. My hair will grow again, and I'll either pin it back, or I'll say your little niece Tawny cut my hair while I slept because she wanted it for her doll. Your niece is quite the troublemaker. Nana will have no trouble believing me."

"Tawny's done worse, I suppose." Carrie pinched her lips shut and stared with a calculating, but disapproving, look. Beth smiled as Carrie plucked the scissors from her hand with a sigh. She could always count on her dear friend to cave when logic and passion were at the heart of her arguments.

Two hours later, Beth sauntered down the stairs and out the door like she'd seen her brother do on many occasions. She enjoyed the feel of the trousers tight against her legs. The harsh scratch of the blue denim a vast difference from the soft cotton of her dresses—not to mention a distinct lack of a bustle strapped to her backside. The sensation of nothing but the rough work pants lent a sort of wicked freedom she could get accustomed to. The satchel swung as she walked, and she ignored the odd looks from the women passing by on their way to the shops—a few of which she recognized from the Missoula Women's Society tea three weeks past. Did they recognize her? Even if they did, she didn't care. In a few days she would be on her way to Bonner to work for the Big Mountain Lumber Mill.

Beth rushed home and snuck up the stairs leading to her room. After she made certain no one was around, she eased the door shut.

She tossed the satchel on the bed, stared into her long dressing mirror, and ruffled her short, spiky hair. Turning to her armoire, she took out an old petticoat and plopped down on the side of her bed to tear the strips of cloth that would bind her breasts. What would the gossiping ninnies of the town think of her now? Scandal followed Beth's family like a hungry dog. Not that she personally deserved the stigma, but with her parents' deaths, and Simon's debauchery whenever he was home, the town gossips painted all the Sanders in the same tainted light. An escapade like this wouldn't come as a surprise.

A knock sounded, and she scrambled to stuff the cloth under her pillow and yank on the hat from atop her dressing table. She pulled the brim over her ears. "Come in."

The door slid open, and her brother Simon peeked in.

"Hey, Lizbe. It's all set through the big bugs at the mill. I thought maybe we could go out and practice tonight. My secret's safe, right? You aren't going to tell the mayor?"

With a sigh of relief, Beth pulled her hat from her head. "It's safe for now. Practice what? And you know I hate that nickname. It makes me sound like I'm twelve."

Simon grimaced as his gaze skimmed her head. "Practice being a man. Meet me by the front door after Nana goes to bed." He studied her a moment longer, and then frowned. "Did you steal those trousers from the twelve-year-old neighbor? You look like a blacksmith's errand boy."

Beth stuck out her tongue as Simon twisted on his heels. She could hear the angry click of his boots as he disappeared down the hallway. She had no idea what he'd planned, but she wasn't about to let his reluctance or insults get in the way. Simon had no clue about the saboteur and catastrophe in the making. Eventually he'd appreciate what she'd sacrificed, after she saved his job, the lumber camp, and the entire town.

Chapter 2

The eerie shadows of Nana's front passageway screamed into the silence of the night. The silvery moonlight illuminated the small windows near the door and gave Beth enough light to know her brother was not where he said he'd be. She hated tardiness. Which unfortunately exemplified the very essence of her carefree brother. Deliberately late to everything, and commanding the attention of whatever room he entered.

It wasn't until ten minutes past nine that Simon sauntered down the stairs as if he had not a care in the world.

"Nana went to bed at eight-thirty."

"First off, little sister, men never act like spoiled young women. They aren't young ladies of the first water." Simon gestured to Beth's hands, faintly illuminated by the small sliver of light. "Behavior like that is not manly. If you want people to believe you, you've got to forget all your feminine habits. Or we can simply go upstairs and forget you ever blackmailed me."

Beth dropped her arms and glared at her brother. "If you would do things on time, I wouldn't be forced to act this way."

"Is that my new vest?" He reached out and plucked a kerchief from the inside pocket. "You may want to avoid any hankies you find."

"Uck!" She adjusted the oversized shirt beneath the vest, and smoothed the material where the inner pocket sat. She didn't even want to think of what had been on that cloth.

Simon brushed past her and opened the door. "Perhaps you should stay home. In bed. Like the decent young woman Nana raised you to be."

"Stop beatin' the devil around the stump," she said in a masculine drawl. "I am going, and you will take me or I'll spill all that I know."

"Your attempt at manly repartee is worse than your new wardrobe. I'm taking you out tonight as a good-faith gesture, and nothing more. If the mayor found out about my affair, there's no telling what he'd do to me. Why can't you be more like Carrie? More amiable and less trouble?"

"You're one to talk. Half the women at Carrie's tea a week ago spent the entire afternoon avoiding eye contact with me. I can only assume it's because of one of your exploits. You're lucky I don't care what they think." She followed him outside and stood on the stoop. Although the clothes gave her the cover she needed, they now failed to provide comfort enough to boost her confidence. What if someone recognized her? Her heart beat faster the more she thought about what was to come. Could she pull off the ruse? She'd never so much as spit on the sidewalk, let alone tromped around in britches.

"You look much more believable in my clothes. Less like a little boy. Not that I'm encouraging this escapade in the slightest, but for us both not to be caught, I need to call you by a man's name."

"Brent," she declared. "I already thought it out." With a turn of the tarnished skeleton key she'd swiped from Nana's armoire drawer, the lock on the front snapped into place with only a whisper of sound. Simon had already taken the stairs and was halfway down the walk by the time she'd turned around. Fort Missoula's Fifth Infantry Regiment marched on the battlefield like boys over a schoolyard compared to the way she charged after her brother. The United States Army held nothing compared to a woman on a mission.

"Where are we going?" she hissed when she caught up to him.

"The Angry Grizzly Saloon, where we will test your manly skills."

To say Simon sauntered through the streets would be akin to calling a hard-case man a donkey instead of an ass. An arrogant strut was a more appropriate term to describe the way her brother traversed the roads. There was no way she could strut like him, but she'd try if it meant perfecting the ruse.

She practiced Simon's walk, which did nothing more than throw him into a fit of laughter whenever she tripped over the rutted street. Blasted man! He had something up his sleeve. The sudden compliance and the ease of his rigid shoulders after they left Nana's house proved it. She'd seen him act this way on many occasions, and it almost always ended with him getting his way. He had formed a plan, but she suspected the result wouldn't be in her favor. She couldn't let him win. Not this time.

"Men really should learn to pick up their feet." Beth followed Simon through the glass doors of the Angry Grizzly. She adjusted the restrictive chest bandage. *What am I doing? No one is going to believe I'm a man.*

Along the front wall, the wooden slab of the bar sat proud—the focus of at least half the patrons, most of whom already appeared to be pissed off their rockers. Card games and drinking tables dotted the room with chairs arranged haphazardly around each one. Following Simon's nod toward a seat in the corner, Beth settled into her chair as he made his way to the bar.

A tall, dark-haired man walked up from behind and leaned on the bar next to Simon. Beth couldn't quite see the man's face, but her heart beat hard at the familiar form. She would know his wide shoulders and confident stance anywhere.

Garrett.

Simon glanced to his right, smiled, and shook his friend's hand. Garrett motioned for the bar boy and called out, "Two straight Jacks."

Garrett sent a piercing stare her way. She slid down in her chair to pull her head into the collar of her jacket like a turtle in a shell. While he'd appeared dapper this morning in his stiff jacket and crisp shirt, tonight he looked like he belonged in the woods. Downright handsome. The same as he did when she'd admired him at the end of each season. *Please God don't let him come over here.* The puffy part of her lip pinched between her teeth. Would he recognize her in britches?

She willed herself to disappear while she strained to listen as her brother and Garrett talked. Alas, all she could hear was the increasingly rowdy drunk at the card table, and the gentle tinker of the off-key piano. The bartender set two beers and three shots in front of Simon, and he and Garrett downed two. Simon picked up the beer and remaining shot, and motioned toward Beth.

She tried to shrink even lower.

Garrett turned to cast a cold stare in her direction. High cheekbones set firm above his rigid jaw gave him the look of a man too refined for Montana, but the stubble on his chin and sideburns on his face proved he fit into humble society well. He looked exquisite in anything he wore.

She couldn't help but burrow deeper into the chair while her heart beat like an ax against a tree trunk. *What am I going to do if he recognizes me?* She chewed her lower lip again, but stopped when she realized her mistake.

His gaze lingered longer than any man's ever had before, and her stomach churned. Did he recognize her? Part of her wanted him to, but the other part begged the Lord above to keep her safe in her disguise.

After a brief conversation with his friend, her brother returned and set a mug of beer in front of her.

With one last glance in her direction, Garrett slid the bartender a handful of money and disappeared into a curtained room with a half-dressed woman. His tall, and quite large, figure disappeared and a strange sensation shot straight to her stomach. Almost as if she swallowed the whole bottle of the whiskey her grandmother kept hidden under her mattress for those rare nights when she couldn't sleep. Her heart sank into that pretend pool of whiskey in her gut and began to break down. In all of her wickedest dreams, never had Garrett taken a lady of the night into his arms. He was supposed to be above such immoral behavior.

But the unease she felt in her stomach had nothing to do with spirits, and everything to do with the man who at one point in time had stolen a glance and polite greeting on a rainy, dreary day, but not so much as a word did he speak to her since. Until he'd whispered her name that morning. *Or had he?* His eyes locked with hers every time the end of season train would come, but he would hurry away as soon as she would turn her eyes down in the customary coy manner.

She felt slighted. How could this harlot on his arm catch his eye while he refused to even give a polite greeting to her? Not that she wished to be a lady of the night, but one real word to her was all she wished for. Was it too much to ask?

Beth slouched in her seat. *Forget about him, Elizabeth Sanders. What you need to concentrate on is the saboteur.*

Simon set down the shot in front of her and quirked half his mouth up in a sly smile. "Drink up. I paid the barkeep enough money to keep us well supplied tonight."

She took a small sip of the shot, and tried desperately not to lose her supper all over the table. The liquid burned down her throat, and she coughed. Did men really drink this stuff?

The smug smile stretched even farther across her brother's face, and he took a long drag of his foamy amber drink, and then lowered the glass. "That was Garrett. Do you remember him? He's a timber beast too. Actually, he's a riverman. There are only a few men in camp crazy enough to go down the river; those of us who are sane are timber beasts."

"Do you two stay in touch when you're in town?" Beth tested the beer. Foam tickled her nose, but the bitter, foul-smelling drink didn't make her want to vomit.

Simon nodded while taking another large swig until half the contents of the glass were drained. Did he plan on drinking his troubles away? *Good God.*

"What else can you tell me about Garrett?" She peeked over the rim of her glass and drank.

Simon waved off her question. "You'll find out for yourself tomorrow. Tonight we're going to work on turning you into a man."

She squinted at her brother, and then spent the next couple of hours sitting in the hard chair, pouring an oncoming slew of shots into a nearby spittoon whenever the bartender walked away and her brother got distracted. All the while trying not to stare at the curtained door where Garrett had left. While she was happy he failed to realize her true identity, somehow the room now felt empty. Tucked into the corner, and secluded from the rest of the bar, her brother began to outline the details of how to be a man. The hours grew long, and she couldn't help but fidget as the evening ticked by with nothing but a few drunken cowhands and one rowdy game of Texas Hold 'em at the green poker table in the corner.

Late that night, Simon motioned to the door, and Beth sighed with relief. If she had to take any more of his meaningless prattling, she'd jump across the table and throttle him just for something to do.

She and Simon had always been close. After their parents had died in a carriage accident, they'd been left alone with their aging grandmother. They had learned to take care of each other. That was until he went and joined the logging company. No matter how hard he fought to make her stay, she wasn't going to sit back and let his life be ruined by the loss of the only thing that truly made him happy: the lumber camp.

* * * *

The moonlight filtered through the clouds and illuminated the streets outside the saloon as Beth and Simon started down the dusty road. They had only gone a block before echoing laughter reached Beth's ears. Simon clutched her arm to stop her and motioned to a couple stumbling down the street in front of them.

"Garrett," her brother said when they drew near.

Beth tensed.

Garrett stood tall and perused her figure with disdain. Why? Just this morning he'd sported a silent yet almost welcome aura. Now, she saw nothing but contempt. Of course, she was dressed as a man. Perhaps her disguise worked better than she'd planned. Beth's defenses slammed into place. The overly friendly harlot sidled closer to him, and he visibly relaxed. The tramp. Perhaps she was the reason his mood changed so drastically from earlier in the day.

"This is my cousin, the one I told you about." Simon gestured toward Beth, and she snapped her thoughts back to the moment, and smiled.

Garrett studied her until her heart started to beat hard. After a tense moment, he raised his head in greeting, but kept his neck stiff with the movement. The harlot moved next to him, and he tugged her closer.

"Simon says you might be working with us this spring." Garrett stood taller, and puffed out his chest. "It's hard work. I suppose you might be able to man the boat. That shouldn't be too much of an issue for you, should it? A weakling like you will only hinder the team and put himself in danger. Best to start where you won't get injured."

"I can handle as much as any man," she said, barely remembering to utter the words in her deepest voice. The haze from the beer made her head buzz, and she shook it off, and deepened her voice even more. "Unlike some, I don't need to buy women to make me feel like a man."

The harlot huffed as if offended by Beth's words. But why would she be? By all appearances, the woman made a living by trading favors for money. She should really learn to accept the truth of her existence.

Garrett glared, and his lips thinned.

Simon gripped her arm in a painful hold and propelled her past Garrett. "Ouch," she hissed.

Her brother turned back toward his friend. "Sorry, Garrett, he's drunk."

"Never a fool man spoke without gaining censure from the audience," Garrett responded.

"How profound," Beth countered, not bothering to act like the man she was supposed to mimic. She shifted her feet, and stumbled, but slid a condemning glare to the harlot pressing her breasts against his arm. "Do the ladies of the night enjoy a clever tongue, or do they prefer more sensible talk?"

Garrett furrowed his brows and stared, as if he saw through her disguise and judged her accordingly. Beth took a step back.

"If you'll excuse us." He turned his attention to Simon. "We need to be getting on before I knock your cousin for a loop." He nodded a good-bye and ushered the half-dressed woman down the street.

"Sorry, Gar. Really," Simon yelled and pushed Beth to make her walk.

She chewed on her lower lip as they hurried home. She knew better than to speak when her brother was in such a state. Simon, however, was never one to stay silent.

"What the hell was that, Elizabeth?" He growled as they marched up the steps to their home. "Garrett Jones is my friend, and the only other person in the camp who will protect you. Do not mess things up with your snippy tongue. In the future, if you're going to get a lickin', you'd better make it worthwhile. Half-cocked insults are not worth it, trust me."

"I don't like to think of any part of my anatomy as snippy. Wicked maybe, but not snippy." She scrunched her nose, but her body swayed with the thrum of a buggy rolling past. Garrett was harder to read than a dime novel in a buggy on Mullan Road. "Garrett seems quite complicated."

"You were a damned fool out there. And no one knows what goes on in Garrett's head. He spent most of his time in England with a cousin who is a baronet or some such thing. You can no better read what he's thinking than a book written with water." He opened the front door and ushered Beth through. "Honestly, I'm surprised Garrett held back and didn't knock you for a loop the way you spoke to him. You're lucky he kept his head about him in front of the lady on his arm, or you'd be sporting a black eye and wounded pride before you even became a logger. You should learn to hold your tongue. For once in your life, control your impulse to cause trouble."

"Does he behave this unreasonable at camp too? I found him to be quite impolite tonight. I certainly saw a side of him I never thought he possessed."

"You really are daft, Lizbe. Way too priggish to pull off this scheme. You're just a woman. Why did I let you blackmail me into this whole mess? In less than a day, we will be on our way to the logging camp where danger lurks in every corner. How the hell am I going to get through the next couple of weeks with you on my heels? No. You're not going."

"What are you going to do when I tell the mayor that his pretty little wife is sleeping with a lumberjack?"

"Join the permanent camp and stay up in the mountain forever, and let you fend for yourself down here. I'll keep my neck, but lose a troublesome sister." Simon stroked his chin. "I could grow a beard."

She threw him a brilliant smile and turned toward the stairs. Little did he know, he didn't have a choice. "I'm going. You'll love having me around… you'll see," she tossed quietly over her shoulder as she entered her room.

"You're not going!" Simon snapped as he walked by her door. Beth grimaced as she waited to hear movement from Nana. When nothing but the tap of Simon's boots heading toward his room filled the air, Beth relaxed. She was going, no matter what Simon said.

* * * *

"Thank you, sir! I don't know how we can ever repay you." Mrs. Ballard, his housekeeper, wiped the tears from her eyes, and Garrett turned to watch as her husband steered their scantily dressed, sixteen-year-old daughter through the door to their chambers.

The girl turned and shot Garrett a look that could kill a grizzly bear. After she realized what he'd intended by buying her from the barkeep, she'd tried to flee. He had to toss her over his shoulder just to bring her the remaining block to his house.

"How did you get her to come home with you?" Mrs. Ballard dabbed at her tears with the long apron attached to her skirt.

"It wasn't easy. She's not going to like me for a very long time. Let's leave it at that." After the talking-to he gave her on the way home, he'd be surprised if she ever spoke to him again. He had divulged information that would embarrass a gentleman, let alone a young woman, but she needed to know what the world was like. How men really behaved.

"I honestly don't know why she keeps running away. I promise we won't let it happen again."

"Perhaps you might consider asking her why she chooses to run around dark-alley establishments dressed as a strumpet and willing to spread her legs for any man who has the inclination," Garrett suggested.

Mrs. Ballard responded, but he didn't really listen. The last thing he needed was to come home from his next log run only to hunt down his servant's troublesome daughter, yet again. God knew he had his own problems. The least of which was Simon's two-bit cousin. Hell, with the young man's small shoulders and weak structure, Garrett doubted he could handle the physical demands of staying on the log while it rolled down the river, let alone dislodge a blockage and fling himself into the bateau before being swept downriver in the tide of crashing logs. But Simon had cashed in a favor owed, and brought the boy to the camp.

Garrett focused once more on Mrs. Ballard as she finished chattering about her wayward daughter. Words he didn't hear, and didn't care to hear. "Just keep her close to home until you can figure out what to do with her." He made his way toward the passageway door.

"We will. Promise," Mrs. Ballard said behind him as he walked into the hallway leading to the front of the house.

He needed a nice stiff drink. The whole evening—no, the whole day—was a mess. Starting with meeting Elizabeth on the street, and ending with his housekeeper's daughter and Simon's cousin. What was it about the boy that made him lose the ability to breathe?

And Elizabeth. Perfect, enchanting Elizabeth. With her carefree ways and ability to talk to anyone with ease, he couldn't seem to get out more than a word whenever she was near. She was so different from him. Throughout the years, he'd gotten to know her through her brother, and all because he was too afraid to approach her himself. She was easygoing and always happy, where he had to analyze life with a critical and pessimistic eye. She moved in the waves of life with ease, and frightened him beyond belief. *God.* Why had his father refused to allow her as a candidate for marriage?

Garrett had begged his father to consider Elizabeth when he'd first brought up the topic of marriage years ago after he first started at Big Mountain. But no. If he were to enter into an arrangement with Beth, his father would cut him off. And all because of the *scandals.* Not that she was involved in any of them, but his father didn't care. Simon had sullied the name Sanders, and now Elizabeth was paying for it. God forbid there was a Jones with a less-than-perfect reputation.

He should go back on his word and secure Beth for his own. Live with the consequences of choosing her over the family. Stand up to his father. Tell him he was going to marry Elizabeth no matter what he said. But Garrett would lose everything. His family, his fortune, and with his father's connections, he'd even lose his job at Big Mountain. How would he be able to support a wife and family with nothing?

No.

He couldn't do that to her. He had to fulfill his side of the agreement. Sacrifice his chance with Beth for one last season at Big Mountain, and a life of misery with the wife of his father's choosing.

Elizabeth.

This morning he'd wanted to ask her how her day was. Engage her in witty conversation that would leave her dreaming of him for the remainder of her day. But no. All he could get out was her name, and even then he'd barely spoken the word. Oh what a fool he became in the presence of Elizabeth Sanders.

The only sound left in his dimly lit home were his footsteps as he trudged into his study and poured a glass of bourbon, swallowing the contents in one gulp, only to refill and take the decanter with him to settle into his favorite seat by the large fireplace.

He stretched out his legs, and the leather on his over-stuffed armchair squeaked in protest as he relaxed into its comfort. He would get Elizabeth and the young cousin out of his head, or drink himself to a stupor.

A log sat in the hearth, waiting to be lit. Stretching a bit farther, he kicked it into the pit and scowled. What he should be doing was preparing for the train ride to the site. Instead, he sat brooding about the next few months. Why did the presence of Simon's cousin irritate him so much?

It wasn't like he was the first young man to want the riverman job, so why did it matter?

He swallowed the bourbon and refilled. Best to focus on what was to come at the end of the spring—his last spring as nothing more than a logger. What was Simon going to say when he found out about the deal Garrett had made?

Chapter 3

Beth peeked into the large, mud-covered railcar and panic rose, threatening to choke her. She curled her nose and tamped back the urge to flee. The place was a pigpen. The large men dotting the inside didn't seem aware of the filth surrounding them. She thought about jumping off the platform and running for the safety of her home, but what good would that do? She was already committed. Was she really going to do this? If she wanted to pull it off, she would need to force her mind away from the muddy shoes of the men in the car and the grime threatening to soil her clothes.

Pull up your trousers and be a riverman, Beth. You can't hide away for the rest of your life.

She searched the car for Simon, but he wasn't there. *Thank God.* He'd left her behind this morning, but she wasn't going to let him win, so she'd come alone. Beth hopped into the car and picked her way through the men to find a spot in the corner.

She'd never betray her brother to the haughty men of Missoula the way she'd threatened, but he didn't need to know that. He would protect her with his life, and she'd do the same for him. That's why she'd enlisted his help in the first place. To shield her when she needed protection, but let her have free rein of the camp. She'd repay him by finding the traitor. Now, if only he could get over the fact that she was *just a woman.*

A movement outside the large door caught her attention and she watched as Simon boarded the car. She pulled her hat low and ducked her head to shield her face. Garrett was noticeably absent. Although her world tilted to odd angles whenever he was around, his behavior last night—and slighting her each time they'd met throughout the years—couldn't be forgotten.

But the thought of him gone from the lumber camp this year made her heart sink to her stomach. What she wouldn't give to spend more time with Garrett Jones.

There were several cars attached to the train that would take the men and Beth to the main camp. Simon had warned her to expect the next few months to be filled with crowded bunkhouses and water closets only the bravest of men would use. Really, he was trying to scare her from going, and it had somewhat worked. She wasn't happy about a community bed or roughage for a toilet, but with each breath she regained her excitement over the experience as a whole.

The boxcar rattled and propelled into motion, gradually picking up speed as more men jumped onto the car, including Garrett. Now nothing could squelch her mood, but she needed to act like a man. Behave like everyone else in the car. She glanced around to take stock of the filthy men. How they sat, their expressions. She would do this.

Beth clenched her teeth as she realized her brother stared straight at her. She tried not to flinch when he scowled and stood to pick his way through the crowded floor.

"I ought to toss you off right now. Let you roll down the tracks and back home." He plopped down next to her. "Why aren't you still passed out in bed after the booze you drank last night?"

"So that was your plan? I knew you were up to something. You won't send me home because I'll keep coming back, and I didn't drink much. I tossed it. Honestly, Simon, I would think getting me drunk to get your way was beneath you."

Simon's upper lip twitched as Garrett made his way to the only space available in the car...directly in front of her. She against one side of the L-shaped wall, and he sitting sideways against the other. She stretched out her feet as far as she could and gave Garrett almost no room in which to set down his perfectly muscled backside. The train jarred, sending him tumbling down onto her spiked boot.

"Ouch!" she squealed, pulled her legs back to rub her shins, and then winced when Simon's sharp elbow slammed into her ribs.

"Watch yourself, *Brent*," her brother scolded loudly enough for only her to hear.

Garrett stared through hazel eyes. Eyes so vexed and clouded they reminded her of an angry fall day. No emotion showed on his face, save for the fierceness of his gaze. She liked reading people, but he read like a bad Gothic novel. Personally, she preferred dime novels.

They were separated by no more than her legs, but heat from his body toasted even her back as it pressed against the cold steel of the wall. How could one man emanate warmth so intense that it scorched the entire boxcar?

She leaned over to Simon. "Is it hot in here?"

He shot her a confused glare and shook his head.

Beth drew her knees up to her chest and squeezed them against her body to gain distance from Garrett—the source of the offending heat. He turned his eyes away from her. *Thank the Lord above!* One more second of his intense, disapproving gaze and she'd catch fire. He greeted Simon, and then leaned his head against the wall.

She tugged her large brimmed cowboy hat down low, settled deeper into the wall behind her, and pretended to sleep. The smoky musk of Garrett's Eau de Cologne drifted past her nose and brought to mind the last ball she'd attended when a large, stuffed puffin of a man asked her to dance and spent the rest of the ensemble flaunting his superiority. Garrett was different. He was a logger. One bottle of the blend was at least three months' pay for a man of his profession. He needed to make up his mind already. Was he a stuffy blowhard, or an easy-to-love logger?

Hours ticked by in the uncomfortable position, and she couldn't help but fidget. With each movement, Garrett threw her a sour look. He'd done that a lot since meeting her outside the bar. Each time it sent sorrow to her soul, but that didn't matter. *You're not here for romance, Beth.* Finding love was for another time in her life. This moment, this season, was for her brother. As long as she kept that in mind, she would get through the summer just fine.

The hard, wooden train floor had to be a torture device from a dark castle the way it ground into her bottom. She squirmed again and stretched her leg to ease the pain. The spikes on her boots hit Garrett's thigh and she winced.

Garrett flinched, but kept his gaze somewhere on the forward wall of the railcar. The muscles in his jaw flexed, but no other emotion showed. The man was as hard as the floor making her backside ache. She supposed he had to be in his profession.

"Sorry," she said, but he scowled. Perhaps this spring was going to be harder than she expected.

* * * *

Garrett tensed when the spikes dug into his leg. Anger rose fast and furious, and he turned a hard stare to Simon's cousin. He couldn't take much more of the kid. Not with the mixture of emotions kicking him in the gut like a bad-tempered mule. There was something about the kid that wasn't quite right. Something that made him feel empty inside—a reminder that he lacked an important ingredient in his life.

The boy shielded his face with that ridiculous hat he wore.

Leaning on one hand, he crouched to stand as the train lurched to slow while it crested a steep hill. Knocked off balance, he fell on top of Simon's cousin. He reached out in reflex to stop his descent, but instead of a bony teenage chest firm beneath his fingers, he felt the softness of two perfectly rounded breasts. Breasts bound by some sort of cloth.

He moved his hands to the floor so he could balance his weight on them, as the *boy* stared wide-eyed with shock. Garrett fought to clear his head of the thoughts running rampant through his mind.

His mood changed fast. He was still mad, but for a completely different reason. He now knew why his gut dropped whenever this so-called boy was in sight, and why he looked so familiar. His breath hitched at how close he'd been to Elizabeth. The woman who on many occasions had smiled at him from across the platform after the end of a hard logging season, and brightened his sometimes dreary day. The woman who haunted his dreams and desires with her dark hair like silk, and a face like a china doll. The woman who made him lose all semblance of thought whenever she was near—a feeling he hated. He could throw himself between logs slamming together at a white-water logjam, but he couldn't bring himself to speak to the enchanting woman who was now dressed as a man, sitting in a mud-caked railcar, bound for the deep belly of an Alpine forest. Now he had no choice but to speak to her. He could no longer duck his way out of the distress of conversation to a woman he could never have.

Beth took a deep breath, and shook her head. Her lips mere inches from his own, and the feel of her breasts in his hands still tingling down his palms. He scrambled to slide off Beth and back to his seat.

Garrett snapped his attention to Simon, who slid his finger over his mouth, indicating he should keep quiet. Garrett wanted to demand an explanation and then make the conductor stop and send her packing. That's what he should do.

Beth hugged her arms around her torso. Something primal tugged deep within his belly. He'd crossed the line with her physically, made her uneasy, albeit accidentally. Still, he never wanted to make Beth uncomfortable around him. But what in Hades name was she doing on his train?

"Later." Simon leaned over and whispered the warning, and then glanced around at the men in the car.

Now that Garrett looked closer, her soft beauty was unmistakable. How did she plan to pull off this scheme when even the dirt on her boots looked feminine and somehow charming?

If he hadn't been distracted by the fact that he was emotionally affected by a boy, he may have realized who she was. Now, he just felt like a fool for falling for her ruse.

The train slowed even more.

How the hell was she going to get through this alive? How would he deal with her around when he couldn't get his tongue to form the words in his mind whenever she stared at him through her long black eyelashes? He couldn't allow it. For his sake, and hers.

The train slowed and the men within jerked when the railcars slammed against each other. Loggers began to jump off with joyful whoops that echoed through the trees. As the last man exited, Simon turned to Garrett.

"Why did you bring her here?" Garrett scowled to Simon, ignoring the warm emotional tug of the woman slowly making her way behind her brother. He'd die if anything happened to her, and here, in the Montana wild, chances were something bad would transpire. He thought the drive dangerous enough when she was male. Heaven knows what would happen now.

"She said she wants to have an adventure," Simon answered. "She blackmailed me, and then snuck aboard when I tried to leave her behind. You can send her home."

"Excuse me!" Beth exclaimed and peered over Simon's shoulder. "I am a big girl, capable of taking care of myself. I may need a little watching over, but I'm no child. Send me home and I'll spill everything to the mayor. Better yet, I'll tell the gossiping Goodall sisters."

He straightened his spine and glared, but his shoulders dropped. "Nothing I've said has changed your mind. Garrett's the riverman foreman, and he's going to say the same thing I did. Go home, Elizabeth."

"No."

The woman was impossible. Exactly how he'd imagined her to be all those times he'd studied her on the platform. Her air of refined control enough to convince one of social graces, but on closer look mischief always flickered in her crystal blue eyes. Challenging one to take control of her fiery ways. A challenge he'd always wanted to take on. But he was a man, leader of the Devil May Cares for hell's sake, and he'd let the fear of a small woman control him long enough. No more.

Garrett too glared at Elizabeth. "Perhaps a wallop would set you to rights."

"You can't do that. You're not my brother."

Thank God! Not only did she render him dim witted when near, but he didn't need another girl full of machinations to rescue in town. He had no sister to watch over, and enough troubles with his housekeeper's daughter. The woman he would marry would be docile and sweet tempered—the perfect ornament for his parlor. The woman he agreed to let his parents choose for him in exchange for one last logging season. Miserable in love, but comfortable in life.

Elizabeth needed to be home in Missoula. Safe. If only she were one of the sweet, docile women his father admired so much. If only Simon hadn't ruined all hope for he and Beth. He couldn't fault his friend completely. Simon was simply doing what men of his age and status do best. Women and booze. That didn't stop his father's judgment, though. There was no way in hell his father would reconsider Elizabeth Sanders suitable for the wife of a Jones, was there?

Garrett stalked past Simon to Beth. Her eyelashes fluttered at the abrupt movement, so he concentrated on her mouth in order to get the authoritative words to move from his brain, to tongue. He softened his voice, but ensured the tone reflected the importance. "You need a strong hand."

She repeated her words in a breathless plea. "You're not my brother, or my father."

"No, ma'am, but I know you almost as well. I've heard about your antics every spring for the last five years. I know for a fact you need a good set down."

"Are you going to let him talk to me like this, Simon?" A slight panic shook her voice.

Simon let out a huff of laughter. "Yes, I am, sis. Because he's right. You do need a wallop. You're spoiled, and God knows I have never told you no before now. If Garrett wants to be the one to put you in line, then he has my permission."

"You're both mad."

"That's why they hire us," Garrett said to the defiant woman. He studied her perfect lips, the bottom one wet where she'd released it from between her teeth. "We don't call ourselves the Devil May Care boys for nothing."

Garrett stilled as she shifted, drawing ever-so-slightly closer to him.

Should she stay here in camp, he could have her for one season. Be near her. For just one season he could collect a lifetime of memories to keep him happy once they parted. There were women in camp. Why couldn't she be one of them? She bit her lip again, and he ached to reach out and touch the silky softness of her mouth with his.

Selfish as it was, he couldn't send her away.

"If this is going to happen, and you stay on, I can't allow you to run rampant, Lizbe. It's too dangerous." He had to find a way to show her who was boss. A way that wouldn't cause her to despise him for the rest of her life. He forced back the resigned sigh deep within his chest. *This is going to be an exceptionally long spring.*

Beth's eyes flashed with defiance. "You can't call me Lizbe. That's my brother's nickname for me."

"I know. As I said before, I know everything about you."

Beth trembled so Garrett softened a bit and stopped herding her to the corner. Her lips firmed and relaxed—an indication of the mixed emotions swelling inside her. She didn't even know how well he could read her mood simply by watching her mouth.

Simon stepped in front of the door, a barrier from the men outside. Catching the movement, Garrett wedged Beth farther into the corner. His fears resurfaced the closer he drew to her warmth. He wanted nothing more than to touch her. Sweep her up into his arms and make her his forever. What he needed to do was leap from the car, disappear in his work, and let her stay in camp with her brother. He scowled at Simon. "You lied to me."

"I know, but I need your help," Simon pleaded.

Garrett gave a resigned sigh. "I'll find her a safe place to work. The bateau, maybe? If I take a position with her in the boat, I can watch over her. I'd say send her to work with the cook, but you know how Aunt June gossips. She might expose her as a woman, and I'm afraid if the men discover her dressed this way, her reputation would be ruined."

Simon nodded. "I might never get her married off if any men found out she was traipsing around dressed like that. Gossip would spread like a brushfire the moment they sent letters home. If she trains hard, she could handle the bateau. She may be a conniving bulldozer, but she's not some frail ninny."

"You talk as if I'm not standing right here," Beth snapped, but he and Simon ignored her.

Garrett tried not to scoff. When had Simon ever cared about his sister's reputation? If he had, he'd have taken care in his own life. Acted like Garrett instead of a two-bit lumberjack.

"She'll be safe in the bateau," Simon continued. "The cook takes a boat down the river with the drive. This is only one step away from the cook raft. If she's in the bateau, she's away from harm and people, and my reputation…and neck…are safe." The lines on his face softened. "I suppose if we can't get her to go home, that's the best we could do. Just take care. She's difficult to control."

Beth gave another sound, irritated at being left out of the conversation.

Garrett faced Simon once more. "The bateau it is." Life on the river was not going to be easy, but at least he'd be there to watch over her. Protect her from harm.

"What's a bateau? Is that the cook boat, or a riverman one? I forget." Beth crossed her arms over her chest. The small movement pulled her shirt taut. Garrett tried not to stare. The damned bands did nothing to hide the roundness of her breasts.

He couldn't answer, but simply stared at the sinfully breathtaking sight before him. One that made his heart race, and stomach feel empty. He shouldn't be watching the display, but he couldn't help it.

"What's a bateau?"

The words snapped his attention back to the moment. "The only way you are going down the river."

Garrett shrugged out of his jacket and wrapped it around her shoulders. Her chest stopped rising with her breath, and the vein at the base of her neck throbbed as he drew close enough to smell the honeysuckle scent of her hair. "You need to wear this. Even with the alterations, you are too obviously a woman. Stay beside or behind me at all times and do *not* talk to anyone." Garrett turned to Simon. "One river ride, and then she's gone."

"First drive and she's gone," Simon agreed.

"First drive?" Beth questioned.

"The first trip down the river. You take it, and then we ship you home." Garrett rubbed the back of his neck. The gleam in her eye belied her ready acceptance. He didn't believe her for a minute.

He turned and jumped from the railcar, holding out his hand to help her down while searching the surrounding area to ensure no one saw his slight in helping this *boy* down. Her face glowed with victory, and he wanted to turn her around and toss her back on the railcar.

He clenched his teeth, his only release for the anger building in his gut.

"Emotion is a sign of weakness. One must always be on guard." He repeated the lesson his mother frequently chided him with when he was a child, not for Beth's sake, but for his own.

She glanced back and frowned. "I was always led to believe that emotion was a spigot for the soul. I'd rather have a clean soul than a surly disposition."

With a curt nod of acquiesce at her retort, he turned to escort her to the center of camp. He must not let her sharp tongue or enchanting charm affect him so. He already doubted all of the decisions he'd made since she entered his life.

Chapter 4

The excitement of the afternoon made Beth want to join in the chaos. Never before had she experienced such an informal and comfortable afternoon. No one in camp seemed to pay mind to social rules, and no one looked twice when she'd tripped over her spikes. So concerned with organizing their own affairs, the loggers failed to realize she was even there.

She smiled.

Men, teenage boys, and the occasional wife or spinster cook ran in all directions—greeting old friends, meeting new ones, and setting up camp. She studied the throng of people for the man she saw at the train platform—the one with the cane and his illusive partner—but with no luck. None of the people buzzing about camp reacted any different from the person next to them. All were excited and happy; not calculating and cross like she imagined a traitor would behave. She frowned. Maybe this wasn't going to be as easy as she'd thought. What did she know about investigating a crime anyway?

A fat-bellied man stood in the center of the crude log buildings and watched the activity. He would bark out an order, but didn't move from his position. Who was he? The man's gaze skimmed over Beth and settled on her brother. He motioned for Simon to join him.

"Be back in two shakes." Her brother ran toward the man.

Beth turned to Garrett. "Who is that?"

"Paul Smith. He's from the Big Mountain Lumber Mill." Garrett's tone was soft and happy. Warm even. It was hard not to be affected by the aura of the first day in camp, and apparently Garrett wasn't immune to the cheery, mountain fresh mood.

Perhaps she could get him to loosen up a bit. She'd always been one to charm the gentlemen of the ballrooms. How different would it be to charm a logger? Hard seeing as she was dressed as a man. She turned a teasing smile on him. "And are you as important as he is?"

"I am to you." His dry tone punctuated the words with finality. She tried not to frown. How was she going to get him to loosen up enough to trust her, talk to her, and carry on a decent conversation? Never in her life had a man spurned her as much as Garrett Jones did. She didn't know how to respond so she kept quiet and let the moment stretch into silence as they watched the loggers. Many of them with visible injuries, which brought to mind her mission. "Do any of the loggers here use a cane?"

"No. Why?" He gave her a curious stare.

If the man with the cane wasn't here, then he must be the one who offered the money. She needed to look for the second man from the platform. The only problem was she had no idea what he looked like. "Just curious is all. I heard there are a lot of injuries in a logging camp."

He nodded. "There are. It's a dangerous place."

Beth's cheek twitched in a nervous smile. Garrett obviously intended that remark to be a warning. "Do all of the men from the train live in the Missoula spring camp?"

Garrett shook his head. "Some are from the Bonner camp, and a few are from the year-round camp. Most of the long-term residents leave during the spring and return in the fall."

"Does each camp have Devil May Cares?"

"Each of the camps here have their structure—timber beasts, river rats, and homeboys. But the long-term camp, they're the ones that have loggers year round, falling trees and bringing the logs to the river's edge. They do not employ rivermen. That's where us seasonal loggers come in. Since we can't bring the logs down in the winter, and the rivers are too low in the summer, we can only ride the logs in the spring when the water is high. We give the long-term loggers a break for a few months, and then take the drives down the river. There's two camps with rivermen. The Missoula camp, and Bonner camp. The Bonner rats take the drive down the river with us, but walk along the bank to dislodge any logs hung up there. It's complicated, but you'll get the gist of it once we get going."

"Homeboys are the men from the towns around here, but what are river rats?"

"They are drifters working for as long as they deem to remain in the area. Stay away from them. The Bonner camp is full of them. They are not to be trusted."

"Are there any river rats in your crew?"

Garrett shook his head. "I am selective of the men I allow on my team. The Devil May Cares are all homeboys."

"When will we go on the drive?" She needed time to find out which of the men had taken the bribe, and who the man with the cane was.

Garrett ran his fingers through his hair and gave a resigned sigh. "I don't yet know. We'll have to talk to Teddy first. He schedules the river runs."

"So *he's* the most important man to me?" She gave a playful punch to the air, hoping to lighten the mood. Garrett stretched his right shoulder muscles like Simon did when he scolded her. What did she say wrong? She dropped her hand back to her side. "Do I make you tense?"

He raised his head, but a strange glint shimmered in his eyes. "You shouldn't be here. It's not good for either of us."

Before she could respond, Simon trotted back to their small circle.

"Beth will be on the first train out tomorrow morning," Garrett said. "I can't risk her life just so she can get a thrill."

"No," she screeched, but checked herself when two loggers turned curious stares in her direction. She lowered her voice and leaned closer to Garrett and Simon. "I'm not leaving. I thought that was settled. I'll bear hug a tree and never let go."

"Gar." Simon turned a warning look to his friend. "Paul said the Bonner camp lost a few rivermen this year, including their leader, and the big bugs at the mill refuse to hire anyone else. Said we had to make do with what we got. Chances are you'll need her to man the bateau on occasion while you work the jams with the boys. As much as I hate to admit it, we might need her."

"Goddamn it." Garrett ran a hand through his hair, and turned his glance to something off in the distance.

He pinched his lips together, but remained silent. Not arguing and not conceding. His face like a fierce storm calculating the best path of destruction. She had a feeling he wasn't finished trying to send her home. She couldn't go. She would fight until her hands were raw if she had to, but she wouldn't go home.

The men held a tense silence as they stared at each other. Men and their silent exchanges. Why couldn't they talk it out like women? Sure women sometimes got so chatty that they ended up sounding like chickadees in springtime, but at least everyone could tell what was happening.

"Mr. Smith said to tell you same as last time. You are responsible for the Devil May Cares," Simon said.

Garrett turned to Beth, and that same breathless feeling she often felt when he looked at her fogged her brain once more. He shifted on his feet and drew closer. "Be warned, nothing happens within the ranks of my men that I don't know about."

"I'll wager you're an extremely hospitable captain," she teased. He simply stared until the moment grew uneasy. Like a child in the midst of a scolding, she dropped her gaze to study the mud on the toe of her boots. Perhaps she should tamp her enthusiasm down a bit. "Warning acknowledged."

"We need to build your strength so you will be physically able to take on the river should you fall in. If something happened to you…" He left the words hanging, but his face read like a blank slate, impossible to cipher, and quite boring. The more she got to know this side of Garrett, the less her fantasies about him enticed her, but then there were those fleeting moments when his eyes softened and she wished he'd let her into his good graces. Not that she deserved his respect after the stunt she pulled, but it was for a good cause. Soon enough he'd see her way of thinking. He moved a fraction closer and all she could concentrate on was his words.

"Each morning after breakfast, you will meet me near the lake until the river run. Be prepared to train."

She gave a slow nod and stared deep into his ever-changing hazel eyes. He held her gaze for a few moments, before giving a slow blink, and turning away. She let go of the breath she'd held during that moment. With one simple look he could rein in her enthusiasm and make her want to follow his every direction—something she wasn't used to doing. Hopefully he wouldn't notice.

With a frown and a shake of his head, he turned to her brother. "What else did Paul say to you?"

Simon flashed a toothy grin and straightened up with pride. "John's gone this year, so I am foreman of the Missoula camp."

Garrett's shoulders relaxed and the furrow of his brows lessened. He slapped her brother on the shoulder. "This job has truly turned into mud if you're in charge." Garrett lifted his head in a silent salute. "Seriously though, the job couldn't have gone to a better leader, Simon. Well done, my friend. You deserve it. You do good work."

Simon nodded. "I've got to get the mail car emptied and deliver the letters to the long-term camps before they leave. Can you show Beth…er, Brent, around?"

"I need to have a quick word with Paul, and then she can follow me about camp." Garrett slapped her brother on the shoulder while he walked past. Beth couldn't help but watch the easy way he communicated with the lumber mill big bug—the man in charge. He smiled and shook hands with Paul, comfortable in the role of leader. This was the man she'd seen on the street the other day, the one she couldn't help but admire. A true leader of men.

After a few minutes, Garrett returned and gave her brother a stiff nod. With a quick show of gratitude, Simon shuffled off, leaving her with the feeling that she wouldn't see him again until nightfall.

Garrett glanced down at her and his mood changed. The smile on his face faded. He cleared his throat, and shifted from one foot to another. A different person than the one who bantered with her brother, and she suspected the other men in camp. She would tolerate his gruffness for the chance to help the people of Bonner and her beloved, yet grumpy, brother. She needed to focus anyway, and find out who had been on the platform that day, hidden around the corner from where she'd sat waiting for Simon.

Garrett motioned for her to accompany him as he made his way through the camp.

Beth smiled and followed. The care he took with each person they encountered was vastly different from the arrogant spirit he showed toward her. He was friendly and caring. Why couldn't he treat her the same? What was it about her that he despised so much?

After visiting with a rough-looking young man with teeth like a mule, Garrett threw her a quick look and turned to the path before them as they circled the camp.

"I find your shrewd smile unnerving. Should I be worried?" The corners of Garrett's lips twitched as if he held back a smile. His face and posture showed haughty indifference, but those brief tells gave her a deeper insight into who he was—the man he didn't want people to see, or at least didn't want her to see.

"Not at all, I was simply admiring how easy you are with your fellow loggers."

"I have known them for years and feel obliged to ensure they are well taken care of."

"Are they all Devil May Care boys?" She studied a young boy busy splitting wood and paused. If Garrett wasn't so keen on walking the camp, she'd stop and help the kid. What an awful existence to be small, yet have the responsibilities of a man. Life was rough up here in the camp.

"No, they are not all rivermen."

"Why do you feel the need to watch over all of the men in camp? Don't they have leaders?"

"Yes, but they are also my friends. And I am the leader of the Devil May Cares"

"How considerate," she paused, and then slid him a sly grin. "Do you always accentuate your words in such a way?"

"Good speech is an essential part of good leadership. A leader cannot expect his men to follow orders if they can't understand him."

"True, but don't your men get tired of trying to understand you? I thought loggers were usually jaunty and easygoing. You on the other hand, are not."

He held out his arms to direct her to the center of camp, but the lines on his face grew severe once more. Her words had made a mark on the man. Instant regret niggled in her chest. Although his attitude today had been less than hospitable, some might argue he simply held a reserve where she was concerned. Which was understandable seeing as she'd blackmailed her way into his life. He didn't deserve such harsh words from her.

A boy she'd never seen before trotted up to them, and held out an envelope. "Message for you, Garrett."

Garrett took the paper. "Thank you."

"Who's that?" Beth watched the boy disappear along the same trail some of the lumberjacks had taken earlier that day after they'd jumped off the train.

"One of the cook's boys from the Bonner camp." Garrett opened the missive, and read it. He pinched his lips tight, and tucked the note into the inner breast pocket of his jacket. Whatever was on the note didn't make him any more agreeable.

"If you'll follow me." His movements were rigid and his face unreadable once more. He turned off the path. "You can take the first week to help the cook. We all do it. Best to get it out of the way so you can then concentrate on learning the river rules."

"You said I would help the cook if I misbehaved. I haven't done anything wrong."

"It's not permanent. It's an extra duty everyone here does." He patted his jacket pocket where he'd stuck the letter. "I have something I need to attend to, and I need to figure out the best way to bring you into the river crew. Having you help Aunt June for the first few weeks will give me some time to do so. You'll still get to train with us, but you'll also be helping the cook. Take care, though—Aunt June can't keep secrets. What you say to her will be made known to the entire camp."

What he said made sense, and if it would help her cause, she'd do it without argument, and shield her secret. She needed to grit her teeth and bake a blasted apple pie…or whatever the cook had planned for the evening. *Damn it.* "So you make the cook rotation as well? You must be very important to everyone in camp, not just me."

"I am no one of great consequence, but I have a good rapport with the cook. Everyone calls her Aunt June. She is my aunt by blood, but has adopted the rest of the men as her family."

"I feel as if I should know Aunt June, but I can't quite figure out why."

"No doubt your brother has talked about her before." Garrett gave a secretive smile. "She seems to adore Simon more than most."

"I suppose that's why. So is it difficult having a woman constantly watching your every move?" She gave a teasing smile, but he didn't see her. His body remained stiff, as if the fact she joked about herself slid past him.

"I hardly notice my aunt. She keeps to her fire and cabin, and I to my job." Garrett Jones was harder to break than a diamond, but that didn't mean she would give up. Someday she would chisel through his pride. Get past whatever reserve he had toward her, and perhaps even grow to like her. After all, he was her brother's friend. In the meantime, she had to find a way to get out of cook duty.

* * * *

"And who have we here?" Aunt June studied Beth until she wiggled in her shoes. After a long, judgment-filled stare that left Beth wanting to chew her lip, the cook turned to pour a pot of steaming liquid into the cast-iron pan heating over the open fire pit. Beth relaxed a bit. The woman's large, maternal frame gave a sense of home, as if one could approach her with any trouble, and she could make it disappear. Beth couldn't help but smile at the woman as she placed the now empty pot on the ground, turned with hands on hips, and gazed at them both. "A little young to be runnin' with the likes of this one, aren't you?" she asked, motioning toward Garrett.

"Can I speak with you in private, Aunt June?" Garrett asked before Beth had a chance to greet the good-natured cook.

"Of course." Aunt June turned to Beth. "Would you mind stirring this, young man?"

Beth nodded and Garrett ushered the cook to the other side of a little cabin sitting nearby.

Adjusting her position to the opposite side of the fire—the side closest to the whispering couple—Beth tried valiantly to hear what was being said, but with no luck. She concentrated instead on stirring the pot. He wouldn't tell her secret, would he?

"This is Simon's cousin, Brent," Garrett introduced when they returned.

Aunt June's eyebrows shot up. "Is it now? I've heard so much about you, young Brent."

"You have?" Beth fidgeted in the overly large jacket and tried to suppress her sigh. By all accounts, Garrett hadn't given up her secret. At least she hoped he hadn't. So who had talked about her to Aunt June?

"Can Brent have first cook duty? I need to train him for the river runs."

"Certainly." Aunt June slid a white, stained rag off her shoulder and handed it to Beth. "Young Brent can start with wiping down the table and then set the tableware on the serving bench."

With what sounded like a stifled sigh of relief, Garrett gave a slight bow to first Aunt June and then Beth. "I have something I need to do. If you'll excuse me, you'll be in good hands with Aunt June. I'll return as soon as I'm able."

The cook nodded, and Garrett scurried away. Beth's stomach knotted as she watched his retreating back. She felt safer when he was near. Being alone in the quest to maintain her guise made her want to run for the train and hide in the railcar until it left. She needed to lift her chin and face the moment in a way that would make Garrett proud.

What sort of thing did make Garrett proud?

She turned her attention to Aunt June and gave an awkward smile. "Is he always this way?"

"Only around women." A strange glint glistened in the cook's eyes, and sent Beth's heartbeat soaring. The trees surrounding the camp seemed to suck the air right out of the clearing. What was the old woman thinking? Had Garrett actually told her of Beth's secret? Aunt June turned her smile to the ground, and then back up to Beth. "Curious how he acts that way around a strapping young lad such as yourself."

After a long pause where the cook stared with what Beth could only call a challenge, she shrugged and continued, "Yes, well, what you need to know about me is that I don't bite, and I don't gossip. Secrets are always safe with me."

Beth's heart beat with alarm. She knew. She had to.

"Why, just the other day I heard a luscious little tidbit that I swore to never tell." Aunt June prattled on as Beth began to wipe down the long, weathered table—one ear bent to the cook's words, but not fully hearing what she said until, "She will be coming in a few days to help me out, you know. It will be her first time in a logging camp. I think you're going to like her. She's a might giddy at times, but has a level head about her."

"She sounds very agreeable." *Heavens to Betsy.* Who was she talking about? *I really should learn to listen better.* She focused on Aunt June's cliché response, but it was too late. The agreeable girl would show up. Was Aunt June going to try to make a match between *Brent* and another girl? Or did she know about her little escapade? Beth tried not to show the small bout of panic turning her stomach into a pit. Complications were not what she needed. For the first time since the train, she was starting to doubt this brilliant idea.

Aunt June heaved the cast-iron pan off the open flames and set it on the ground with a thump. "We're gonna need a few more dishes for this hungry bunch. Run into my cabin and fetch the spare tin before the rest of the men come thundering in here."

With a nod, Beth tossed the rag over her shoulder and did as ordered, keeping one eye on the older woman as she walked away. She still didn't know if Aunt June was always cheerful, or if she knew the secret. Either way Beth wasn't going to give any fuel for the gossip fire.

The little cabin was decorated with a rough female touch, but pleasant nonetheless. It was a logger's world bejeweled with feminine trinkets and delicate doilies over the horizontal surfaces. A small bed stood in the corner covered in a colorful hand-sewn quilt.

A ruckus sounded through the trees outside, so Beth grabbed the stack of plates and tin bowls and hurried to the table near the fire. Excitement bubbled in her stomach when she recognized the gentle mayhem of rowdy men in the distance.

Aunt June set the large pot at the end of the serving table and wiped the sweat from her forehead with the back of her sleeve. The rumble of shouts grew louder as the men began to race into the camp.

"Don't you worry about these boys. They tend to plow in here at mealtime like bulls down Main Street. Despite their manners, they're all angels."

"Except us Devils," a thick man shouted as he clambered onto the middle of the bench.

"Yeah, Aunt June," another logger bellowed. "Don't let Gar hear you call him an angel. God knows we have a hard enough time keeping him on this side of death."

"Why's that?" Beth adjusted her voice to an even deeper tenor, hoping no one saw through her disguise. Aunt June smiled down at the pot of food as she stirred. Beth furrowed her brows. By the sly smile on her face, she knew a secret she wasn't yet willing to tell.

The first man who spoke leaned on the table with his elbows and raised his head in greeting. He kept his thumb rested on the side of his chin with fist open before his face—as if sizing her up. "He's a risk taker. He's always the first to ride into danger and the last to come out." He eyed her. "Name's Wallace…Wall for short. What'd you say your name is?"

Beth cleared her throat and moved to help Aunt June dish up the vittles. "Brent."

"Where are you workin', Brent?" Wall asked.

"With the Devil May Cares."

Several of the men surrounding the table snickered.

"Ain't no way you're a Devil boy," one of the men toward the end of the table called out.

"He is too. Heard it from Garrett myself." Aunt June plunked down a bowl on the serving table, the contents splashing on the gray weathered top. "Now, all of you boys get over here and get your supper. I'm no serving slave."

"That there's Blue." Wall motioned toward the man who'd made the Devil-boy comment. "Over there's Dick, and Clint. There's a few more of us due in a few days. We're all Devil May Cares. The rest of these jacks are timber beasts."

"Come get your supper, boys. It ain't gonna stay hot forever." Aunt June plopped down another bowl on the table.

Beth glanced over the dozen men shuffling into line, their rough-worn clothes hidden beneath layers of dirt.

"If you haven't already seen him," Wall continued, "Garrett will be along in a while. He's our leader." The grumble of hungry men sounded behind Wall's words as he took his place in line.

"I've met him." Beth handed out the bowls as the men filed on by.

"And he agreed to let you ride?" one of the timber beasts asked.

Wall nodded sideways toward the man. "That's Luther. He was in line for the job you got."

"This here is Simon's cousin," Aunt June let out, shooing a lingering logger down the food line.

"S'that so?" The corner of Luther's lip lifted in disgust as he grabbed up his bowl and sat at the table. "So we have to bow to you too?"

Beth shook her head. "I don't—"

"Oh, bosh, Luther," Aunt June scolded.

"Don't get yer back up, Luther." Wall took his food and headed toward the table. "You know damned well the Devil May Care job wasn't yours, and Simon will be a good boss. Way better than ol' John was. We're lucky he shucked outta here this year. Simon will take care of you beasts better than that mudsill that done left."

Luther dipped low over his bowl and shoveled a sloppy spoon full of stew into his mouth. Brown liquid dripped down his chin, but he didn't bother to wipe it clean as he scowled at the tabletop. Beth felt bad for him. She didn't mean to disrupt anyone's lives but Simon's and Garrett's, but there was no way to change the course she'd started.

* * * *

"Where is he?" Simon asked as Garrett shifted his weight onto his right foot. "If it's important enough we needed to leave Beth alone with Aunt June, the damned fool could at least be on time."

"He'll be here." Garrett checked the dense trail, barely visible under the straggling vegetation. The note he'd received made him nervous. Something was in the air, but God only knew what. "It's not like anyone knows who Beth is, let alone the fact that she's down there."

"Why'd you leave her alone with Aunt June anyway? Do you want to get her discovered?" Simon shuffled his feet.

Perhaps he did. Truth be told, he didn't know why he'd handed her over to his aunt, or how he felt about her being there in the first place. Maybe it was in secret hopes that she'd get caught and sent back home, but it may be that he needed to get his head straight so he could mull over the situation, and the tone of the letter gave him pause.

The selfish part of him wanted to spend what little time he had with her, but the rational side needed her to be tucked back home in Missoula where he could fight to forget the way her blue eyes sparkled like the top of Seeley Lake on a sunny day whenever she smiled.

Garrett stiffened at the crunch of footsteps.

"I didn't know if you'd gotten my note." A pinch-faced logger he recognized from the Bonner camp approached. "I didn't want anyone else to know we were meeting. Best keep this between us." The man extended his hand. "Name's Jessip."

"What's so important we couldn't speak in camp?" Garrett shook the logger's hand.

"There's something brewin' from some of the other logging companies. I've been offered a job of sorts. One that pays mighty well, if you get my drift."

"What sort of job?" Garrett eyed Jessip with care. He didn't miss the hint in the man's voice, but he wasn't about to pay for worthless information.

Jessip stood quiet.

"Out with it," Simon snapped.

"I'm not at liberty to say."

Simon took a threatening step forward. "We don't—"

"How much?" Garrett asked.

"They offered me a thousand dollars, but I'll take five hundred, and you get me a contract for a steady job."

Garrett extended his hand. "You've got yourself a deal. I'll contact the mill, put in a good word, and request a contract. It should come through, as long as the information is important and legitimate. The money I can't give you until the end of the season."

The man spit in his palm and shook Garrett's offered hand. "I'll look for you at the Missoula train depot after the pay is handed out."

"What do we need to know?" Simon asked.

"I've been tasked to make things happen around camp, you know, to stop the logs from getting to the mill."

"Why?" Simon looked ready to spit nails.

"They didn't say." Jessip smoothed his left eyebrow with his forefinger. "They said they'd give me a thousand to stop the logs from going downstream."

"Find out," Garrett commanded. "You'll get your five hundred and a contract, provided nothing happens to the logs."

With a smile that lifted only the right side of his face, Jessip agreed. "I'll send you a notice when I know more. We can meet here again."

Garrett raised his head in silent accord and watched as the man tipped his hat and bid his adieus. Both Garrett and Simon stood silent until Jessip was no longer within earshot.

Garrett started down the trail.

"What do you want to do, Gar?" Simon sped up to keep pace.

"Keep an eye on the camp. If anything at all happens, we meet up with Jessip. I don't know if we can trust him. A thousand is a lot of money to turn down."

"Why would someone want the drive to fail?" Simon veered off the trail near the cabins and picked his way through the forest vegetation, headed toward the cook fire.

"I don't know, but I'm going to find out."

"Hopefully the man has enough honor to keep his side of the bargain. If someone is trying to sabotage the drive, we could use an inside man," Simon said before entering the firelight of camp.

Garrett answered with a nod and followed. With any luck, they had stopped an attack. He cursed his bad luck. First Beth, and then a saboteur. The other logging companies had to choose this of all years to plan an attack. He'd wanted to go out silently, and without notice or fuss. He had a gut feeling that bad things lay ahead.

Chapter 5

"Where have you both been?" Beth chided when Simon and Garrett trudged into camp. How was she supposed to find the traitor if she was paired off with a matronly woman who wanted to do nothing more than watch Beth's every move? At least with Garrett, she could search the entire camp for anything untoward. He'd watch over her no matter what, regardless of his gruff ways and resistance.

The fire illuminated their forms as they walked through the center of camp and headed toward the tracks. She followed them to the open door of the railcar just outside the reach of the firelight near Aunt June's cabin. Darkness now blackened the creaking trees and silhouetted a few stray loggers. To her left the firelight licked the low-hanging branches and the men's faces who sat around the fire ring. She turned her gaze back to Simon. "You missed supper. I almost set out to look for you."

"Never traipse the forest alone." Garrett reached in and grabbed her bag from inside the railcar.

He tossed it to Simon, who handed it to her with a scowl. "I'm not carrying your luggage, *Brent*. You're a man. You take it."

Through the moonlight, Beth made out the disapproving glare Garrett sent her brother. She pursed her lips to stop from smiling. He was a gentleman used to the rules of society, and not the easy way she and Simon behaved toward one another.

"I'll carry it." She reached for the bag, but Garrett snatched it up first. She took a small step toward the bag. "I don't plan to shirk on my duties as a man."

The shadows on Garrett's face changed and once again he wore his usual scowl. He moved the bag away from her reach, but kept silent. If her brother were to sport a constant glare and frown the way he did, she'd tease him without mercy. But on Garrett the surly look made her heart melt. What was wrong in his life that made him want to keep the world at a distance by casting such a sour expression?

He reached in to grab the other two bags, tossed one to Simon, and then marched toward a small cabin on the outskirts of camp. "She'll take a corner bunk, next to you. I'll take the single cot near the door."

Beth scrambled to turn and keep pace with the large men. Once she caught up with her brother, he gave her an elbow to the ribcage. She felt more than saw him gesture toward Garrett, and she understood. At least she thought she did. Although Garrett was one of the leaders in camp, he opted to take the bed most didn't want. Beth tightened her lips to hold back a smile as memories of Simon's stories surfaced from when he was a camp greenhorn. The men back then had not only made him take the cold, lone bunk, but had even hidden the bed in the trees behind the cabin and forced him to sleep out in the cold under the canopy of evergreens.

She was about to nudge her brother and remind him of the story when a little log building emerged from the darkness, its doors open to reveal an even darker shade of black, as if welcoming them to their new home with a foreboding grin. A flicker of light flashed in the window to the right as someone lit a match. Light illuminated the inside and made the house shine like one of the jack-o'-lanterns she and Simon would carve on All Hallow's Eve.

"It doesn't look big enough for all the men." She strained to keep step with Garrett and his long strides.

"This is one of the temporary lodges," Garrett said. "There are three more for the Missoula camp. They're designed so that we can take them apart and move camp once the trees are all downed in this area."

"Oh," she managed to say as she hurried to follow. Her heart beat hard. She knew when she started she'd have to share a cabin with men, but now it was real. She ran a quick hand over her stomach to try and stop the nausea threatening to make her vomit. "I should take my bag inside myself."

With a small huff of agreement, Garrett handed her belongings to her and then walked through the door. His shirt illuminated with the light from the cabin as she followed him through.

The ambiance in the room warmed with the small flicker of the candle. Ten bunks crammed into the room, with one lone cot along the wall next to the door. A few crudely made log chairs sat about the room between the beds as if waiting to be used. Three men stood unpacking their belongings, their packs tossed haphazardly on the gray-striped mattresses.

"You won't mind if I take this bunk, will ya, Luther?" Simon slid by her and elbowed past Luther to toss the logger's bag and stack of shirts on the next bunk over.

Luther turned a dark shade of red, yet he seemed to emit a shadow of gray when he turned an icy stare to Simon and Beth.

"Don't touch my belongins," he warned, one corner of his mouth curled into a snarl.

"No need to get your back up. I didn't mean nothin' by it. I just need to keep the little shave tail where I can mind his business is all, between me and the wall."

"What's a shave tail?" Beth whispered to Garrett.

"Someone like you. Unexperienced," he responded, not taking his eyes off the altercation near the bunk.

"I don't like people touchin' my stuff," Luther growled.

"All right. We won't touch your stuff." Simon turned and raised an eyebrow only she and Garrett could see.

Luther jerked his pack open and yanked his belongings out to toss them on the mattress, all the while keeping one glaring eye on the small group. Simon turned his back to the angry logger, so Beth shifted, bringing them in a small circle.

Garrett cleared his throat and relaxed his shoulders. He motioned with his head toward her. "Brent should be fine on the bottom. Keep an eye on Luther. He seems off this spring."

Simon nodded. "I think he's still pissed that he got passed up for the Devil May Cares."

Both men slid a condemning stare toward her.

"What?" She shifted her eyes back and forth between Garrett and her brother.

"If you didn't blackmail me," Simon said, "Luther would work for Garrett."

Garrett shook his head. "Not necessarily. I don't know if I trust Luther."

"But we wouldn't be in this mess with Beth," Simon continued. "He's the better man for the job...no, he's the only *man* for the job."

He was right. What had she done? She'd intruded upon not only her brother's life, but Garrett's, and now ruined Luther's chance at his coveted job.

But she couldn't tell Simon how guilty she felt or she'd risk both men grabbing her up right there and tossing her on the first train home. Whether Garrett trusted Luther or not was beside the point. Perhaps after this ordeal was over she could help convince Garrett to take the disgruntled logger under his tutelage to become a riverman. At least if she helped get Luther onto the crew later, she wouldn't feel as bad taking his job now.

"What does she have on you anyway?" Garrett asked in a voice so quiet she had to strain to hear over the noise of the men behind her.

Her brother shuffled his feet in the powdery dirt of the floorless cabin. "Ah, you don't want to know."

"Oh for heaven's sake," Beth chimed in a more womanly tone than she'd intended, and then lowered her voice when Luther turned to glare at her once more. "I found him in a…precarious position with a woman."

"Is that the whole of it?" The space between Garrett's eyebrows creased and he gave the same look as her brother sported. Men seemed to have only two expressions, outright angry and happy for the moment.

"She was married to someone of consequence." Simon tipped one side of his mouth in a wry smile. There was the third expression men sported: guilt.

"Ah." Garrett nodded. "I believe you're right. It's best I not know. You're certain the secret is worth risking your sis—Brent's life?"

Simon rounded his shoulders and slouched as if resigned to his fate. *He should be.* The woman in question was the old white-haired mayor's nineteen-year-old wife. The woman he ordered from New York City in one of those mail-order bride flyers the passenger train brought in last year.

"Let's just say if the man was to find out, I would spend the remainder of my days in the hoosegow, staring at the gallows."

Garrett turned a questioning look in her direction. She nodded. "It's true."

"Say no more. I don't want to get involved." Garrett turned to his bunk and shoved his pack beneath his bed.

"Hey, Gar," one of the three other men in the room called. Beth turned and recognized Clint as he sat down on his bunk. Like Garrett, the man sported broad shoulders and a sturdy frame, but he lacked the underlying sense of passion and power that Garrett exhibited. Clint leaned over to rest his elbows on his knees. "Is the shave tail gonna take Dick's job in the bateau?"

"As soon as I train him he will." Garrett pointed at Dick. "As long as you don't mind being a log jumper."

Dick shook his head.

"Just to be absolutely certain," she said. "The bateau is the boat the rivermen use, right? Not the one the cook does. I think I kept getting the two mixed up whenever Simon would tell me of his adventures here."

Clint and the other man, whom she recognized as Blue, burst into laughter, as Simon shot her a vile look. Her heart started to beat fast. She tried not to chew on her lower lip at the slip up, hoping she didn't just give away her secret. *Good Lord.* It was way more difficult to check her womanly habits than she'd thought.

"Shave tail," Blue called, and turned his back to dig through his belongings. "Maybe he should start with cuttin' the firewood for camp. He can work with the Miller boy from the Bonner camp." Clint laughed. "Better yet, have the Miller boy row the bateau, and let the shave tail do the firewood."

Blue laughed at his friend's joke, but her heartbeat slowed to a normal pace. "So it's the riverman boat?" She squinted toward her brother.

How would a man behave in such a situation? She wasn't certain if Clint and Blue didn't like her, or were razzing her like Simon and his friends had done at the schoolhouse yard when they were young. Beth gave a pleading glance to Simon.

"You brought this on yourself by sounding like a confused ninny." He narrowed his eyes in a warning she didn't fail to miss.

"I didn't sign on to cut firewood." She gave her best impression of a man not afraid of anything, although her stomach jumped to her throat. It was possible she couldn't physically handle the arduous tasks of the riverman, but she was hell-bent on trying. "I signed on to be a Devil May Care."

"We'll see, shave tail." Clint's voice dripped with unmistakable challenge. That was one hurdle she was anxious to leap over. Beth would prove herself to Garrett and his men. She couldn't fail. The lives of not only her brother, but the dozens of families relying on the survival of Big Mountain Lumber Mill, depended on her success. Whether they knew it or not.

* * * *

Beth lurched upright in her bed as a terrifying screech echoed throughout the cabin. "What in heaven's name is that?" *Blazes!* She'd forgotten to talk like a man. She cleared her throat. With any luck, the slumbering men hadn't noticed.

The men in their bunks grumbled.

"Shut the hell up!" someone yelled from across the room.

Beth relaxed. *Thank God they're too tired to realize my little slip up.*

"It's the train headed out," Simon mumbled. "It means we have one more hour of sleep before we have to wake up. Go back to bed."

"Blast." Beth jerked back the covers and scurried into her boots. She tucked in the blue work shirt she'd bought with the button up square bib adorning the breast, and threw Garrett's jacket over the top. "Aunt June told me to be at the fire before the train leaves."

"I want biscuits and gravy today," Simon said sleepily as he turned over in his bed. "Eggs and bacon."

Darkness shrouded the room. Beth made her way to the door, but bumped into a hard body. The faded hint of Eau de Cologne drifted on the breeze from the crack in the window, and she knew Garrett stood before her. He steadied her like he did that first day on the street. He bent his head low until she felt his heat graze the side of her neck. His breath tickled her skin and made her stomach flutter when he whispered. "Wait for me."

She nodded even though she knew he couldn't see her through the night, and then forced her knees to carry her as she made her way outside.

A few minutes passed before he quietly slipped out of the cabin door, easing it shut behind him. He turned to her. "I'll walk you to camp."

She nodded again, not wanting anyone inside to overhear. Garrett started down the trail, and she followed.

"How did you sleep?" he asked once they were far enough away from the cabins not to disturb the occupants. The tension eased from her shoulders the farther away they drew from where the men slept.

"As well as can be expected." She tripped over something sticking out from the ground, but caught herself and continued to follow. "I'm not used to crude cots with straw-stuffed bedding."

"I can have a feather mattress brought up for you if you'd like."

Beth smiled. The man who yesterday wanted her gone, now offered to provide her with comforts not afforded to any other loggers. Although the thought of a soft mattress was tempting, she wouldn't give in. What would that look like to the rest of the crew? "I'm all right. It might look suspicious if I get a soft mattress, and everyone else sleeps on straw."

The light of the fire illuminated the base of the tall pine trees and Garrett stopped short. "This is where I leave you. I need to go check things over down by the water. I'll see you at breakfast. And Elizabeth..."

Her heart started to beat at the way her name rolled off his tongue.

"Take care. If anything were to happen to you, Simon and I would be hung out to dry."

She nodded and turned toward the fire. In the crisp mountain morning, her breath puffed out before her face as she entered the camp. The fire threw light over the small cooking area in the dark morning hours. Drenched in a golden sheen, Aunt June bent over the flames, tossed a log into the fire, and then moved over the cast-iron pan. Her elbows popped out of the dark silhouette, and her shoulders dipped as she worked.

Beth leapt over the shadowy form of the protruding tree root she'd seen yesterday and sprinted into the firelight, the thought of Garrett awake and yards from where she stood fresh on her mind. *You're not here for romance, Elizabeth*, she scolded. *Get your head straight.*

"You're late." The cook handed her a wooden spoon and motioned toward the sizzling pile of eggs. "You can't be late for things if you wanna be a logger."

"I know. Sorry." Beth stirred the eggs. A pop from a second pan cooking over the fire sounded, and Beth peeked into the bacon-filled cast-iron pot.

"Don't say sorry to me, *boy*. You'll be answering to the dozen hungry men wonderin' where their breakfast is before long. Once you're done there, you can start the gravy. I need to check on the biscuits. They need to be the right shade of brown for your, er, cousin."

"Did he put you up to this breakfast?" Knowing Simon, he used his dimpled smile to convince the plump cook to make his favorite meal. "You don't have to bother yourself for him, you know. He's already got enough women in town wrapped around his finger and eager to satisfy his ego, he doesn't need one at camp too."

Aunt June giggled. "That boy can charm the trinkets off a gypsy." She disappeared into her cabin as Beth took the bacon out of the pan and tossed in a handful of flour to start the rue. Aunt June returned with the biscuits by the time she'd added the remaining ingredients and was stirring the gravy.

The cook peeked over her shoulder. "Excellent job. Most men don't know how to fry an egg on a cook stove, let alone add the proper ingredients to make gravy."

"My...my mother taught me," she said in quick defense. Hoping her knowledge of food didn't give away her disguise.

The older woman eyed Beth for a moment before giving a sly smile. "Sun's startin' to show its face. Only a few more minutes before the men start tricklin' in. Best get the tins set. I'll take over the stirrin'."

By the time Beth placed the dishes and utensils on the table, the first logger lumbered into the area and plopped down on the bench. She glanced over and recognized Wall.

"You always outdo yourself on the first day of camp, Aunt June. I know the Devil May Cares will be here shortly. They wanted to be the first in line."

"Where's Simon?" Aunt June asked, dishing a plate full of eggs, bacon, and biscuits slathered in gravy, and placing it before the logger. "He's usually the first to the table in the mornin'. I don't want him to miss out on my special breakfast. I made it for him."

"Don't know. Luther took my spot in the Devil May Care cabin. I had to bunk with them damn beasts. Smelly bunch. I don't think a one of them has discovered the use of properly laundered socks."

"The rivermen are supposed to have their own bunkhouse, separate from the timber beasts?" Beth asked, as another logger lumbered up to the serving table. Beth dished him a plate while Aunt June set down fresh milk.

"No," Wall said. "We just sorta follow an unspoken rule. The bunkhouse by the creek is for the Devil May Cares, and the others are for the timber beasts."

"Simon's not a riverman," she supplied, and then snapped her mouth shut. *God.* Why did she keep talking? Someone was bound to see right through her if she kept up the girlish behavior. She needed to stay invisible. Blend in. *Fat chance of that happening.* Maybe they'd ignore the prudish talk and pass it off as social awkwardness.

"There's some men who are part of our crew without being a riverman. Simon's one of them."

"I'm the only one." Simon and the rest of the Devil May Cares rumbled into the cook camp with a crew of timber beasts hot on their heels. "Pissed about losing your spot, Wall?" Simon teased. "Shoulda set up your bunk earlier."

"A deadbeat river rat from the Bonner crew needed a lesson. I had to clean his plow."

"D'ja beat him good?" her brother asked.

"My left hook did. His eye swolled up like a whore on payday."

It took all of Beth's will not to react as a lady would at such language. She'd never in her life heard a man talk so in her presence. Her face heated.

She locked eyes with her brother who must have realized her discomfort and looked fit to explode in a bout of laughter. *I swear. The man is bound to see me fail.* She glared. At the least he took great joy in her discomfort.

"Watch your language in front of the lady." Garrett's voice boomed from the other side of the fire. The men all turned to watch him walk into camp—thank God—if they hadn't looked the other way, someone would have noticed her wide-eyed stare of fear. "I'll beat any man who can't hold their tongue in front of Aunt June."

Beth stared at the tin in her hands and waited for her face to cool, grateful for the gentle mountain breeze.

Garrett adjusted the sheath to his large deer-antler knife, sliding it along his belt to settle at his back so he could sit. Simon, the only man who hadn't turned toward Garrett, quivered with a silent chuckle and dipped his fork into his eggs, shaking his head. She'd honestly thought Garrett was talking about her when he entered, and she was secretly thrilled.

"How long 'til the train comes back?" Aunt June dished Garrett's plate and set it before him while he took a seat at the end of the table.

"It should be back Friday or Saturday. They're picking up a shipment of tools." Garrett dug into his meal as Beth sat across from him and began to eat.

"I need another bunk and a mattress in my house for my goddaughter. She'll be coming on the train and taking over the duties of mess cookin'. That way you boys can concentrate on your work and we women can make you those hearty meals you're fond of."

"I'll send out for the mattress on the next train." Garrett gave a quick glance in Beth's direction, and she blushed.

"I'll build the frame for you this afternoon, Aunt June," Wall offered as he ate.

"Thank you, Wall." She turned to Simon. "What about you?"

Beth chuckled as her brother swallowed hard and stared, the whites of his eyes bulging. "I would, Aunt June, but I got all these responsibilities now. I don't know if I have the time."

"We'll all help you out so's you don't have to worry about that," one of the timber beasts called, followed by cheers of agreement and a few snickers. "Go ahead, Aunt June, he's all yours."

The cook raised one eyebrow, and her eyes twinkled. "I'll wait for you at my cabin after I'm done here."

Garrett finished his meal and stood, catching Beth's eye. "When you're done, meet us at Seeley Lake. You'll start your training by splitting logs. I'll show you how when you get done here." He motioned to his men, who crammed what remained of their food into their mouths, and stood.

"What are you looking at?" she asked her brother as he sat staring at her. "You get to make furniture today. At least I get to be a logger."

"Not until the dishes are done. Best get on them." He gave a triumphant smile, and whistled as he stood and walked away, following Wall and Aunt June.

Splitting logs wasn't ideal, but it was a start. At least she'd be able to watch the men while they worked. What did they do when they weren't making a drive down the river, anyway?

Chapter 6

Garrett tried not to stare as Beth leapt over a tree root and continued to skip toward him and the rest of the crew. Wisps of her jet-black hair had escaped from its confines under her wide-brimmed hat while the jacket he'd given her hung almost to her knees, giving her a look that made his heart drop to his stomach. She was irritatingly naïve, but with a determination that made one believe she could achieve anything she wished. But why the lumber camp? Why now?

"Ah, good, you're here," he said as she neared the group. "This is Michael. He'll show you how to cut firewood while the rest of us go check on the raft."

"The raft?" she asked.

Garrett pointed to a sectioned-off area in the lake filled with logs waiting to be taken downstream to the mill. "The wannigan is the floating cabin over there. That's the cook boat, not the raft. When the logs that float down the river are tied together, we call that the raft. Once the timber beasts fall the trees, they take them down skid row, and then slide them down the chute. Then they are placed on the rollway to wait. When we're ready for a drive we release the logs into this section of Seeley Lake and bind boom logs to one another to keep the rest of the logs together. It makes it easier to get past the lake. Once we reach the river, we release the logs so the river can take them to the mill near Bonner. This load is almost ready for the go-ahead from Teddy, and then we'll take it down. Your job will be to assist me in the bateau until you're ready to handle it on your own." He pointed to a boat sitting a few yards from the bank.

"When will I train for that?"

"Soon." He wished never. It had taken weeks to forget her face the first time he'd met her on the train platform in Missoula, and each time they'd returned from a season after that, he'd distanced himself before being forced to engage her charming wit. Now, whenever she turned her dimpled smile to him, his chest tightened, and it took all of his strength just to breathe normally. She disturbed his destined path, and he couldn't have the distraction, or her.

Garrett turned to watch as the rest of his crew meandered down the bank, leaving him behind. Michael moved to get another ax from the other side of the small woodpile. "When you finish here, come over to the raft."

Beth eyed him. "You're talking differently."

"What do you mean?" But he knew exactly what she meant. Beth made him nervous, and yesterday when he realized it was she on that railcar and cleared his initial shock, he reacted like years of boarding school and London parties had taught him. With a reserved aloofness designed to allow him to face the challenge with a calm head and effective tongue.

"Not stuffy and refined."

"I'm focused."

She gave a slow nod as if she didn't quite believe his response. Thankfully, the Miller boy chose that moment to return and hand her an ax. She reached for it. The weight of the tool jerked her shoulder down until the head plopped on the ground. Garrett reached out to grab the ax before it injured her, but snapped his hand back, and flexed his palm at the desire to touch her. To help her. He needed to treat her like he would one of his men. *Oh God, the men.* How would they react if they knew her true identity?

She turned a nervous glance toward him.

He nodded in encouragement, but he really wanted to take the burden from her hands and into his own. "You'll do fine."

"I'm not frightened." Her voice quivered with forced confidence.

"Excellent. We'll be right over there." He pointed to where the men gathered in front of the raft.

After she gave him a nervous smile, he took leave. His tense muscles eased the moment he walked away from Elizabeth. All he wanted to do was feel her. Caress her hand to see how soft her skin was. He couldn't, especially since Michael had watched them with a curious stare. This guise couldn't last. Not with the tug of longing he felt whenever Beth was near.

The boisterous noise from his crew grew in intensity as he neared. They were excited over the start of the season. So was he. The tumble of a half-hearted fight between two of his men rippled through his core. This was what he'd looked forward to when he started the season. Camaraderie and easy banter, not traitors and women disguised as loggers. At least he could enjoy this moment. This one last start of the season challenge between his men.

"Who wants to go first?" Garrett asked and leapt on the top of a floating log to balance with expert ease.

"Dick and I need a go. I got a beef to settle with him from last year." Wall followed Garrett's lead and appeared to walk on water as he jumped from log to log, stopping at a large trunk near one of the boom logs.

Dick gave a lopsided grin and followed Wall onto the raft. "You lost fair and square. I can't help that I have a surer foot, or a better right hook."

"You chiseled your way through," Wall claimed, taking a wide stance to rock the log and causing Dick to wobble.

"Give in, Wall." Dick readied for the log roll by adjusting his stance and holding out his hands. "I got the bulge over you. I man the bateau. I don't have land legs like you bank walkers."

"I barely walk the bank. I ride the logs, not some flat-bottomed boat." Wall shook one of Dick's outstretched hands. "Let's go, then."

Wall set the log in motion, and Dick began to run in place as the men on the bank cheered. Garrett couldn't help but laugh as Dick gained control of the log and Wall wobbled. There was no better morale booster than the start of the season challenge.

"How fun! Do you do this every year?" Beth's words were almost drowned out by the cheers as Dick stumbled, but quickly regained his footing. Garrett snapped his gaze to the troublesome woman now standing beside him.

"Why aren't you chopping wood?" He shifted to stand next to her, shut her off from the rest of the men.

"The boy had to leave. He said he'd come get me when he needs me again. I guess he didn't trust me alone."

Garrett stretched his neck muscles. He didn't trust her alone in the woods either. The woman would be the death of him. "What about cook duty?"

"I'm done with that for now too. I'm all yours until someone else comes to get me."

A battle between sending her packing and allowing her to stay raged in his head. At least they weren't doing anything dangerous. No harm would come of her watching. "It's a friendly competition. Each year the men compete for their place among the crew. First a log roll, and then a cockfight. The winner gets the distinction of taking the position as foreman of the Devil May Cares. I have never lost."

"Never?"

He shook his head. Many a man had tried, but his stature gave him a leg up from the rest of the men. This year was different. What a moment for the woman of his dreams to break into his life—just in time to see him get beaten down. He had to lose so the winner could take over as leader of the Devil May Cares. "Not so far. We'll see what the day brings."

"May I have a go?"

"No." There was no way she could stay on for even a second.

"Can I at least walk on the logs?"

"Not yet. I'll take you out on the boat after supper tonight." The boat was about the only thing she could handle. At least then she'd keep quiet about helping, and he'd get to ask her about the moon-shaped scar on her arm. The one he focused on whenever he forced his gaze away from her eyes.

She nodded and adjusted her demure stance, crossing her arms over her chest as she watched the men. Garrett turned as well, and forced back the smile threatening to stretch across his face. This felt good, her next to him, comfortable in the wilds of the forest. With her spunky bravery, she was the sort of woman who could make a man happy. Content. Share the love of the mountains with him. Be near him without the need for meaningless prattle.

Wall took the lead once more and within seconds knocked Dick into the water. Cheers rose from the men on the bank, and Beth jumped up and down with excitement. It took everything he possessed not to smile in response to her enthusiasm.

His pulse raced when she drew closer to him as she moved around in the buzz of merriment. The more time he spent with her, the more he wanted to be with her every moment of the day. He gave a sly glance at her face, and his spirits dropped. He must keep her at arm's length, and not only for appearances around camp. It wouldn't be fair to toy with her emotions when he was destined for another. Elizabeth was nothing but a dream.

* * * *

Beth sat on a nearby log to enjoy the competition, as each riverman took their turn challenging the next until all that remained were Wall and Garrett. On occasion, she'd remember the manly pose she was supposed to sport, and would adjust her position. She hoped it worked. The last thing she wanted was someone finding her out.

Garrett motioned with his head for her to follow, and then wandered into the forest with Wall, leaving Beth to walk with the rest of the crew. "What now?"

"Now's the best part. They fight." Dick took the lead as he dried off with his shirt and shrugged into his heavy coat.

"Wall is a pugilist," Clint boasted. "Never had a chance at Garrett, though. This'll be one hell of a cockfight."

Beth took care to remember not to chew on her lip like she was apt to do when nervous, instead she copied Blue's stance as he shouted words of encouragement to the fighters. Two men brushed past her when she slowed. She should take the opportunity to scope out the men, see if she could identify the traitor among them.

"Don't worry, shave tail," Clint teased. "You'll get a chance next year, once you bulk up a little. Can't have you gettin' knocked out before you even spin a log. Unless of course, you want to? We can have a row after Garrett and Wall if you'd like."

The hope in Clint's voice made her tense. Did men go about their day for the sole purpose of finding someone to knock fists with? Was this where male camaraderie went to cultivate, or die? If the female gender behaved like men did, the world would surely come to an end.

Garrett's dark hair peeked above a chokeberry bush just off the trail. The path veered to the right and opened up to a small clearing.

"Ah, there you are." Garrett held out the spare jacket he'd worn since he'd given her his large wool coat. Beth took his coat, and snuggled deeper into the thick warmth of the wool she wore and remembered his chivalrous move. It still smelled like him—a slight note of pine and wood shavings, with an undertone of Eau de Cologne.

The men circled Wall and Garrett as they rolled up their sleeves and shook hands. She studied each man, concentrating on the sound of each voice as they spoke, but no luck. Each man spoke with a mountain slang, but not one had the same distinct timbered drawl as the man from the platform. The cold, nauseating pangs of nerves made her want to press her palms against her stomach. Did she think she could come and locate the saboteur on the first day? Hardly. Her plan was dicey at best, but she had to try.

The two fighters began to arc around each other until Wall threw the first punch. She almost believed Garrett's neck had broken as it slammed back.

He gave a wicked grin, swiped at the blood trickling down his chin, and lurched forward with a left jab, followed by a hard right hook.

Wall stumbled with the impact, but righted himself as Garrett threw another jab.

They continued until Garrett stumbled, and Wall pounced like a mountain lion on a carcass. Beth held back a squeal as Garrett fell underneath his opponent, and Wall began to beat him ruthlessly.

"You have to stop them." Beth yanked on Dick's sleeve, and then jerked her hand back when she realized her mistake.

"Are you a hard case or a ninny, Brent?" Dick asked. "Garrett's the best fighter we have. Wall ain't no match for him, and Garrett will never back down. He's just beatin' the devil around the stump is all."

Clint chimed in, "Stay down, Gar. Let him get a couple good punches in before you knock his block off. 'Bout time we had a real show."

"Yeah," Blue agreed. "Whip him, Wall!"

The encouragement must have worked, for Wall shifted over Garrett and began to slam his fist into Garrett's face. Blood squirted out of his mouth, coloring the dirt beneath their rolling bodies.

Beth wanted to scream and ran to yank at Wall's jacket in an attempt to dislodge him from Garrett. But a loud whistle echoed through the trees like a train through a desert canyon. Relief spread through her gut. She hadn't gotten the chance to once again draw unwanted attention. Thank the Lord above. The men all stilled and turned their heads toward the sound. Wall, with fists raised and ready to strike, lowered his hands and clambered off Garrett, reaching down to help him stand.

"Who?" Garrett asked, although she suspected he spoke to himself. Beth's heart sank. Whatever the whistle meant wasn't good.

The men launched into a run toward camp, leaving Beth to follow in confusion.

Her legs burned with each long stride as she ran to catch up with Garrett. "What's going on?"

"Something has happened at one of the sites." He slowed and gave a quick glance in her direction. She saw the worry in his eye a split second before he turned back to the path.

They didn't take the usual route to camp, but veered to the right and headed up a steep trail. A large clear-cut area came into view with a small crowd in the center gathered around something on the ground. Garrett picked up speed and disappeared into the group of men.

Beth fought her way to the center. A large man lay crumpled in the grass with a bone sticking out of his forearm as if it were merely a twig broken in half. His skin was white, and his eyes rolled back in his head, but his chest still rose and fell.

She tried not to heave the little bit of breakfast she'd eaten this morning as Garrett kneeled next to the man and ran his hands over the body.

"What happened?" he asked.

A tall, gangly logger with brown teeth spoke. "He was in the middle of the back cut when a widowmaker fell. He tried to get away, but he wasn't fast enough. A branch as thick as Tiny Pete's leg fell on him and sort of crushed half his body." The man motioned toward a logger the size of a bear. "The bulk of the branch missed his head by an inch."

"Take him to Aunt June. She can care for him until the train comes to take him to town." Garrett stood. "You boys go make a stretcher."

The men gave a mumbled agreement and separated.

When the crowd cleared, with the exception of a few stragglers, Beth slipped through to stand next to Garrett. "Who is he?"

"A faller from the Bonner crew." He turned to the tall brown-toothed man. "I'm going to warn Aunt June. Have the boys bring him down when the stretcher is ready, but don't forget to bind his wound first. We don't want it to break further."

The man nodded, and Garrett motioned for her to follow.

Once out of sight of the crew, Garrett grabbed her hand to tow her behind him. His fingers tingled in her palm, and he squeezed. "The widowmaker is but one danger of the forest. I was a fool for leaving you with only Aunt June or Michael to watch over you. Aunt June is reliable, but she too has an adventurous spirit, albeit a bit more checked. Had you wandered into the cutting zone while you searched for the raft, you too could have been injured or killed. From now on, you do not leave my side unless Simon is with you."

A knot formed in the back of her throat, and she had to take a deep breath to stay the tears forming in her eyes. The vision of Garrett kneeling next to the wounded man played in her mind. The calm way he'd checked the man for life, the automatic deference for his word, the loyalty his men showed for him proved they all looked up to him. His autocratic demeanor was a guise—one she could see right through. He was a generous and kind man to those he loved, and he loved this camp more than anything else in his life.

Chapter 7

"The raft has *what*?" Garrett paced in front of Blue. Beth hid somewhere behind him. Her small frame flinched every time he spun around to head in a new direction. His heart melted each time he saw the fear in her eyes at his movements, but it couldn't be helped. Sooner or later she'd find out what sort of leader she'd signed on with. His brash ways weren't favored by women, but he was fair to his men, and they responded by working hard. "Where are the logs?"

"I don't know," Blue answered. "The Bonner crew told us the barrier was cut on the raft, and some of the logs are floating out into the lake."

"Cut, not broken?"

"Yes. Cut."

"Bloody hell!" Garrett headed in the direction of the raft, trusting that Beth would follow, and not worrying one whit about his language. Usually he'd take care in front of a lady, but today he hadn't the fortitude for niceties.

He didn't need another accident, especially one that would prevent him from getting the logs to the mill. Was Jessip responsible? He thought he'd seemed genuine enough when he asked for the steady job, but maybe the lure of the thousand dollars got the better of him. "How many logs escaped?"

"I haven't counted. Enough to put the Bonner crew on alert."

"Find Simon," he ordered.

"I'll go." Beth moved to do as he asked.

"Not you. Blue. You stay by me." The last thing he needed was her getting lost and wounded, or worse. From now on she was his shadow, even at night.

Blue ran off, leaving him and Beth alone. Garrett grabbed her hand to tow her behind. The rapid thump of his pulse leveled off at her touch. She did something to him. Grounded him, and allowed him to think clearly whenever her soft skin touched his. When he'd taken her hand the other day, it was out of pure need to get her walking faster, but he'd liked the instant wave of serenity he felt when they touched.

Never in his life had a logging season been so difficult, and only a week had passed since they rode the train up the mountain. The woman warming his palm was the reason. Since she showed up in camp, nothing seemed to work. He suspected the traitor stalking the trees held only a little responsibility in that aspect. Garrett couldn't get his mind in the right place. Any other year, he could have identified the traitor, had him arrested, and already taken down one drive. Not this year. This year a woman shook his world enough to crumble his mountain of confidence and turn it into a whitewater river.

The trees opened up to the lake, and he let go of her hand to take the lead.

"What the hell happened here?" he asked the group of men gathered on the bank. Four men, all Devil May Cares, waged war against the logs with boats and peaveys as the wood fought to break free of the raft's confines.

"Someone cut the anchor line holding the boom logs." The Bonner man who answered lifted a piece of line, sliced through.

"How many have we lost?"

"About a hundred, maybe two. It must have been cut sometime last night while we slept."

Garrett cussed under his breath. He kept one eye on Elizabeth as she moved toward the water's edge and watched the mayhem. A large chunk of the raft was missing and would cost the mill at least a month's worth of pay. It had to be Jessip. Who else could it be? "Who found it?"

"Peter, from my crew," one of the Bonner boys said, stepping forward through the men. "Said he come down this morning to take a piss and noticed a log slipping out."

"Tell him thanks." Garrett ran his hands over his face. Where the hell did Jessip work? He needed to pay the man a visit.

"What's going on?" Simon asked as he ran up behind him. *Oh, thank God.* Garrett needed to focus. The only way to do so would be to leave Beth with her brother.

Garrett excused himself from the group. Yanking Simon to a secluded area off the path, he checked over his shoulder to ensure he could still see Beth as she huddled with the men—afraid, by the look on her face. He turned to Simon and gave a quick account of the incident.

"Shit." Simon pursed his lip and turned to watch the men working to tie the outside boom logs together. "Jessip."

"We need to talk to him. Now."

"I'll go find him." Simon slapped him on the shoulder as he rushed past, heading toward the Bonner camp.

What was he going to do with Elizabeth now? Drag her around while he confronted a potential criminal? Garrett massaged his temple and moved in the opposite direction to gather Beth, and then intercept the letter he'd sent to the mill earlier in the day, requesting the contract. With any luck, it hadn't gone out on the morning train. He'd have to leave her in Aunt June's care again. There was no other option.

* * * *

Elizabeth tossed a bucket of dirty water into the dense vegetation behind Aunt June's cabin, and studied the trail Garrett had disappeared to after he left. She knew he was in no mood for tomfoolery, so she did as ordered and stayed to help Aunt June. Although every time she drew near the edge of the clearing, she'd study the trees for Garrett's return. Her mind drifted to the fear and anger in his eyes when he'd watched the logs glide into the middle of the lake. She'd wanted to reach out and caress his cheek. Show him he wasn't alone. She would have helped, but in doing so she would have overstepped her role. So she simply watched and obeyed.

A twig snapped from halfway up a small hill behind the cabin. Garrett appeared from around a tall quaking tree, his shoulders as rigid and tense as before. Not a good sign.

"Let's go," he barked as he walked past, leaving her to follow. Aunt June simply watched, her brows furrowed in concern, but she didn't stop him from taking Beth away.

Beth's legs ached as she struggled to keep step. "Where are we going?"

"Up. We'll stop at the cabin first. I need to grab a few things."

Finally, she might get to tidy her bed and stow her belongings before the men came back. She entered into the small abode, and hurried to her bunk. She stuffed her bag below her bunk, and moved to make the bed, only to snap her hands to her chest as she yanked back the blanket.

"What is that?" Beth took a step back, as Garrett leaned over her bed to stare at the slimy green creature now housed in her covers.

"A slug." He plucked it from her pillow and tossed it out the open window.

She'd heard of the revolting creatures, but never encountered one herself. They didn't often plague the town she lived in. "How'd it get here?"

Garrett's lips twitched as if he held back a smile, but his back remained stiff. "Most likely the men put it in here. A slug in the bed is a typical trick they play on the shave tails that come into camp. You can expect more things to happen, but I'll try to make them keep it to a minimum."

"No, no. They are fine." She tried not to bite her lip. If the pranks didn't get much worse than this, she could handle it. Slimy and wet creatures, she could deal with. Anything with teeth, though, was a different story altogether. She lifted her chin with false bravado. "I signed on to be a riverman. I can handle it."

"I'm still going to talk to them later. Right now, we need to go." Without waiting for a reply, he turned and trudged through the open door.

Once again, she followed. Her shins burned from the long strides and ill-fitting boots, but she wasn't about to complain. Not with his clipped tone and stern expression. What happened between when he left her, and when he returned that made him move with such urgency?

Her nerves hummed while she followed Garrett as he picked his way up a rough trail leading to the top of a large hill. The higher they climbed, the thinner the air seemed to be. An omen to the danger of the woods, or perhaps it was the dense sensation of a land undiscovered by man. Either way, it was eerily calming. Red strips of torn cloth marked the safe paths through the trees. "Did you put those there?"

"No. I had Simon do it. That way you won't go wandering where you can get hurt." The tense way he carried his shoulders eased the higher they climbed. Did the crisp spring air affect him the same way it did her? Had the morning not started out with the missing logs, a day such as this could make one never want to leave.

"How long until we ride the rapids?"

"A week or two," Garrett said over his shoulder as they climbed. "Today we're going to The Deck. That's what we call the area between The Grove, where they're cutting the logs, and the chute. I need to see if Teddy saw anything this morning from the hilltop, and we can find out when the first drive is going to be."

Beth nodded and followed closer. Today she would finally get a chance to see the logging operation in action. Watch the men. Perhaps even identify the traitor. As they crested the top of the trail, a buzz of activity penetrated the fog of exertion assaulting her brain. Faller teams dotted the mountainside, and she kept her gaze steady. Any one of these men could be the man from the platform. Their spiked boots helped them jump from one log to the next. The thud of hammers on wedges, combined with the grating sound of crosscut saws biting into the wood, sounded through the forest.

Two men cut at a tree, then leapt back as a third called out the warning, "Down the Hill." The signal rang through the forest. The voice wasn't the one she'd heard plotting against the company. She noted the man's face, mentally eliminating him from the list of suspects.

The tree screamed its protest as it plunged to the ground with a loud thump.

"Why not timberrrr?" She sped up to keep pace. The back of her hand brushed against his when he slowed to turn toward her.

Garrett sucked in a quick breath, tapped his offended hand against his leg, and took a moment before responding. "No self-respecting timber man would be caught dead yelling that."

"I thought all loggers used the term."

Garrett laughed, his tense shoulders dropped a fraction of an inch. "You have a lot to learn. For one, they don't call themselves *loggers*, they are timber beasts." He motioned toward the tall, dirty man working the horses. "And this is Teddy, we call him our chute monkey. He brings the logs from The Grove to the chute and sends them down to the lake."

"The man we're going to speak with?"

Garrett nodded his response. "He also decides when the raft is ready for the drive."

Teddy was a lanky, gawky looking man in his mid-twenties, good-natured judging by the smile he tossed their way. She could see kindness in his eyes. His team of horses looked as long and ragged as he did, but with the power to pull an incredible amount of weight over rough terrain.

Beth and Garrett walked up to the man, and Garrett greeted him with a slap on the back.

"This is Brent. Simon's cousin," he introduced.

Teddy inclined his head in greeting, and Garrett turned him around to speak, leaving Beth alone in the middle of the field. Searching the grass, she set her sights on the gorgeous sets of mismatched horses tied to the slip-tongued wagon.

Beth made her way to the four steeds. The two front animals looked alike, with dark brown shaggy fur while the sorrel horse on the back right contrasted with the large and powerful white draft horse. Beth stared longingly at the beautiful pale animal. What she wouldn't give to have such an animal for her own, should she ever be in a position to own one herself. Perhaps the man she married would spoil her with her own buggy and horse.

As she got closer to the team, she reached her hand out and stroked the horse's muscular, white neck. She talked softly to the beast and twined her fingers through the soft, but durable mane. She circled the horse as much as she could, needing to get closer to the beautiful creature. The white gelding flicked his tail and it caught in the large bolt in the center of the wooden beam of the tongue. She waited to see if his tail would dislodge. It didn't.

She placed her hand on the white horse's rump, stepped onto the tongue, and reached down to free the horse tail. The animal shifted and wedged her between his butt, and the sorrel. Her breath grew shallow, and her heartbeat kicked up when the powerful animal pranced and sidestepped in response to her intrusion.

The white horse slammed into her side and smashed her against the front of the wagon. Pain pierced her lower back, and her heart beat hard and fast against her ribs. She was going to die. *God, Elizabeth. Why do you do such foolish things?*

Spooked, the sorrel pranced to the right, and the tug of the axle caused the white gelding to resist and panic. Before she could jump clear, the pale horse thrashed, yanked, and tried to buck to break free. Beth held on to the wooden frame. The wood beneath her feet splintered when the horse kicked toward her. She squished against the front of the wagon and clung with a white-knuckle grip, trying to brace herself. All she could do was cling. Cling to the wooden structure and cling to her life as she tossed back and forth, bashing into each of the horses.

The harness that connected the panicked horse to the wagon snapped and whipped past Beth's face, barely missing her tender skin. Within a heartbeat, the second connection cracked, and the frightened animal broke free of its confines and bolted. The mare tore down the trail, the long reins whipping in the air. The wagon shook as the remainder of the animals fought to break free and follow.

Beth eyed the now empty space, gauging the distance she'd need to leap. She bent her knees to jump as someone yanked her from the perch. She landed with a loud thump in the vegetation, a safe distance from the wagon and team.

She glanced up to see Garrett, face fierce, but fright tinted his eyes like a storm over the mountain top. He towered over her as her heart began to slow.

"Get up, boy." Teddy Barns stalked toward her after settling the remaining horses. "The horses didn't lick you enough. I'm gonna finish the job." Across the field, men dropped their tools, and started after the fleeing horse.

Teddy grabbed the front of her overly large jacket near her throat and plucked her from the ground like she was no heavier than a babe. Her feet dangled in the air as Teddy wound his arm back, prepared to issue the promised beating. Beth closed her eyes, ready for a lickin' she knew she deserved.

It seemed like time slowed as she waited for the pain, but all she felt was Teddy release her jacket and the hard ground as she once again landed on her butt.

"I'll do it," Beth heard Garrett say. She opened her eyes as she clutched the ground in her fists, as if the little crushed plant in her palm could stop the moment.

Garrett released the white-knuckle grip he had on the front of Teddy's shirt, but the chute monkey shook his head. "Hell no, Garrett, this flunkey broke my harness and spooked my horse."

"He'll pay for it. A week's pay should cover the expense. Brent isn't a wet-nosed flunky," Garrett replied in a mild tone. "He's training to be a riverman."

Teddy paused for a moment and stepped back. "Fine, I'll use my spare harness, but I expect you to teach this river rat a lesson in touchin' another man's belongins."

Garrett nodded at Teddy, grasped Beth's upper arm, and picked her up. She tripped along the trail as he led her farther into the forest. "What kind of fool thing was that? I'm gonna whoop you a good one, boy," he growled as they stomped through The Grove and headed deep into the forest. The men chopping trees stopped and watched.

She followed him up the path until it became no more than an animal trail. Angry vibrations emanated from Garrett. They were getting farther into the trees now. She couldn't see or hear any sign of habitation. Except the occasional bird call or scurry of a frightened animal, there was no sign of humans anywhere. They were alone.

"What the hell was that?" His voice sounded calmer than before, but still shook with a vibration of anger. "You could have been hurt...or worse."

"I know." Her voice sounded small, even to her. "The mare was beautiful. I didn't think she would spook. They looked tamed and calm."

"What would your brother think if the whistle sounded for you? He'd be devastated."

She didn't have a response. He was right.

Garrett studied the trail in front of them without speaking, or even glancing in her direction, as the path grew narrow. They continued the climb without a word. She knew from dealing with him the last few days that his pinched-lipped silence meant he was upset. She'd really messed up this time. He'd never forgive her, or let her stay.

Just when she was about to insist on stopping for a break, they entered a small clearing. In the middle sat a small, roughly built cottage surrounded by tall grass and smiling white daisies. The serenity of the meadow helped to ease the tense back muscles she'd sported since realizing her mistake with the horses. She didn't want to make the blunder that would put her on the first train home, and she had a feeling she just did.

He neared the cottage and faced her. "I think you should reconsider your determination to ride the river."

"No."

"I can force you."

She blinked a few times to stay the tears caught behind her eyes. Her voice cracked in a weak whisper. "You wouldn't."

"Beth." The simple word sounded pained.

"I've got other reasons to stay," she said. Anything to convince him.

"What?"

"I…I can't say. It's important, though."

"If you can't give me a reason, I will put you on the next train down the mountain. The camp is no place for a lady. You're going home." He grabbed her hand, tugging her toward the trail.

"Someone's trying to ruin the company!" she blurted out. *Blast.* She showed her hand, but if that's what it took to stay, she'd let him in on all her secrets. Well, most of them.

He hesitated and turned to her. "What?"

"I overheard someone at the platform after Simon got home from the pre-season meeting with you and the big bugs. Someone's out to destroy Big Mountain. I know who he is."

Garrett stiffened. "Who."

"He has a deep drawl."

"You said you knew who he is."

"I do. I saw him," she lied. "But I don't know his name."

Beth chewed on her bottom lip as the lump in her throat dropped to the deepest pit of her stomach and made it ache. He had to let her stay. The more she got to know him, the more she wanted to bring the saboteur to justice. He loved this company as much as her brother did.

"If I could meet everyone—see who they are—I'm certain I can identify the culprit." She dropped her shoulders and tilted her head, a silent plea that always worked on her brother. "Please, Garrett. I need to stay. I promise. I'll take care in the future. I won't get into trouble. You'll be there to watch me."

Garrett pressed his palms over his eyes and then jerked his head back up and threw his hands to his sides. "You can stay, but you will remain with Aunt June as camp cook."

"No. The men already think I am a Devil May Care, and I won't meet anyone in the Bonner camp if I'm hidden in the cookhouse. I'll stay in the bateau during the drive. I promise."

"What do you plan to do once you find the traitor? You can't even heave an ax properly let alone take on a riverman."

"I'd planned to tell Simon."

"Why didn't you do that to begin with?"

"I didn't want to risk his life."

"No?" Garrett scoffed. "Just your own, right?"

"Please? I need to do this. Do you realize what will happen to Bonner if they lose the mill? So many children will be without homes, without the means to buy clothes. If I can help to keep even one baby fed, alive, I will move this mountain to do so. Can't you understand?"

"I can." He stood silent and fixed his gaze on her. "You would stay here to help save a company you don't have any connection with, other than your brother, for the prosperity of others?"

"For the lives of others. This place is important to Simon, and you. Why would I not help out if I knew something was amiss?"

With a deep inhale, he inched closer. He reached up with hooded eyes, and pinched a stray lock of her spiked hair between his fingers. The heat from his hand made her vision blur and all she could see was his face.

Silence stretched as the air seemed to thicken.

"You have a good heart, Elizabeth Sanders." He lowered his head closer until she could feel his breath mingle with hers. Was he going to kiss her? She stared at his lips, hovered over hers. They squeezed together mere seconds before he stepped away, and cold air replaced the warmth of his breath—a cold she felt down to her soul.

He cleared his throat.

"Uh...this is a place we can go to get away," Garrett said and motioned to the small abode in the center of the flowers.

"A cottage?" She turned to the small house. "How did you find this?"

"Your brother and I made it our first spring here. Quaint, is it not?"

"What is it called?"

"Called?" Garrett shook his head in confusion.

"It seems a little too whimsical to not have a name. Don't you think?"

Garrett dipped his chin a fraction of an inch and gave her a stare that made her stomach flip. She swallowed harder than she'd expected, her tongue dry. He waved toward the abode. "We never bothered naming it. Would you like to do the honors?"

"Hmmm." Beth cocked her head to one side and stared at the building, partly to break away from the growing need to radiate toward him, and part to judge the entirety of the scene. "It feels as though a fairy tale could take place in this meadow. How does Mother Goose's Cottage sound?"

"Like a princess would be welcome to grace the bed within." The tenor in his voice wove the words like silk over a velvet carpet. The thought of both sinfully pleasant fabrics brought visions no decent woman should possess—especially since Garrett stood like a conqueror, square in the center of said visions.

Loggers do not wear silk.

Not even loggers of the female kind. Namely, her.

She took a deep breath to steady the beat of her heart as he stepped toward her. His eyes darkened like a storm above a mountain peak, and pulled blessed moisture back into her parched mouth. He stopped close enough to warm her entire body with his heat. He flicked his hand toward her, stopped, clenched his fist, and then dropped it to his side. Beth's heart all but stopped short when he cleared his throat and turned to wave toward the cabin. "Loggers, on the other hand, may not be so fortunate."

"Why not?" Beth also focused on the solid structure. As if the swirls and dips in the wood could answer his question, and make sense of the moment they'd just shared.

"Aren't loggers always the villains in fairy tales?" he said in a tone she could only describe as a manly, forced chipper. Not his usual drawl. Curious.

If he could pretend the moment wasn't profound, then so could she. "Heavens no. The timber men are always the heroes. Everyone knows this. Why else would they be featured in such a romantic story?"

"Romantic?" One of his eyebrows perked up. "I didn't know stories about wolves trying to eat children were romantic."

"Well, maybe not all fairy tales, but most." She smiled.

"Mother Goose's Cottage it is then. As long as I can be the hero in whatever story takes place here." The silk was back in his tone, but luckily without the velvet carpet. To be honest, the whole thing confused her to no end. This was Simon's friend, Garrett, for heaven's sake. A man too refined to speak her name on the sidewalk. Yet she was quite certain he was flirting with her.

She'd played this coy game before, but never had it filled her heart with more joy than it did today.

"Perfect. Now all we need is a princess." She walked into the sea of flowers, and spun around to watch the colors mix. She needed to cool her fiery skin, and what better way to do so than to make distance and feign delight in the foliage.

Her twirl halted when a large hand snaked around her middle. She gasped and stopped. Garrett's face hovered mere inches from her own. In that moment, she wanted him to kiss her. To take the sensation she'd felt moments ago a step further. Would he?

"You are the closest thing to a princess these woods have ever seen," he said, the silk and velvet now weaving a tapestry in his voice. A blasted tapestry to hide the secrets he kept hidden behind pretty words. A moment of passion, perhaps? Would it be wrong of her to give in to one kiss should he be so inclined?

Her breath caught in her lungs. Her mind swirled as his hand caressed her cheek bone. This was real. Garrett's touch tightened her core, and spread heat to every inch of her body. The fire in his eyes made her stomach churn in alarm, yet somehow it excited her. She'd been kissed before, but never by a man like Garrett. And never had she wanted it more than she did right now.

She stopped breathing, evident by the stillness of her chest. Garrett couldn't help but study the path his hand took down the soft contours of her neck to dip into the crevice of her collarbone. She tilted her head, an offering. She needed to deny him. Make him stop...for her sake.

By the small of her back, he pulled her closer and lowered his lips to hers, needing to taste her as much as he needed to breathe. Her lips were as soft as he'd imagined. Warm and pliant beneath his, they begged him to take more. The scent of honeysuckle drifted and mixed with the surrounding smell of the flowers in the field. She could be his if he wished—the way she leaned into him as they kissed proved as much. He should claim her for his own.

Instead, he drew back and nestled his face into the hair above her ear. "'And even silence found a tongue. To haunt me all the spring long'... I'm sorry, Beth. I guess I'm not the gentleman I believe myself to be."

She drew back, confusion written on her face like the ink stained swirls of a hundred-year-old book. He shouldn't have kissed her, but when she'd spun round, an inherent need to touch her itched his fingers. Only the softness of her skin beneath his could set his mind to right after her brush with death filled every fiber of his being with rage. The woman could send his world spinning, and stop it dead in its tracks in the same confusing moment.

A whisper of a frown creased her porcelain face, and she took a deep, shuddered breath. "I've heard that poem."

"It's John Clare. The name of the poem, I will never tell."

"Did you bring me all the way up here to quote pretty poetry?"

He dropped his hands and stepped back, needing to put distance between them. He couldn't have her so he shouldn't toy with her emotions in such a way. As much as he wanted to claim her for his own, he could not. "No. I needed to clear my mind after your little incident down there. This is where I go to think."

Beth chewed on her lower lip. "What did Mr. Barnes say?"

Garrett stared down into her crystal eyes. Heaven above, she tempted his resolve. Her swollen lips begged him to take them once more. He concentrated on her eyes, but even the blue depths only allowed him to gain enough mental control to answer her question. "He doesn't know when the logs will be ready after the incident this morning. It could be weeks, maybe even a few months."

Beth nodded, her face unreadable. He needed to pretend she was a spirit—nothing but the whisper of a woman, untouchable to him. He'd already proven he couldn't control his impulses while she was around. He had to do something to keep his mind off her and his lips to himself. He would only break her heart. If pretending she was physically beyond his reach would work, then so be it.

"What do we do until then?"

Garrett pivoted and started down the trail. He waited for her to catch up before glancing back to see the disappointment show on her beautiful face. Did she want him as much as he did her? Did she love him? To find out that she felt something for him would be too much. If he could have had her for a wife, stolen her heart the way she did his, only to lose her because of his father's pride, would be too much to bear.

No.

Focus on the task, he mentally scolded himself. "We help the timber beasts. There's plenty of work to be done. Someone always needs a hand. We'll have a meeting with the boys tonight. The shave tails usually train for the drive at night, which we will do, but during the day we'll help with whoever needs a hand."

"Are there many shave tails who need to train?"

"No, just you. I'll be personally taking you through the ringer. When the time comes to take the river, you'll be ready for the bateau."

"I may seem frail in my gowns at home, but I'm no wilting miss," she boasted, tripping over a raised tree root and falling flat on her face. He flinched toward her as she fell.

"I can see that," he said, picking her up off the ground. A mistake. The line holding together his resolve tightened to its breaking point. He wanted to kiss her again. Taste the warm flavor of her mouth. Savor it.

"I can walk." She wriggled out of his arms, only to crumple straight back to the ground, clutching her ankle. "I lied. I think it's twisted."

"Let me have a look." He took a deep breath to check his wayward thoughts and bent down to adjust her leg so he could unlace the spiked boot and slip it off. He ground his teeth together against the urge to run his hands over her calf to see if her skin was as soft as her lips.

She yelped in pain when he pressed on her ankle.

"Sorry... It doesn't look too bad. I'll carry you down until we get close to where they're working, and then you can try to walk again and see how it feels." God, he was a glutton for self-punishment.

"You don't think it's bad?" She put her boot back on and laced it loosely.

He shook his head. "I've seen worse. It's not even swollen."

He swiftly swooped her up into his arms and started down the hill. Her round, soft breasts pressed against his chest when she slid one hand behind his neck, tangling her fingers in the hair at the base of his skull. The warmth from her small fingers tingled against his head and demanded his attention. Even with the fight to leave her alone raging through his body, her touch calmed the anxiety he'd felt tearing apart his insides. He needed her. Forever.

"Thank you," she whispered. Her breath tickled the base of his neck, and he remembered the feel of her mouth beneath his mere moments ago. He tucked that memory away as he descended the mountain with her wrapped warmly in his arms. His mother's lesson replayed in his mind: *A man who wears his emotions for all to see is but a fool in the eyes of a woman.*

Chapter 8

The ear-piercing squeal of the train as it rolled to a complete stop echoed off the building and trees surrounding the cook fire. Beth limped off the trailhead, following Garrett. He'd set her on her feet when they'd drawn closer to the camp, and she worked through each step until the pain was tolerable. The feel of his warm lips against her mouth flooded her thoughts, and refused to ebb. The moment her feet hit the ground her lungs could once more hold air, but the memories remained. He liked her. At least enough to kiss her. That she did not expect to experience up here on the mountain.

She tried to force away the daze she felt as she walked into camp. A mess of disorder drew her attention to the train as men jumped from the railcar and scattered. Beth wandered to where the cook stood watching the chaos with hands on hips.

The older woman flashed a look at her before settling her eyes on the rumpus at the tracks. "Ah, good, you're back. Glad Garrett didn't keep you busy all day. The train came in and my goddaughter should be onboard. Would you like to meet her?"

"I would love to," Beth lied, and faced the train as a tall blond woman emerged from a fancy caboose attached to the back of the usually dirty train.

"*That's* not her." Aunt June frowned and, with her eyes, followed the woman's progression through the camp.

"Garrett," the woman called when she neared, and headed in his direction. She sidled up to him and kissed him on both cheeks the way the French women from the bakery on Mullan Road did whenever they greeted people. Beth fought the need to copy Aunt June's critical glare.

"Funny. She doesn't sound French," she mumbled to herself.

"She's not." Aunt June shook her head in disapproval.

Beth frowned when the woman looped her arm through Garrett's elbow and stood spine straight. Who was this woman? A mere hour ago there'd been no one on earth but her and Garrett, yet now he stood next to a woman who behaved as if she were the sole reason for his existence. The woman turned to study the mill of people as if they were her loyal subjects.

Garrett flicked a glance in Beth's direction, and then down at the ground. Guilt was evident in each clipped movement. Beth was a fool.

"I'm positively ecstatic," the woman sang as they ambled closer to Beth and Aunt June. "I wanted desperately to see how this all works so I begged Papa. With a little persuasion"—she batted her eyes at Garrett—"he finally let me come. Of course, Aunt June is to be my chaperone." She sent Aunt June a sweet smile, and then turned back to Garrett. "Your father lent me the railcar to use for a home. It's much more comfortable, you know." She giggled. "Put me to work, Garrett. I've come for an adventure."

Beth's mouth ran dry from the air, and she realized she'd let it fall open at the sight of the woman. She snapped it shut. What did this woman mean to Garrett? By the way she fell on him the moment her feet touched the damp forest ground, she'd come for more than an adventure.

"*I've* come to help Aunt June." Carrie's voice permeated the fog of jealousy in Beth's brain, and she snapped her gaze to where her friend stood staring at Garrett and the blonde. Carrie turned up her nose in disgust, flipped one hand through the air, and then faced forward. "To hell with adventure."

"Carrie," Beth exclaimed, gave a quick survey to ensure no one realized her mistake, and then faced her friend. "Where'd you come from?"

Beth shot Aunt June a nervous look.

"Oh, she knows," Carrie confessed.

"True right I do, my dear." Aunt June winked. "And people say I can't keep a secret."

"When? How?" Beth asked.

"I wrote her the minute you left my parlor. I couldn't have you traipsing up here all by yourself." Carrie turned her attention to Aunt June and started to walk into her cabin. "Imagine the trouble she would get in all alone up here. I figured if she was going to get into trouble in the forest, at least she'd chosen to do it in your camp."

Aunt June clicked her tongue and laughed.

"How do you know her?" Beth followed the two women into the tiny home until they were completely shut off from the rest of the camp.

"I told you before that my godmother worked at a lumber camp." Carrie turned to Aunt June, "I swear, she never listens." She set down her bag on the bed. "June was my mother's dearest friend in school."

"Why didn't you say something?" Beth asked Aunt June.

"It was more fun this way." She chuckled. "Plus, you were determined to do things your way. I knew you wouldn't listen."

Beth's heart jumped with joy. She had found this adventure to be a little more trying than expected, but with Carrie here she could accomplish anything. She couldn't wait to show her Mother Goose's Cottage. The slugs. How the men competed for balance on the logs.

Beth sobered as reality intruded upon her thoughts.

They weren't here simply for enjoyment. They had a task. "You must help me find out who is behind the sabotage."

"That we will," Aunt June answered. "Once Carrie told me of your discovery, I decided to keep my ears open as well. Men tend to forget I'm around when they're elbow deep in elk stew. So far I've only heard a little bit of chatter, but you aren't going to like it I'm afraid."

"Why?"

"The only tidbits I've heard include your brother, Beth."

"There's no way Simon is involved."

"That's what I thought. Ain't no way that angel of a man is anything but honest." Aunt June shook her head. "Ain't no way. Only problem is, one of them Bonner boys came whisperin' something fierce to Luther. Going on about how Simon is getting knee deep involved in something. Then that Luther said he was going to take care of it."

"Take care of it how?"

"God only knows," Aunt June whispered. "But whatever happens, I hope it spares him and that handsome face of his."

Beth couldn't disguise the worry she felt. No doubt her look mimicked the one Aunt June wore as she stared at the ground.

Carrie tapped her finger on her chin. "That's it. You two seem a bit too emotional here. We need someone with a clear mind to make our decisions in the scheme. I'm taking over this spy operation. Aunt June, you keep butting into everyone's business. Beth, keep an ear open for talk amongst the men. I'll try to charm information from the men, and we'll report back to each other. We need to flush the culprit out before anyone gets hurt."

"Don't you be charming these boys too much," Aunt June chided. "Them's loggers, not city gentleman. I don't want to have to hear it from your mama when you end up hitched to a river rat…or worse."

"Of course not, Auntie. I'm a lady. The only man I'm getting hitched to has to at least have two carriages and a mansion on Higgins Street."

"Atta girl." Aunt June smiled, and then turned to Beth and lightly shoved her toward the door. "Now off with you. You have some wood to cut for tonight's fire. I see how good you're getting with that ax. Chop me a few extra pieces, and maybe I'll make a pie for after supper. Your brother loves my pie."

She was getting good with the ax. Since the day the boy Michael had shown her how to swing the thing properly, she'd taken every opportunity to chop. Her muscles screamed in protest every night as she lay weak in her bunk, but it was worth the pride she saw in both Aunt June's and Garrett's eyes. Maybe now Garrett would let her start training for the river.

* * * *

"What are you doing here, Victoria?" Garrett asked the blonde hanging on his arm. To keep from making a scene, he'd waited until the camp had cleared before addressing the issue plaguing him since the train had rolled in. Things were starting to go well with Beth. He'd gotten over his fear of talking to her, and had even kissed her. He shouldn't have, but he wouldn't take back that moment for all his springs as a logger. When he'd carried her down the mountain he'd decided to beg his father again to consider Beth for him.

Now, Victoria, with her light skin and equally pale hair, piled high in the flawless coif, stood before him. She was the perfect example of what every Jones should be, but he wasn't. His soul belonged to the mountains, and hers to the status his name would give her. He wanted to live simply, where she wanted the house on the hill. He wanted Beth. Not Victoria, the woman who he'd known his whole life. The woman who his father had joked about Garrett marrying on more than one occasion. There was no doubt why she was here. She'd come as a symbol of his father's decision.

"I told you. I've come to learn about this operation. Your father was kind enough to lend me his personal railcar for the stay, so I figured why not. It will be great fun, don't you think?"

"What do you plan on doing here? You aren't built to survive in the forest, let alone ride the river or even chop wood."

Victoria laughed and waved toward the camp. "Oh no, silly. I'll help out here, and watch how you men do things. I need to know the logging process if I'm to help my future husband run the mill once my father retires, but I wouldn't be caught dead doing such mannish work. That other woman who came on the train with me said she was coming to help the cook. I'll lend them a hand. Things around here could use a lady's touch."

"How long do you plan to stay?" *Hopefully not long.* What was he supposed to do with two incorrigible women? Beth, and the feelings she evoked when near, were hard enough to deal with. The last thing he needed was Victoria and all of the fears that surfaced with her arrival. With no wifely prospects, and no time to court, he'd agreed to his father's suggestion for an arranged marriage. He'd made a huge mistake.

"Oh, I don't know," she answered. "Until I get bored, I suppose."

Garrett snapped his focus back on Victoria. "You must stay in camp. You cannot wander off."

She waved off his concern. "I wouldn't dream of it. I plan to be by your side or here in camp. There are too many wild things in the forest."

"Garrett." He heard Simon call and turned around as his friend neared. "I need to speak with you."

"Of course." Garrett turned to Victoria and bowed his head. "If you'll excuse me."

With a proper curtsy from her, he turned to leave, but stopped. "Tell Aunt June that I sent you. She'll get you set up."

He followed in Simon's wake as they picked their way toward the lake.

Simon peered over Garrett's shoulder as if checking for something, or someone, and then leapt off the trail over a small brush, motioning for Garrett to follow. When vegetation shrouded them in secrecy, Simon spoke, "I finally found Jessip after you went up to talk to Teddy."

Damn. If he hadn't been so focused on Beth, he would have been able to talk to the man and demand answers. "What did he say?"

"He heard about the cut boom log and wanted to let us know it wasn't him."

"Then who was it?" *Who cut the damned rope?* The question had burned in his mind since they found the scene.

"I don't know. I'll keep my ears open."

"Keep your eyes open as well. If someone is trying to stop the drive, they aren't done causing accidents. The last thing we need is a fatal disaster." The safety of the men was a priority in the Big Mountain Lumber Mill camp. Throughout the company's history, there had been three fatal catastrophes, none of which could have been avoided. Big Mountain would not stand for a death caused by the negligent greed of an inside man.

* * * *

"Isn't Garrett a fine man?" the blond woman asked and drew close to where Beth and Carrie stood. Beth stacked the cut wood near the cook fire and tried not to be noticed when the woman extended her hand like a queen to a subject. "I'm Victoria Harrison."

"We met on the train platform, remember? You climbed in the fancy caboose, and I rode with the crew." Carrie smiled and, with exaggerated movements no doubt geared toward shocking the prim woman, shook her hand in a very unladylike way. Beth snickered, but kept her focus on the wood.

"Oh...yes," Victoria said hesitantly, and yanked her hand to her chest. "I remember. But I was talking to your beau here." She extended her hand to Beth. "I'm Victoria. Garrett's...well, goodness, I suppose you could call us *friends*. If my parents have anything to do with it, though, we'll be wed by the end of summer, and running this operation together."

Beth forced a smile and shook her hand, but in truth she wanted to dunk the ninny-headed wench into the dirty wash bin.

"What do you do here?" Victoria asked Beth.

"I'm a riverman."

Victoria squealed. "You work for Garrett? Oh, how delightful. I'll bet it's great fun to watch him work all day. I'll bet he's an excellent boss." She giggled. "You know, sometimes I wish I were a man so I could chop wood and ride the river. You know all those masculine things they do."

"Sometimes Brent wishes he were a man, too," Carrie said and stifled a laugh with the back of her hand.

"Oh, aren't you wicked." Victoria giggled with Carrie, completely ignorant of the inside joke.

What a ninny head. Beth turned back to stacking the wood and couldn't help but loathe the cackling hen before her. Not that she had a reason to. So Garrett had kissed her unexpectedly. One kiss didn't mean anything. It was probably because of the enchanting atmosphere of the flower-speckled meadow at Mother Goose's Cottage. Somewhere with the lasting fog of her dreams, it meant something more.

"If you'll excuse me." Beth picked up the ax from a nearby stump. "I have to be getting back to work. There's still a few hours left before dark."

After a regal nod from Victoria, Beth took her leave. If she had any luck at all, she'd find the men at the raft and would be able to get a start on actually training for the drive.

She fled before Carrie could find a reason to make her stay. She gave a forced gloating smile and ran through the brush, taking a shortcut to the trail. Her empty chest ached. Hollowed out by the promise of tomorrow destroyed by the reality of today.

The quarter-mile trail wound through the dense trees at the base of the hills and away from the main logging site to open up yards from the bank of Seeley Lake. She appreciated the few moments she'd had with the women of camp, but when Aunt June watched over her, as directed by Garrett, she felt stifled. With Garrett and Simon, she felt protected, but free.

She emerged from the trees as a log flew down the chute with flames whipping out from behind as it fell and landed with a frightening crack. The wood tumbled down the rollway to rest with a pile of logs waiting to be added to the raft.

"Someone run up there and tell Teddy to grease the chute!" Simon shouted from where he stood next to Garrett. "Damned man never greases the chute. I swear he thinks wood is flameproof. He's all horse and wench."

Garrett shifted and turned a slight shade of red. Odd. He'd never before seemed embarrassed when she was around. Arrogant, maybe. Playful at times, but never uncomfortable. Was it the kiss that made him nervous, or the arrival of Victoria with all her bewitching plans?

"We have a few hours left of light," she said, hoping he'd understand her silent suggestion. She licked her lips to keep from biting them. She needed one more moment alone with Garrett, and what better way to do that than to train for the log drive.

The color in his face faded, and his shoulders dropped a little. He motioned toward the shoreline. "We can take the bateau out. You'll need to get used to maneuvering the boat."

"What are the rest of the men doing?"

"Since the drive is delayed, they're finding other jobs around the camp. Most are helping the fallers and buckers. You and I will work to get you physically ready."

Another flaming log shot down the chute.

"Goddamn it, Teddy!" Simon roared and started up the hill. "Grease that damn chute!"

She followed Garrett to the bank where a long boat, mirroring a split peapod from her nana's garden, sat waiting.

"Get in. I'll push it out," he ordered.

She did as directed and before she knew it, they were swaying with the waves. She watched the easy way he handled the stick, the calm approach to maneuvering the boat when needed, and the way he stared at the water. Not once did he glance up in her direction. He prodded at the bottom of the lake with a long pole, and propelled them forward. "This is the peavey. It's perfect for the shallow waters of a river, but only works so well in a lake."

When the water became too deep, he slid the pole into the boat and took up the oars. They rode in silence until he stopped somewhere in the middle of the water.

"You're going to need to be able to row in case something comes up and I can't be the point man in the boat. Watch how I do it." He demonstrated, still keeping his gaze everywhere else but on her.

If he wanted to pretend the kiss never happened, then she would go along. Except she didn't want to pretend. She followed his gaze over the water to watch the shoreline slide past her vision in slow motion. The kiss had happened, and it shot fire down to her stomach and out through her fingers. A feeling new, raw, and a bit frightening.

Best to concentrate on the training. She turned to watch him work the boat. She could do that, no problem. Garrett's shirt grew taut around his chest with each movement. His muscles rippled beneath the worn fabric. This wasn't going to be easy, but it looked doable. With Garrett as her guide, she refused to show weakness. She'd prove her worthiness as a riverman, and woman. He offered her his seat with the wave of his hand. "Now you take us back in."

The boat rocked violently when she stood. Beth grabbed on to the sides as she wobbled to the back of the boat and picked up the oars. She dipped them into the water, only to have the force of the pull cause the oars to flip and smack the side of the boat as if they were the wings of a gangly duckling trying to fly. "Sorry."

"The boat's not damaged. Just keep trying."

She did it again. This time she dug deeper. "It's going!"

"Good. Now try to make it go straight."

The horizon began to spin and she glanced at the water to find they moved in a circle. She bit her lip and focused hard on the task.

After a few minutes of concentrated silence, Garrett interrupted. "You're stronger than you look."

"It's from years of washing my brother's dirty clothes. It's a back-breaking duty. He's a filthy man."

"I hardly think laundry is enough of an undertaking to give you strength to row a bateau after days of splitting wood. Most women would have shirked the moment they had to heave an ax."

"I'm not most women. I'm getting good at the ax."

"I noticed." His face flushed, and he sat quiet for a moment before speaking again, "Where'd you get that scar on your wrist?"

Beth looked at her arm. "The carriage accident that killed my parents."

"I'm sorry. Had I known it was such a personal subject, I wouldn't have asked."

"No. It's fine. To be honest, I barely remember it, remember them. I was only five when the accident happened. This is all I have left of them." She took one last look at the mark, and then dug the oars into the water to row toward the shore. He reclined back once more, the awkward silence thick for a moment before she interrupted the peace. "Tell me about your family."

"My father is consumed with his job," he said. "And my mother with her place in society. I was raised to be concerned with both."

"You seem to love what you do."

"I do, but I won't be doing it much longer. This is my last season here. I haven't told anyone this, and I'm not certain I should now, but if you're anything like your brother I know you can keep a secret. After the rivers get low, I will take over my father's business."

"That's good, isn't it?"

He gave her a smile that didn't reach his eyes. "I prefer to be on the river, but duty calls, and you can't ignore duty."

She studied the notch in the wood on the seat in front of her. Her own reservations of her future churned up with the gentle rock of the boat. "No. You can't ignore duty."

"Why do you want to ride the river so bad with the Devil May Cares?" His voice changed to one of concern. "Why won't you content yourself with riding the cook boat?"

"I need to find the traitor. I can't do that if I'm stuck in the Missoula camp. If I'm with you, I can see the men from the other camps as well. Just because the man was at the Missoula train station, doesn't necessarily mean he lives in our camp."

"I suppose you're right, but do you see why I am worried? I can't even count the broken limbs I've mended on the drives, let alone the battered bodies I've tended to at night. We risk hypothermia and death, on top of surface wounds. I couldn't bear to see a body as pale and perfect as yours beaten and bruised from wayward logs. I'd feel like I haven't done my job as a man."

"I won't blame you for anything happening to me. I understand the risks I'm taking and the position I'm putting you in, and I am sorry. I can't go back now, though. Not with the traitor stalking the camp. I couldn't face my life at home knowing I was a failure here."

"What is awaiting you at home?"

"Duty and honor. Like you."

"Two fools striving for a semblance of heaven, but destined for something else."

Beth dug both oars into the water and finally brought the boat straight. If Garrett could relate to her reasoning, or at least understand, then she wouldn't feel so guilty. If he were indeed destined to give up the life he loved for the life he was destined to have, then he too needed a season to remember. Perhaps she could help him to get just that.

Chapter 9

"For the next week or two, we'll be helping the timber beasts replenish the logs that were lost when the boom was cut." Garrett stood tall, a small movement that never failed to cause his men to pay attention when he spoke. "We need to get a raft down the river, and soon. We can't do that if we don't have the logs. I'm not going to send a half turn to the mill. It's a full load or none at all."

A ripple of movement swayed through the crowd of men, both Bonner and Missoula teams, as they nodded their agreement and firmed their jaws. At this moment, he couldn't be more proud of them. There was nothing more important than their pride, and pride demanded an exceptional job in whatever task they took on. That was why they were chosen to be rivermen, and why they were the best in the industry. Pride.

"The shave tail will work with me so I can train him. The rest of you pair off as you wish. We'll report to The Bull of the Woods today and work until he says we aren't needed anymore. You've all had a go at those jobs when you were wet-nosed loggers. There's no reason you can't show the timber beasts a thing or two while you work."

Crooked smiles played at his men's lips. They were all seasoned lumbermen and loved to show off, which was the reaction Garrett hoped to get by ruffling their feathers with a challenge. With skills to match their determination, the rivermen and timber beasts could replenish the raft in no time, and the logs would be on their way to the mill within a fortnight.

Garrett signaled for the men to precede him up the trail, and then he followed. His only worry was Beth. She could barely heave an ax. There was no way she would be able to chop down a hundred-year-old pine.

Spotting her in the throng of men, he picked up his speed and grabbed her forearm. Urging her back with gentle pressure, he slowed to a walk that would put the men far enough ahead that he wouldn't be overheard. "You stay with me at all times. The Grove is incredibly dangerous. You and I will find The Bull, and then we'll claim an area far enough away that we'll be out of sight from prying eyes."

Beth's vein pulsed at the base of her neck, a sign he came to realize was her only nervous tell. Garrett tried to hold back a smile. It was a good thing she didn't gamble. She would lose everything at the tables.

They crested the top of the hill and found The Bull on the outskirts of The Deck, talking with the team controlling the horses. Garrett neared, and The Bull turned to him with a grunted greeting.

"My men are here to help," Garrett said.

"So I see. With your help, we can get double the sticks to the water's edge. We should get the raft replaced in no time."

"How are the new steel wedges working?"

"I just passed them out this morning. We'll find out today."

Garrett nodded. The steel wedges sent up from the mill should speed production and save the loggers' backs—at least that was the opinion of the vagrant timber beasts he'd met in town before the season began.

"Brent and I will get started, and we'll see you at quittin' time."

The Bull gave a halfhearted salute and turned back to the horses.

Garrett did a quick survey of the men working around the site, handed Beth the wooden sledgehammer and wedge from the supply wagon, grabbed a few more tools, and then headed up a trail leading to a tree far away from any other faller team. "Falling a tree is a taxing job. I'll do most of the work."

"I'd like to help. I didn't come all the way up here to the heart of the forest so I can be coddled and pushed to the back."

"All right. You can help." Garrett turned away from her and smiled. One thing was clear, the woman had guts and a large amount of determination. A woman like that would stand next to a man during even the worst of times. A woman like her was exactly what he couldn't have, but someone he desperately wanted. "But if you need a rest, take it. Don't push yourself too much. You've been through a lot already the last few days."

"Don't worry. I won't try to be a hero."

Off in the distance a group of men stood huddled around a man near a large pine. Beth stopped. "What are they doing?"

"My guess is making a bet. A good faller can place the tree anywhere he wants within a few feet. Oftentimes the men will wage a week's pay on the accuracy of the faller."

"Do you think he'll make it?" Beth asked, gesturing toward the man now chopping a slice from the large pine tree.

"Wall was the best faller on the team before he became a riverman."

"That's Wall?" She squinted to try to see the man clearly from where she stood.

"Watch." Garrett turned to the group of men as Wall chopped the face of the tree. After the back cut, he slid in the steel wedge and took up the wooden sledgehammer, only to have it bounce back and almost hit him in the face. Wall adjusted his grip.

"He's getting tired." Beth commented.

"No. It's something else. I think it's the wedge with the maul. They aren't working together. I'll have to let Simon know so he can figure out what to do next."

After a few well-placed hits to the wedge, the tree fell, and the men burst into good-natured shouts and congratulated Wall with slaps to the back of his shoulder.

"I take it he won the bet." Beth turned to him.

Garrett simply nodded and motioned for them to continue. Once at the tree, he tossed down his load, and Beth did the same.

"We'll use the ax to cut a slice out of one side of the tree. Sort of like an odd shaped triangle." He turned the ax in his hand as he studied the bark. "And then we'll do a back cut, and then use the wedge to tip the tree."

"Where should I stand?"

"Stay behind me. If I run, you run, but don't head out toward the forest. Watch the tree and run sideways. That is the fastest way to avoid being crushed beneath the pine."

"Okay." Beth's voice was shaky. Her nervous confidence melted his heart. A man would never get bored with her around.

Garrett began to chop the slice out of the side of the tree. He was halfway done when Beth stopped him with a gentle hand on his shoulder. "Can I have a go?"

He handed her the ax—handle first. "Can you heave it?"

She nodded.

With a smile, he stepped back as she swung the heavy ax and attacked the base of the tree with all the subtlety of an angry bear, but she was good. As good as any man of her small stature could ever be. He let a smile stretch across his face when she gritted her teeth and wrinkled her forehead in concentration. Silly as it was, he could watch her determined expression for the rest of his life and never grow tired of it. How different she was from the prim Victoria. Never one to make too many expressions for fear of wrinkles. Once Beth whittled the trunk down to where he needed it, he cleared his throat to get her attention.

"Now we need to do the backcut. This is where it gets difficult." He picked up the long saw and walked to the other side. "We're going to use the saw, take up both sides, and move it back and forth. This is a might tricky 'cause the one we got stuck with is a misery whip. Miserable to use 'cause it's duller than a wallflower. Are you up for it?"

Her perfectly plump lips turned up in a smile that proved how truly excited she was over doing this job—a task that would tax even the strongest of men. Elizabeth Sanders had guts and grit to rival that of a hard-pressed cowboy. Oh what he wouldn't give to see her smile like this every moment of her life. His thought drifted to Victoria, tucked safely in camp, away from danger. She was boring, but perfect in every other wifely aspect. However, he hated being bored.

* * * *

Beth peeked around the small clearing as she neared the outhouses. Yesterday she'd chopped down a tree with Garrett. It had been the most exhilarating time of her life—the giant tree slamming to the ground simply because she cut it. No wonder men liked this sort of work. It made them feel invincible.

Now, she had to find a decent lavatory. For the last few weeks, she'd managed to use the one with the moon—designated for women—but today the men lingered nearby. She couldn't let them know she wasn't the man she pretended to be. She'd have to use the one with the star. Beth scrunched her nose at the thought and tried not to dance as she scurried through the door, almost puking when it shut behind her.

Therapeutic papers littered the ground with what she hoped were muddy footprints. Flies buzzed around the soiled wooden seat, and a large brown spot in the shape of a three-legged horse stained the walls. She gagged at the smell and ran back out. When her brother had mentioned a dirty outhouse before they came, he wasn't exaggerating.

"Why would you go in there?" Blue called. "You're damned brave if you go in there. We all just piss in the bushes, or use the women's, but don't tell Aunt June. She'd tan our hides a good one."

"Thanks." She gave a halfhearted smile and rushed into the much cleaner women's toilet. She was in the middle of doing her business when the wall next to her began to thump, and the outhouse began to shake.

What the hell is going on? Male laughter floated through the moon-shaped hole.

"Just push it over," Dick shouted.

"No way. If we get it dirty, Aunt June will whip us with her spoon. We'll just tip it."

She grabbed onto the walls to steady herself—pants tangled around her ankles—as the small building shook. Her heart pounded against her ribcage. This was it. She was going to get caught, and in the most embarrassing way. She had to get her pants up and get out!

"What in Hades name is going on over here?" Aunt June's voice boomed through the thin wooden walls. Beth sighed with relief and hastily yanked up her britches, tucked in her shirt, and stepped outside. The old woman stood next to the men and glared.

"The shave tail used the outhouse we made for the ladies. Ain't no man gonna go around acting like a woman and not get razzed for it."

"Not on my watch. How long has it been since you boys cleaned out the men's toilet anyway?"

Wall scratched his head. "I can't rightly say, Aunt June. A while, I guess."

"A while, you guess? Well, I guess you boys earned yourself privy duty. I didn't have you make men and women's toilets so you could use the bushes. Get yourselves on in there and clean it out. And while you're at it, move both outhouses over there." She pointed to where she wanted them placed.

"Aunt June." The men grumbled like a group of young boys scolded by their mothers. "We're rivermen, not chambermaids."

"I expect it will be done within the hour." She gave a wicked grin and marched toward the camp.

"Hey, shave tail," Wall called out. "You get to scrub the shit pit."

Beth couldn't help but widen her eyes, without a care if the men saw, when she thought of the nasty waste piled high below the lid. There was no way she could clean it.

Beth turned and ran after Aunt June.

"Thanks," she breathed when she caught up to her.

The old cook emerged through the brush next to her cabin and chuckled. "No need to thank me. I wasn't about to let a silly prank destroy the one luxury I have out here."

Aunt June plucked a bucket from the ground next to the side of her house and handed it to Beth, and then grabbed a handful of torn rags from inside her cabin. "Off you go, now. Don't forget to run down to the lake and fill the bucket with water."

She gave a humored smile that made Beth's stomach drop. The cleaning of an outhouse waited, and no one was going to prevent it from happening, not even Aunt June.

Like a child doing afternoon chores for her mother, she trudged to the lake, filled the water, and lumbered back to the crude privies.

"Hurry up, shave tail!" Blue yelled when she neared. By the time she returned, the men had dug two holes and were in the process of shifting the outhouses over the fresh pits. "We want to be able to wash up in the lake before chow."

Once they moved both toilets, she plopped the bucket down between the weathered buildings, and prayed that Garrett would come and rescue her. What was he doing, anyway? After lunch that day, he'd ordered her to stay in camp with Aunt June, and disappeared with her brother. She wanted to go back out on the water like she'd done the last few days.

"Shit pit!" Blue called out and handed her a water soaked rag. "Get as far in as you can, all the way up to your shoulder. When we're done filling in the old pits, we'll be back to help."

The men all chuckled and walked away as Beth turned her face down in disgust. How was she going to get through this?

She yanked the blue handkerchief from around her neck and tied it about her face, sucked in a deep breath to boost her determination, and marched into the women's outhouse, gagging as she walked through the weathered door. She stepped back outside to catch a breath of fresh forest air, only to watch Wall and the other rivermen turn and laugh at the sight of her. She couldn't let them beat her.

Beth pulled up her pants, and trudged back inside, ready to prove to herself and the rivermen that she could handle whatever task they threw her way. Even the outhouse.

* * * *

"Who do you think is behind the attacks?" Simon asked as he hacked away at the base of a large pine tree. He stopped and leaned on the handle, breathing hard from the exertion.

"Someone who needs Big Mountain Lumber Mill to fail. My guess is it has something to do with the new contract to Boilson Mines." Garrett lowered his eyes to a concentrated glare, took the ax from his friend, and continued where he left off. "The thousand will come to the man who actually destroys the company when the season ends and Big Mountain fails to keep good on their contract."

"So this is all about the contract?"

Garrett nodded. "The big bugs from the rival mills are behind the thousand-dollar prize money, and probably more. Ever since Big Mountain signed with the Boilson Mining Company, the mill's had nothing but problems."

"We need to find out who the other person is before anything big happens." Simon took a shot at the ax again. "I've been poking my nose around and asking questions like you suggested, but so far no one's talking."

"I figured as much. I paid the Bonner kid, Michael, to keep an eye out and report anything suspicious to me. I'm watching the operations closely as well. Hopefully the kid is inconspicuous enough to overhear something that the culprit might otherwise not say in the presence of an adult. I've an idea to at least prepare us in case something does happen, but first we need to talk with your sister." Garrett stepped away, and pulled on his friend's shirtfront to get him to do the same, as the tree fell. "There's one for Teddy to take. Let's go find Beth."

Garrett heaved the ax over his shoulder, and rushed down the trail.

"Okay," Simon said slowly. "What does she have to do with all this?"

"She knows something, and we need to know what."

Much to Garrett's relief, Simon followed the rest of the way in silence. The last thing he needed was his friend digging too deeply into his and Beth's relationship, and finding out he'd stolen a kiss from her, and then come down the mountain to find out his father had sent him a potential fiancée, bursting all thought of asking for Beth's hand once more. *God.* He felt like a fool. A failure. A woman like Beth deserved better than a liberty-taking coward like him anyway. He had to control himself around her.

The scene before them when they entered the meadow would have been comical, if it weren't for his growing desire for Beth. She stood in the midst of the men covered in filth, holding a bucket and pile of rags. Her chin quivered, but she made a valiant attempt to appear unaffected as the men razzed her. The same way they did to any man wishing to be a part of the Devil May Cares. Except she wasn't a man. She was Beth. Had any one of his men known her true identity, they'd trip over themselves to give her the moon, right after they ganged up to beat the tarnation out of him for allowing her to be on the river crew.

"What's going on here?" he demanded. A quick glance at Simon, and Garrett knew he had to take control. The man was hell-bent on defending his sister and ready to pound the first man to speak. One thing was certain, even though Simon couldn't be trusted with the farmer's daughter—or even the mayor's wife—he was fiercely loyal to his sister.

"We're just teaching the shave tail here the ropes." Wall and the Devil May Cares chuckled at their shared joke. "Your cousin needs a good whoopin', Simon. He's a little weak in the shoulders." Wall punched the back of Beth's shoulder and caused her to topple forward. She caught herself with her hands before her face hit the grass. She struggled on to her knees. Her small shoulders shook as she stayed in that position, head bowed, and no doubt fighting back tears.

"Mush-headed bastard!" Simon shouted and jumped onto Wall with fists flying.

Wall ducked, but not fast enough. Simon's fist slammed into his jaw, sending blood spurting on the green grass as the two men toppled to the ground.

Beth stood to watch, and flinched several times as if she planned to intervene, but thankfully didn't. As long as she stood back, the men wouldn't look twice at the tears streaming down her filthy cheeks. He needed to get her out of the meadow before the men took notice.

A quick study of the occupied men, and Garrett grabbed Beth's hand to tow her a few feet into the brush. The vegetation gave him enough coverage to run an eye over her body.

"My clothes are ruined." Her voice shook with the tears she now let fall. "I tried to do what a man would. I tried to fight my way out, but when they tipped me upside down over the hole. I...I swore at them. I punched Wall, but I don't think he felt it. He didn't flinch or try to whip me for punching him." She gave an angry growl. "Those mudsills."

"Follow me." If it had been a man in her position, he would laugh. Hell, he had laughed in the past when they did that to others. Normally he'd tell the shave tail to muck up or go home. Testosterone-filled days made events such as what just transpired an everyday occurrence, but she was a woman.

He led her to the edge of the water, and moved the ax to his other hand when he let go of her fingers. "Stay here until I get back."

He waited until she nodded, and then ran to the cabin, leaning the ax against the post of his bed as he walked inside. Normally he wouldn't touch the personal belongings of a woman, but this couldn't be helped. He ripped open the top of her satchel and grabbed what he needed.

He'd almost made it out of camp when someone called his name. He turned as Victoria sauntered up to him. "Where have you been? I'm utterly bored. I tried to help Auntie June, but she shooed me away." Victoria's bottom lip jutted out in a well-practiced pout. She looped her arm through his and leaned into his side. In town, he'd been more than happy to escort

Victoria around at the request of his parents. He'd taken her to balls and teas, even once to the county fair, but now he desperately needed to get back to the lake, and her presence was more of an annoyance than anything else.

"When I return, we'll take up a game of poker."

She released his arm and clapped excitedly. "Oh, yes, that would be positively wicked. I'll be just like the woman who won the poker tournament on the Louisiana paddle boat last year." She tapped her index finger on her rose-petal-pink lips. "What was her name? Miss Masterson. She was a wicked, audacious woman. Don't you think, Garrett?"

He dipped his head once in response to her meaningless prattle. "If you'll excuse me, I have something pressing I need to attend to." And being away from her was one of those things.

"Of course. Business awaits." She gave a regal nod so he did the same, and ran to the lake where Beth tried valiantly to hide behind a large bush. Tension ebbed from his core at the sight of her—even covered in human waste, she was more the woman he envisioned when he thought of how his life should be. Not the woman he'd just left at the camp. Fate was a jealous shrew with a thirst for vengeance.

"Come on then. Hop in the boat. I'll take you somewhere you can wash up."

"A bath?"

"Yes."

Standing tall, she took a deep breath and started toward the bateau. The ever-present determination she sported restored as she trudged to the water's edge and climbed in the boat. She sat with a pin-straight back like a princess awaiting a carriage ride to the village—only a princess wouldn't be caught dead in a pair of Simon's old canvas pants and spiked boots, an outfit she somehow wore with elegance. If the men on his crew hadn't figured out by now that she was a woman, they were daft fools. How would they react once they found out?

Chapter 10

The hard wooden seat dug into Beth's tailbone as she tried to touch the boat as little as possible while Garrett rowed. Her clothes were stained with things no woman should have to encounter, but she supposed she'd brought this on herself. "Where are we headed?"

"You'll see," was all he said. He dug the oar into the water, turning the boat toward a distant shore.

The scene as they floated north following the lake's shoreline calmed her and let her relax enough to enjoy the silent serenity of the tree-speckled, emerald-green mountains. Garrett gave her a sad smile. Well, she didn't want him to feel sorry for her. She had to man up. They rode in silence, except for the gentle lap of the water against the side of the boat and the screech of an eagle off in the distance.

She studied the sun to gauge the time as they rode. Half of an hour ticked by before he angled the boat into a small cove across the lake from the logging camp.

Garrett leapt into the water and pulled the bateau onto the shore enough that it wouldn't escape into the lake without them. "There's a nice little area past the tall grass where you can bathe." He reached into the bottom of the boat, pulled out the handful of clothes, and unfolded them to reveal her bar of soap. "I won't look, promise."

"Thank you."

"I figured you haven't had the luxury since before you came to camp. My mother used to say that a woman's reputation is as unsoiled as the bath she took that day. I know you're not supposed to be seen as a woman right now, but I figured you'd like a little more than a sponge bath in the outhouse." He slid his gaze over her dirty clothes.

"How did you know that's how I've been bathing?" Beth bit her bottom lip. She'd made a habit of sneaking into the outhouse with a wet rag at night in order to avoid the prying eyes of the men, certain no one knew about her clandestine outings.

"It's my duty. I swore to watch over you, and I can't do that if I don't know where you are."

"You followed me?"

"For your protection."

She smiled and motioned toward her filthy clothes. "I'm going to—"

"Of course," he cut her next words off, and extended his hand in the direction she should go. "I'll be here."

A quick look back down the grass-covered trail proved he didn't follow, so she stripped off her clothes like she would if ants had taken residence in her britches. She chewed on her lips when she plucked the bar of soap from the pile of fresh clothes. She'd chosen her most masculine soap when she came, but it still smelled of honey and lemon. A fragrance the men might notice, especially since most of them smelled like the inside of a hog barn.

She'd chance it for a bath.

The cold water gave her goose pimples, but she didn't care. She dipped down until the surface covered her breasts. With a sigh, she leaned back and let the cold water soak her body.

After a while, the water grew unbearable, so she washed and dressed. It was truly amazing how one little action, such as taking a bath, could boost her confidence and determination.

Garrett squatted by a fire built in a small pit made with large rocks. She neared, and he stood to wipe his hands on his pants. "I figured you would want to burn the dirty laundry. I can send for another pair of clothes, since you only brought the two pairs."

Beth peered down at the pile of soiled cloth, wrapped in her long-john underwear—the only article of clothing that was even remotely clean. Garrett's jacket she held with two fingers. "I've ruined your coat. I'll buy you a new one when we get into town. I promise."

"Burn that when the fire gets hot enough. You can have this one." He took off his last coat and waited for her to toss the pile down on the ground, and then he wrapped the jacket around her shoulders.

"Thank you." She smiled. She wasn't used to the small considerations. If she were here with Simon, he'd simply let her suffer in her one set of clothes. It was nice to be taken care of in the little ways. Simon had always charged in and beat the tar out of anyone who threatened her, but he never thought of the little things in life. "That would be wonderful. Thank you."

He tipped one side of his mouth up in a half grin, yanked a deteriorated log near the fire, and sat. "I'm sorry things aren't going as well as you'd like. There's a lot about this summer that is unusual, to say the least."

"Like what?" The tone in his voice made her heart melt with the need to make whatever troubles he had disappear, and she'd been one of those troubles since she'd come.

He tossed a small stick into the fire and shook his head. "Nothing you need to worry about."

"I find talking out my problems helps me deal with them."

He gave a crooked smile. "All right, but you've got to swear not to tell a soul. At least until I figure out who's behind it, and what to do."

"I swear," she promised.

"There's a bounty of sorts out for the log drive this summer."

"What do you mean?"

"I've some inside information that some of the other mills have offered to pay a thousand dollars to anyone willing to stop the log drive. It seems there is at least one person in the camps willing to do just that." He tipped his head toward her. "And the information you gave me at Mother Goose's Cottage confirmed everything we've been told."

"Who else has told you about the plot?"

"A man named Jessip from the Bonner crew approached us, but I don't think it was him. He's the one who let us know about the deal in the first place. I've a feeling that whoever's behind the mishap is about to do something drastic; something that could have dire repercussions on the company, or even kill one of the loggers. Even the slightest misstep up here could lead to utter disaster. A huge incident could have catastrophic consequences."

"You're certain Jessip hasn't been causing the accidents?" If she could get near the man, hear him talk, maybe this whole mess would be over. Maybe she could go home. But then she wouldn't be able to wake every morning and see Garrett. The man who had stolen her heart with a kiss, and then grown distant the moment Victoria had slithered into camp.

"As certain as I am that you look quite endearing with your hair spiked like that." He didn't make eye contact with her when he spoke, but kept his gaze on the dirt between his feet. *Thank goodness.* Her cheeks flamed with a heat as hot as the fire in the pit, and her heartbeat doubled in speed.

"So he's already almost killed someone with the widowmaker?" she asked.

"The widowmaker was an accident. The boom logs, now those were intentional."

"How can I help? If I can do anything to expose the traitor, I will. I'll do whatever you ask."

"You're a rare woman." He spread his legs out in front of him and relaxed against an old tree branch that jutted out the top of the log, but the vein at the base of his neck pulsed frantically. "What can you tell me about the man you saw on the platform?"

Beth circled the fire and sat next to him on the part of the weathered log that wouldn't cave under her weight. Did he still have feelings for her, or was he nervous to be alone with a woman who wasn't his fiancée? More likely the latter. If she were engaged, she'd not want to be put in a difficult situation like the one she just put Garrett in by allowing the men to best her at the outhouse.

Stop it, Beth, she mentally chided herself. Chances are he was anxious to get the traitor, and it had nothing to do with her. She shook her head to clear it. "His voice wasn't deep, but not high pitched either. He had a very slight accent, but only on certain words. Like he was from the North."

"A lot of the men are from the North."

"Far North." She pinched a blade of grass between her fingers and began to tear it apart. "Sorry I can't tell you more."

"And his features?"

"It's difficult to say." *Because I didn't see him.* She left that last part out. What if Garrett knew she didn't actually know what the man looked like? He'd put a stop to it all and send her packing. She had to play along with her lie or risk everything she'd worked for. Only problem was, she hated lying to him.

Garrett ran his hands through his hair, and then dropped them to his lap. "You may remember something else later. We'll keep an ear out. If I hear someone that has a voice with a deep timbre and a northern accent, I'll let you know."

"A medium timbre," she corrected, but uncertainty niggled in the back of her mind. Did she still remember the voice? She thought she'd never forget, but now she didn't know. How long could she pretend to have seen the man before Garrett realizes she's only telling half of the truth?

"Right." He nodded, curtly. "A medium timbre. If I remember anyone matching that voice description, we'll go have a casual conversation with him, and you can see if he is the one you saw."

He doesn't believe me. She fought the need to bite her lip. "What do we do after we identify him?"

"*We* do nothing. You go home. I will take care of it from there. I don't want you getting any more involved than necessary. I wouldn't be letting you dig your pretty little nose this far in if we had any other options."

"You think my nose is pretty?" She touched the tip of her nose with her middle finger. Never before had a man complimented her nose. Such an odd feature to praise, but flattering, nonetheless.

His answer was a blush that made his tanned skin color. She recognized the feeling. It mimicked her own. Although he'd fought her coming, he'd let her in. Accepted her as much as he could into his world, and kissed her. A kiss she would never forget. Would he do it again?

"I know how difficult it is for you to let me help." She tossed her soiled clothes into the fire. The fabric sizzled, and the flames licked at the material until black holes burned through the middle and spread. "You're used to being the one to carry the burden of others, aren't you? Have you always been so protective?"

"I find people tend to need looking after whenever I'm around. It's a natural reaction to want to help."

"Not all people find helping others an important aspect of life."

"Would that all people believed life was worth protecting, then maybe the world wouldn't be in a constant state of turmoil." The lines on his face grew taut. The look not one to encourage a romantic moment like that in the meadow.

Her rapid heartbeat slowed. What sort of woman would she be if she encouraged him to kiss her again when he was beyond her reach? *Keep it together, Beth. Focus on why you came.* "I can't argue with logic so profound. It's endearing."

"Most people don't think me endearing." He poked at the fire with a stick. "The only people who enjoy my company are my servants and my team. I tend to put others off. I can be a bit controlling at times."

"You don't say." She playfully bumped him with her shoulder. "Some people need a firm hand to guide them."

He gave a slow smile, and his eyes clouded as if he harbored a secret. He flexed his hand and grasped it with his other. "Do you need a firm hand to guide you?"

"What do you think?" *Oh, God.* What was she doing? *Leave it be, Beth.*

"I think you do. You need someone who can guide you, but let you be who you are without getting into trouble."

Silence flowed like molasses in winter between them until Garrett stood and walked to the other side of the fire. The only sound she heard was the rushing of her blood past her ears. Why couldn't she forget the way his lips felt over hers, or the strength of his hands as he carried her down the mountain? Maybe she was a ninny after all. Just like Victoria and the rest of the husband-hunting women back in Missoula.

Dawn Luedecke

Garrett ran his hands through his hair, and turned to face her. "About the other day at Mother Goose's Cottage."

He stopped talking so she waited patiently for him to continue. Her heart pounded in response. The other day she'd wanted the kiss. The one memory carried her through the pain of the last few days with Victoria dogging Garrett's every move in camp. She was lost.

Garrett studied the ground and then the treetops, but remained silent.

"Yes," she prompted, not knowing what she wanted him to say. He loved her? He was sorry, and to move on? Something.

"Why haven't you said anything to me about the incident? I thought you would have at least slapped me or berated me, told your brother and had him challenge me. It was a mistake to kiss you. I shouldn't have taken advantage of you like that, but I couldn't stop myself. I needed to feel you beneath my hands. Taste your mouth." He took a step closer. "I still feel that need. The urge was too great last time, but you have to prevent this from ever happening again. I don't know if I can stay away from you like I know I must."

"Oh." Her breath grew shallow. What was she to respond to such a statement? How could she stop him when she didn't even want to? The kiss had been like a boot to the gut, but in a pleasant way. Until Victoria had shown up. When she'd laid eyes on the buxom blonde, an unpleasant heel—like the one Victoria wore when she got off the train—slammed into her gut. "By the tone of your voice, I thought you were going to apologize like men are apt to do in such circumstances." She gave him a reassuring smile. "I didn't think it appropriate to interfere with you and Victoria. I'm not that kind of woman."

He drew back and creased his eyebrows. "Victoria?"

"Yes, Victoria."

"You've got it all wrong, Beth. Victoria and I are more like brother and sister. We've known each other since we were knee high in knickers. Victoria is no more in love with me than I am with her. I can promise you that."

"But yet you are set to marry her anyway."

"Who told you that?"

"Victoria."

Garrett collapsed down on the log next to her and quietly cursed. Her heart mimicked the movement and slid to her stomach. By the way his shoulders sank, Victoria told the truth. "I'm sorry, Beth. It's my father's arrangement. I wasn't convinced that's what she was sent up here for, but if Victoria believes so then it's true. She is my intended."

"She seems to be a bit more enthusiastic about the arrangement than you."

"I agreed to a business deal, that's all."

"Business deal, or no, Victoria is smitten to the core."

"She is a sweet girl, but lives in her own world full of fancy parties and fine things. She doesn't know what she wants, and never will."

Beth made no attempt to argue. It was commonly known among the women of Missoula that a man could no more ascertain the feelings of a woman than he could the source of the sun's heat. It was more likely that Victoria had feelings for the intense man before her, but that he didn't know. Even though a light shone brighter in Beth every time he looked at her the way he did right now, she couldn't compromise herself if destiny had another plan for Garrett.

Could she?

Chapter 11

"Don't do it, Garrett." Aunt June rested her fists on her ample hips. "You've already taken your uncle Marcus in twice and what has it gotten you? Wrinkles and a drained bank account."

"I don't have wrinkles, and my bank account is fine." Garrett paced in front of Aunt June and Victoria as they stood before the doorway of the cook cabin. It had been an hour since he returned with Beth and handed her over to her brother's care, only to learn that his troublesome relative decided to prevail upon Garrett's life once again. As if he didn't have enough problems.

"Yes, well, *my* bank account is not," Aunt June snapped. "Your father refuses to take your uncle back, and I refuse to let him into my home again."

"If I don't give him a place to stay then he will be homeless."

"Aunt June is right, Garrett." Victoria took a step closer and looped her arm through his, peering up at him with a look of concern. Her voice conveyed a sardonic calm, as if she were a mother quietly persuading a hard-case child. "Your uncle is nothing but a deadbeat bunko artist. He's a genius at getting everyone else to support his lifestyle."

Garrett looked over to where his uncle leaned against a tree and chatted with Carrie. Garrett knew that posture. It was his, 'No woman can resist me,' stance. In his gray-haired, flabby-skinned state of being, he somehow managed to believe that he was the stallion of the barn, even though he hadn't shaved or had a shower in at least a month.

Carrie stood in front of his uncle like a rigid statue while he oozed all the charm of an ungreased wagon wheel.

"He's family. You outa know, Aunt June, he's your brother." Garrett watched his uncle as the old reprobate brushed up against Carrie's bodice.

The poor woman cringed and took a step back. Garrett dropped his gaze to the pebbled ground in shame and then to Aunt June. "Unfortunately for both of us, we have to help out family, no matter what."

"Ain't true." Aunt June furrowed her brows even deeper. "I gave up on him a long time ago."

With a quick whistle, Garrett made eye contact with his uncle and raised his head to call him over. At least he could save Beth's poor friend, Carrie, from an uncomfortable situation.

The old man trotted toward them and then slid to a stop. "Did you see that woman over there? Whew, what a fine specimen." He eyeballed Carrie and then turned his attention back to Garrett. "She said she wasn't being courted."

"Thanks, but I'm not interested," Garrett let out, knowing full well what his uncle meant. "Perhaps Simon could show her around." Garrett turned to Aunt June, and shuffled her a few feet away from his uncle so they wouldn't be overheard "Where is he?"

"Off causing trouble, no doubt." Her dimples showed when she gave a grin—a feature that at one time in her life had been her greatest asset, and maybe still was. She claimed a past of charm and beauty, and said a coy smile and fluttered lash never failed to get her a dance or stroll with the most sought after gentlemen of her time. Alas, she had chosen a life of adventure over love. Even now, with the inheritance left her by her parents long ago, she could retire to the city and fall in love or simply exist in peace, but she chose to stay here and cook for the lumberjacks. She reminded him a lot of Elizabeth with her carefree independence, and penchant for trouble.

"I think you like my friend, Aunt June."

She sighed. "If only I were thirty years younger. I'd wrangle Simon and make him a decent man. I suppose I'll have to settle with picking up Marcus from the gutter every year or two."

"If you're done with me, then. I'll be over talking to the womenfolk," Marcus called, and took a step toward Carrie.

Aunt June stomped over and slapped his uncle on the back of the head when he ogled Carrie once more. "My goddaughter is off limits to you."

Marcus snapped his head away from Aunt June's hand, and flinched toward her with fist clenched, but caught himself. He scowled. "Don't ever do that again."

"Or what?" She stepped forward and glared. "You'll hit me back like you did your sons when they were boys? You lay a hand on my goddaughter,

whether in anger or lust, and I'll hang your man parts from a tree branch…
with or without the rest of you still attached."

"Aunt June," Garrett scolded, shocked at such language from the
matriarch. "Marcus is a changed man, for the most part. He hasn't laid
a finger on anyone since. Besides, he always ensured the boys were
taken care of."

"You can't be serious, Garrett!" Aunt June turned an icy stare on him.
"Are you defending him?"

"No…no." He shook his head. No way was he defending his lowlife of
an uncle. Ever since Garrett was younger, he'd always seen through his
uncle's greasy charm and straight to the drunken fool he truly was. "I'm
simply trying to calm the situation."

"You're playing *advocatus diaboli.* Don't," Aunt June said. "He doesn't
deserve your respect, or your good will. He is bane to our family and a
scallywag to the rest of the world."

He gently grabbed Aunt June's arm to escort her to the edge of the
cabin in secrecy.

"Ah, taking her to task are you, Garrett. Good lad," Marcus sneered.
"Take a switch to her. God knows Mama never did."

"You know nothing about Mama. You never did." Aunt June pivoted
as if to flay Marcus, but Garrett caught her around the waist and urged
her to twist back around.

"I'm not playing the devil's advocate. I'm trying to ease my own
conscience. If I let him go without a home and something happens to
him, it's on my head. At least this way if he messes up, I can feel comfort
knowing I did my part."

"You're making a mistake, but you were always one to do things your
own way. Just know that I won't have anything to do with him. He can
find his own meals. He's not welcome at my table."

Garrett agreed. If that's what it took to keep the peace, then his uncle
would have to find his own food. They were in God's country, there was
food ripe for the picking…or shooting. "I'll let him know."

They returned to the group where his uncle fidgeted uncomfortably.
"Where shall I put my things?"

"There's an empty bunk in the first cabin on the right. I'll show you."
Garrett flipped his hand for his uncle to follow and headed in the direction
of the loggers' cabins. *God. How in the world did this season get so
out of control?*

Marcus stepped closer as he struggled to keep step. "Hey, Gar, I met
a man in Bonner who works for another logging company. He's a good

guy. We got to talking about this wood business. Did you know he's been traveling around the countryside from job to job? Can't seem to keep in one place for more than a season on account of all the crooked sheriffs and such. He'd been in a few scrapes, but he's a really good guy."

"Is there a point to this story?"

"Yeah. Could you maybe take him on as well? He was sayin' that he wasn't happy where he is."

"I don't make that call. Paul Smith does. I don't even think I can keep you on. I'll let you stay until I can get word to Paul. He will have to make the decision. If your friend wants a job he can apply at the mill."

Marcus fell silent long enough to draw Garrett's attention. He followed the path with his eyes cast to the ground and face scrunched in concentration. Garrett knew that look. He sported it whenever he was plotting something. There was no telling what, though.

Garrett opened the door to the only cabin with extra bunk space. "You can stay in here. There's a spare bed in the corner. Until I talk to Paul, you'll have to work with the timber beasts. You can go talk to Simon after you're done and see where he can put you to work."

"Much obliged." Marcus tipped his worn-out cap and tossed his small bag on the bed.

Garrett left before he could ask for anything else. He stretched his neck and shoulders to ease the tension that had spread since his uncle had rode in on the tired old mule. With all his earthly belongings in the saddle packs, Marcus had no doubt come confident he could stay at the camp. *No surprise there.* No matter who he prevailed upon, he was confident they would provide for his necessities, and he laid guilt on anyone who denied him.

Garrett entered the camp. The mule sat where Marcus had left him— reins dangling in the mud.

"Can someone take care of that animal? I think Teddy has room in his stalls." Garrett shouted to the small group of men gathered around the cook fire waiting for the evening meal. God knows his uncle hadn't planned on taking care of his own mount.

He glanced around for the train conductor and found him in the midst of a group of men deep in conversation. Garrett hailed him over. He jotted down a note about his Uncle Marcus with the stub of pencil he kept in his breast pocket, and held out the supply list and the letter he'd written to the mill about Jessip. He'd opted to wait until he knew the Bonner logger was legit, but he could wait no longer to send it. "Can you take this to the mill when you leave? Wait for them to bring the supplies, and don't come back without them."

"Sure thing, Gar." The conductor shoved the letters in the inner pocket of his jacket, and then turned back to his group.

Garrett massaged the knot that formed at the base of his skull. He needed to relax, and there was only one thing that could make it happen.

He gave a quick scan of the camp for any sign of Simon and Beth. He wouldn't try to kiss her again—he couldn't lead her to believe they had a future together—but he needed to be close to her. Perhaps even steal a touch. The mere smell of her freshly washed hair made the mountains grow peaceful once more. The adventurous spark in her eye made him relish the moments he had left in the camp. The warmth of her body near his made him feel whole. She brought peace to his threadbare soul.

* * * *

"Are you certain Garrett said to meet him out here?" Beth balanced on the rounded trunk of the log beneath her as it teetered. She slipped, but caught herself before she tumbled into the lake. Something felt off about this whole situation.

Luther jumped from log to log next to her like a frog on a lily pad. "Yep. He said to help you out here and tell you to wait near the boom logs. He'll be down in a bit."

"Do you know what training he has planned?"

"It's a…a lesson in balance." His face twitched, and he studied the clouds, the tree line across the lake, and the log beneath his feet. Anything, it seemed, but her. Why was he so wary? There's no way he could know her secret, right? He fidgeted. "So's you can ride a log without falling into the rapids."

"How long until Garrett gets here? It's starting to get dark. I can't imagine we'll go out on the water tonight. Why did he send you to get me? You aren't a riverman."

Luther's faced turned red, and his chest swelled with a deep breath. "Just pick a log along the edge and get settled. He'll be there shortly."

She picked her way across the wood strewn pond and chose a log that looked as if she could straddle it without problem. Dipping her legs into the water on either side, she wiggled back and forth to settle into her seat.

She studied the horizon from her new level as she teetered on the log that seemed to want to do nothing more than roll over. The tree line where Garrett had taken her to bathe earlier looked even farther away from this vantage point. She'd wanted him to kiss her again while they were tucked away in a secret place. He sent a tingle down her spine and flutters in her stomach whenever he looked at her the way he had next to the fire. For a moment, she'd truly believed he would kiss her. She'd even prepared to attempt to deny him like he requested, but then he'd backed away and stood to ready the boat. Much to her disappointment and relief.

Luther moved behind her and growled, "I don't understand why you got the riverman position. You're built like a piece of prairie grass after a dry summer. No meat on your bones."

The log wiggled, and she clamped down with her thighs and clung to the trunk with her hands. After struggling for a few minutes to stay upright, she finally gained her balance and glanced over her shoulder to Luther, but he was nowhere to be seen.

The log shifted, and she turned toward the boom logs just as her log broke free and floated out of the raft into open water.

"Luther!" she shouted and frantically searched the logs where she thought he stood, only to witness the side-winding snake vanish around a bend in the trail leading to camp. The log teetered again, and panic stuck in her throat like a ball of molasses.

"Blast!" She scrunched her nose at the foul expression. It somehow felt wrong on her tongue, yet seemed to be the perfect word for her situation. *What in the blazes am I going to do now? I don't even have a paddle.*

Another glance back, and the shoreline grew distant. The log angled toward the mouth of the river and grew parallel to the shore far enough out that she couldn't swim to safety. The trail of logs behind her made her want to cry when she realized the current held her tight in its grips.

"Help!" she yelled and jerked her head toward the shoreline. The bank lay empty. A quick search of the hill above the chute proved fruitless as well. The men had already left for the evening. They were probably all sitting down to Aunt June's chicken and asparagus pie, and here she was bound for God knows where.

The log picked up speed as it neared the mouth of the river, and she screamed for help. Looking back over her shoulder, she realized it was too late. No one could hear her.

* * * *

Garrett slammed the door to the cabin shut and headed toward the lake, almost running into Luther. He moved to the side to let the timber beast past. "Have you seen Brent?"

Luther answered with a shake of his head and gave an easy smile. "If you can't find him, do I get the riverman job?"

Garrett kicked one side of his mouth up in a forced smile. Luther's joke made his stomach drop. "Sure. If Brent is gone, then you can have his job." *Beth had better not be gone.* Could the careless prank this morning have made her think twice about staying in camp? Had she gone home on the train? There was no way she went back to Missoula on her own.

Where in the hell had she gone without him? After Aunt June sent Simon to summon him to the cook cabin, he'd left her standing near the bunks with Simon plopping onto one of the few chairs in the room.

Now, Simon sat at the chow table with the rest of the crew and threw his head back to laugh at something one of the men said.

Garrett locked eyes with him, stopped, and motioned for his friend to meet him in the thicket. Once his friend stood, he continued down the trail, veering off into the brush where he and Simon frequently met when they didn't want to be overheard.

It took only a few moments before Simon's large frame hurried through the brush. "Was Jessip here?"

"No. Have you seen Beth? I left her with you in the cabin, but she's not there now."

"Oh that. She's probably using the outhouse or something."

Garrett shook his head. "I don't think so. Not after what happened this morning."

Simon touched his bruised eye. "Yeah. That was quite the row. I would have taken Wall's head off, if it wasn't for the other river boys yanking me back. Thanks for getting her out of there."

"So you haven't seen her since the cabin?"

"No. She left the bunkhouse to use the bathroom. When she didn't return, I figured she'd met up with you."

Garrett pinched the bridge of his nose and closed his eyes. This woman was proving to be even more difficult than he'd initially thought. He fell silent, as he usually did when he needed to think, rather than react.

"We need to find her, just to be certain," he stated once he gained his composure.

Simon turned. "I'll take the outhouses."

"I'll check the lake." Garrett headed toward the path with Simon trailing behind. "Meet back at camp once you've found her."

"Right." Simon ran off in the opposite direction.

Garrett took the trail as fast as he could. She was instructed to stay with him, Aunt June, or Simon. She wasn't at camp. Where the hell did she go?

He stopped for a second as he registered the scene before him. The boom logs had once again been cut, and at least half of what had remained of the logs from the last incident now made a trail toward the river. How long had the raft been open?

Fixing the boom logs by running over the top of them would be way too dangerous at this point, so he ran to the bateau, threw it into the water, and began to row to the trouble spot. Large tree trunks bumped against the hull and made the boat rock dangerously. Digging the oar deep into the water, he used the skill taught by years of practice to maneuver between the rocketing debris, and slide the bateau into open water. It took only a few seconds to pull up next to the damaged boom logs.

His muscles flexed and stretched to their limit as he worked to get control of the opening and tie it together. He fought against the power of the current as it claimed the logs in its powerful tentacles.

Once finished, he stood and assessed the damage. All the hard work the men had done to rejuvenate the numbers from the incident before were pointless as over half the raft now drifted down the river. Who would do this, and how did no one witness the offense?

Bloody hell! Garrett tried not to punch the side of the bateau as he took up the oars and started toward the bank.

A better question was where in the world was Beth?

Yanking the boat to shore, he ran back to the meeting place as Simon passed the cook fire, headed in his direction.

He met up with him near Aunt June's cabin.

"She's not here, Simon!" Garrett paced in front of his friend in the center of camp for everyone to hear. He didn't care. Fear clenched at his chest and made a lump the size of a monkey fist catch in his throat. "Where the hell is she?"

Simon raised his palms out in surrender, the golden glow of the campfire shined off his slightly tanned hands. "I don't know, Gar. I'll wager she's fine. Probably went off somewhere to be alone."

"No. I can feel it in my gut. The logs were loose. Beth is missing. I can't help but think the two are connected." He stopped pacing and turned to his friend. "You don't think she cut the boom logs open, do you?"

"No. My sister may be one of the socialites in town, but she's not brainless like most of them."

"What the hell is going on?" Aunt June stomped her leather-soled toes against the pebbles on the dirt, making a clicking sound loud enough for Garrett to hear. "What do you mean where's Beth? Aren't you two guarding her?"

"Who's Beth?" Wall asked as he and the other rivermen made their way to Garrett. They all stood with backs straight and chests expanded. Wall continued, "You're in a right fit state, Gar, and that's never a good sign. What happened, and who is Beth?"

"What?" Carrie elbowed her way into the small crowd formed around him and Simon.

"Beth is my sister," Simon confessed, "and right now she's missing."

"We've never seen your sister before," Blue called from the back of the crowd.

"Brent is Beth." Simon stood taller and puffed out his chest.

"What are you saying?" Wall shook his head in confusion.

"She was posing as a man so she could work as a logger." Simon's chest rose with a deep breath. He clenched his fists and shifted his feet. "The logistics aren't important. We need to find her."

"Goddamn it, Simon. Why the hell didn't you tell us?" Clint shouted as the rest of the men mumbled their displeasure and shoved to get a better look at the center.

"Having a woman on the crew is bad luck!" Luther yelled.

Garrett silenced the men with a wave of his hand. "We can talk about this another day. Right now, there is a woman missing in the woods, or God forbid on the water. She was last seen in the cabin, but left presumably to use the outhouse. Did anyone see her right before chow?"

Luther raised his hand, his face blank with indifference. "I saw her over by the lake. She was on the raft. Didn't know she was a woman, though, boss. I swear. If I had, I would have told her to get off the raft. The river ain't no place for a woman. I'll bet she's the one who's been cutting the boom logs. Just like a woman, always causin' problems."

"She *was* on the raft?" A whistle like the one that warned of a disaster in the trees went off in his head.

Luther nodded. "Last I saw."

"Did you happen to see her, or anyone else, cut the line to the boom logs?"

"Na. I was only passin' through on my way to chow."

"Goddamn it! She's got to be down the river. Pray she's down the river, and we don't find her body washed up on the shore." He shoved his way through the men to head back to the lake.

"Where are you going, Gar?" Simon emerged from the throng of men.

Garrett stopped and skimmed over the crowd. Carrie's shoulders shook for a second before she burst into tears.

"Take care of her," he told Simon. "I'm going down the river."

"You can't." Wall stepped up and stopped him by placing a hand in the center of his chest. "There's only a few minutes left of dusk, and then it will be too dark to see. You'll get killed."

"She is going to die out there if I don't. I can't let that happen. Everyone will be out in the night until she's found. Everyone." He made his point by accentuating the last word. He had to find Beth. He would die if anything happened to her. She was his soul. He passed a glance over the stone-faced Victoria. At this point he didn't care if she discovered how he felt about Beth.

"Garrett," Aunt June whispered, placing a hand on his forearm. "I'm sending someone to notify the mill. If they stay on the path and ride through the night, they can get there in time for the morning whistle."

He nodded. The men at the mill needed to be on the lookout for Beth—or her body.

Chapter 12

Beth shivered as she trudged through the knee-high water toward the bank. The log she'd clung to for the last few hours finally entered flat water and floated close enough to the bank for her to leap off and swim to shore without getting crushed by a nearby log.

The late spring weather and run-off from the snow-capped mountains made her shiver. She wished she'd somehow managed to maneuver the log to the beach instead of swim. She was soaked, alone, and probably close to death.

She stumbled up the incline and hugged herself as tightly as she could. What was she going to do? The darkness had settled in long before she stumbled onto the bank, and now the sounds of the night made her want to swim back onto the log and ride it the rest of the way down, although her screaming muscles told her that even if she did catch another log, she wouldn't be able to hold on any longer.

Picking up a long stick, she tried to stop shivering as she poked at a bush. A large tree stood next to the dark vegetation with what looked—through the haze of night—to be a hole in the trunk, and one big enough for her to take shelter while she figured out what to do.

She poked the bush again, only to jump back when it shook in response.

The gentle chattering coo of a raccoon and putter of small receding feet filled the night, and the knot in Beth's throat dropped back down to her stomach.

She prodded the bush once more. Without hearing another sound, she turned to poke at the hole in the trunk. When no animals slithered or skittered out, she settled down in the crevice and pulled her knees to her chest to hug the warmth back into her body. She needed to get dry and stay warm. She needed a fire.

Tears filled her eyes.

How in the blazes do you make a fire?

She'd always seen her brother do it in the fireplace at home, but never actually built one herself. What did he say to do? Light a matchstick? She didn't have one. What else did he say? A fire steel? She didn't have one of those either. She did have wood readily available, and lots of it.

She scurried out of her shelter and searched the dark ground for rocks for the fire ring and kindling. Once her pile was high enough to provide an adequate fire, she sat back down and built a stone ring at least half the size of Garrett's earlier that day.

Piling the twigs in the center, she chose two large pieces and rubbed them together.

She worked the sticks until her arms burned like they had enough heat to shoot flames from her fingers.

She gave herself a quick break, and then started again.

She didn't know how much time had gone by, but the tears she'd pushed to the back of her eyes spilled like a waterfall. It was hopeless.

She tossed down her sticks and curled up into a ball, making herself as small as possible in the hollowed-out tree trunk, grateful for the small amount of warmth Garrett's large coat allowed. There was no telling what creatures moved about in the branches and leaves above her head, but as long as they didn't have fangs or a hunger for human supper, she would deal with it. She wasn't afraid. Never afraid.

Except right now.

She drew her legs closer to her chest once more and gently sobbed. Why had she done this? She wasn't as strong and able as a man, no matter what she'd believed. She wasn't a riverman. She was a socialite. Her nana and brother had given her the best gift they could. They made her a lady of the first water, coddled by those she loved, and given whatever she wished for in life. Why did she think she could pull this off?

Dear God. Please help me live through tonight.

A loud noise behind the tree made chill bumps run down her spine. Whatever was out there, wasn't a raccoon.

* * * *

Garrett used the peavey to push his way through the dark water. The only thing visible along the bank was the slightly darker outline of the trees against the starry night sky. Any movement hidden in the dense thicket was masked by the blackness.

"Beth!" Simon shouted from the front of the bateau. He had demanded to accompany him on the trip down the river.

In truth, his friend's presence was reassuring, like between the two of them, they would find her. No one else in camp wanted or cared for her as much as they did. The only problem was the damned blackness. They couldn't see two feet in front of the boat, let alone a few yards into the trees on the river bank.

They'd floated almost all night with no luck. Garrett slumped into the bottom of the boat in defeat. "Maybe we should pull up on shore. Walk a little ways to see if we can get a better sense of things. I've been riding this river for years. I know it as well as I do my childhood bedroom, but I have no idea where we are on it right now."

"Only until you get your bearings, and then we float again. If Beth did ride a log down, and is still clinging to it, there's no telling how far she's gone." His friend's voice cracked, and the pitch changed as if he forced back tears. "I can't lose my sister. I was a fool for letting her come. I cared more about my reputation in town than her safety. What a brother I've been. My parents died because of my foolish behavior and now maybe my sister."

"You've never spoken of your parents before." Garrett leapt from the boat and pulled it to shore. With luck they would find Beth soon, but in the meantime he needed to distract his friend—or perhaps even himself—from the tense emotions swirling around them in the pre-dawn mist.

Simon climbed out. "I was young, I think nine, when my parents decided to take us huckleberry picking near Rattlesnake Creek. A neighbor girl'd just gotten a new pup and invited me over to see it. Mother and Father didn't care and took their time with the berries. I got mad, and when they weren't looking, I started to walk down the mountain toward Missoula. Well, I didn't tell them or nothin', so they got frantic looking for me. Pa took a corner a little too sharp for our buggy, and they wrecked. Beth was the only one who survived."

"Beth said something about the carriage accident once when we were training." What else could he say? His friend had always met life with a smile and confidence the size of the mountain they logged. Never would he have thought such a tragedy existed in both Beth and Simon's lives. What strength they must possess, not only the physical kind, but strength of mind and heart.

"What I need to concentrate on now is doing right by my sister, but first we need to find her. Do you know where we are?"

Garrett did a quick search of what he could see in the night. Not much. He was hoping for an odd rock formation, tree bent a certain way, something to signify where they'd landed along the river. Nothing. His shoulders dropped. "No. I think we may be near the rock cliffs, but I'm not certain."

"Do you want to search upstream, or down?"

"Let's leave the bateau here and go downstream. It will be light in about an hour, and we'll turn around and come back up. Just in case we missed her."

Simon started to follow the river and called out, "Beth!"

They both paused to listen. Silence.

The more time that passed without finding Beth, the deeper Garrett's heart sank into a lake of despair. She had to be alive. He couldn't lose her.

Simon sighed, and they continued to follow the river.

"What's going on with you, Gar?" Simon asked after a few moments of quiet.

"What do you mean?"

"I know things are difficult this year, but you seem distracted. Different. You usually have no problem fixing problems."

How much should he tell his friend? He didn't want to spend the next few months talking about leaving. He wanted to enjoy what little time he had left. "I won't be coming back next year."

"What? Why?"

"I will be settling down in town and taking over my father's business."

"But you love being a Devil May Care."

"I do." The one thing in his life he valued as much as he did his family was the loggers he worked with. Walking away from the spring camp would be hard, but necessary. He wouldn't be far away from the mountain, but he would no longer be a part of the crew. No longer have a reason to see Beth at the end of the summer, standing on the platform, waiting for Simon. If she was alive, that is. "I'm trying to find my replacement."

Simon moved ahead of him as the trail thinned. "Is that why you let Wall lick you when you fought? I wondered why he bested you."

"If it wasn't for the whistle, he would now be the leader of the Devil May Cares, and I would be sitting in the bateau wondering why I let your sister stay."

Simon walked around a bend in the trail and disappeared from sight for a split second before a chilling scream filled the pre-dawn dark.

Garrett yanked his blade free of the sheath on his belt and ran toward Simon. He rounded the bend as a large mountain lion tugged his friend's body into the vegetation off the trail.

Without thinking, he followed. The dim light of the new morning did nothing to help as he fought his way through the brush.

Blade out in front, he leapt into a thick patch of the white-tipped bear grass that dotted the ground beneath the trees. He could hear Simon's screams in the trees. Although the terror of the sound made his blood pump faster, the cries meant he was still alive.

Early morning light began to slide over the scene around him. He tried not to panic as he followed the bright red trail of blood.

A roar from the mountain lion sounded, and then silence.

His blood pumped like a runaway train, and he ran ever faster. The stench of blood and animal filled his nostrils, and he knew he was close.

The cougar screeched and hunched over in the grass. A twig snapped under Garrett's shoe, and the animal turned a predatory stare in his direction. Simon moved his arm as he lay beneath the animal's chest, and relief loosened the knot in his stomach. He was alive. God, what would he have done if he had lost Beth and Simon in one fateful night? He'd fight to the death to protect his friend.

The cat stepped off Simon, and faced him full on.

Garrett adjusted the blade in his hand so his grip wouldn't fail him when he tried to kill the beast.

With only a flinch of the cat's tanned fur as warning, it attacked.

Garrett sliced the blade through the air as the mountain lion bore down on him. The blade vibrated as it pierced the animals shoulder, but it didn't stop him. Garrett stumbled and fell backward onto the ground as the cat descended. Pinning him down.

His eyes were hollow and soulless. A hungry gleam shone in the black slits of his pupils as he bent toward Garrett's jugular.

Garrett's muscles strained with the animal's weight. For a split second he felt like giving up and letting the cat take him. The deep groan rumbled in the cougar's chest as he crushed Garrett beneath his massive body.

It felt as if each of his ribs were one more twitch away from snapping like dry tinder.

The cougar stopped, and his ears flicked. Garrett heard a small thud at the same moment the animal's fur twitched. Another thud, and the cougar jerked toward Simon.

Taking the distraction, Garrett reached up and, with his fist clenched around the hilt of his knife, sliced as deep as he could through the mountain lion's neck.

The cat shuddered and slumped over him as warm blood poured over his face and chest from the mortal wound.

"Simon!" he shouted and shoved the animal. After a few minutes of struggling, he managed to slide the cat's body over enough to wiggle out from his dead weight. "Simon?"

"I'm alive." Pain infused his friend's voice. "I think."

Garrett leapt to his feet and ran to his friend, running his hand over his body to check the injuries. "You're covered in blood. Where are you hurt?"

Simon flinched when Garrett ran his hand over his shoulder. He screamed in agony, "There!"

A low growl split the air like a whip, and both men snapped their heads to the trees lining the other side of the opening where a fearsome brown bear lumbered out of the shrouded dark of the forest.

"He must have smelled the blood. We have to go." Garrett glanced down at the blood soaking Simon's shirt. "Lean on me. We have to go. Now!"

He struggled to stand with Simon leaning most of his weight on his shoulders. His body jerked with each unsteady leap they took as they did what they could to run toward the river. Animals were unpredictable, especially the ones who searched for blood.

They picked their way through the forest and emerged on the small animal path they'd taken earlier. Garrett turned them so they followed the river upstream. "Let's go."

Simon struggled to talk while he panted, "I don't think he's following us. I think he came for the mountain lion."

"Let's hope." Garrett moved off the trail and spotted the bateau tied to the rock where he left it. "There's the boat. Get in. I'll row us to the other side of the river, and check your injuries. Then we'll figure out what to do next."

His friend's head wobbled on his shoulders when he attempted to nod. Garrett gave a quick prayer that all would be well with Simon. It had to be.

Chapter 13

Beth's nose itched worse than it had when she'd been ten and Simon had stuck the Chickweed in her face, but she couldn't move until the large brown animal left. In the early morning sun, she stared at the rotted shelter she'd stayed in during the night, and cringed. Bugs of some kind skittered about hollowed out trails and down the surface of the decomposing, cavernous trunk. The warmth from her body fused with the elk's body heat. If it wasn't for the animal's chosen bed last night right in front of her natural shelter, she would have died during the cold dark hours, but the warmth from the elk's body filled the small space and warmed her like a blanket. God had certainly answered her prayers.

A tremor shot through the animal's skin, and it leapt to its feet and ran. Flashes of brown flew by past the opening as the rest of the herd followed.

She wiggled her arm out from under her body and flexed her hand. The numbness she'd felt all night turned into painful pin-pricks as she worked the blood back through her fingers. Now that it was light, she could finally try to pick her way back to camp.

A twig snapped, and she stopped in her tracks, and listened. A squirrel skittered from the ground and shot up a tree. She relaxed.

The sun sliced through the leaves to her left, but the large gap in the canopy of trees the river provided would allow her to catch her bearings and figure out which way to go.

She waded shin-high into the water, not daring to go farther. She craned her neck to see upstream. The familiar peak of the hill across the lake from camp was dark against the cloud-sprinkled sky. She faced the mountain and mentally calculated the distance to camp from the peak, and then turned in the approximate direction. If her calculations were correct, she could cut through the forest and walk straight to camp, as long as she didn't stray from her straight line. If that didn't work, she would back track and follow the river, which would take a lot longer, judging by the amount of time she floated last night.

Beth studied the sun to try to gauge the direction she would take. With any luck, she would be there by dinner.

The trees enclosed her in shadows as she picked her way deeper into the forest. Each creak, every crack or thud that sounded, sent fear sliding down to the pit of her stomach, but she knew it was nothing but the voice of the forest.

She walked until her legs ached.

Two, maybe three hours had passed before she stopped to gauge her direction. She checked behind her. The path she'd taken seemed straight enough. She should be hitting familiar terrain soon.

The ground beneath her shifted when she stepped onto an animal trail that descended the hill. Pebbles cascaded to the bottom of the ravine as her foot slipped. She landed on her backside and followed the pebbles.

Sticks jabbed into the meaty part of her butt, and she struggled to stay upright as she tumbled down to the bottom to land in a trickling creek. Water splashed in her face. She stood and cleared the droplets from her eyes. She slowly climbed out of the water and circled around to the thickest part of the bank, but she couldn't quite make out where her straight line to camp had been.

With one last look up the hill, she made the decision to try to make her way to the river and follow it upstream. Was anyone even searching for her? Her brother surely was, but what about Garrett? He was probably relieved to be rid of her. She'd done nothing but cause him unnecessary strife, but he'd still allowed her to stay and even protected her...or tried to, anyway. It made her feel even guiltier for lying to him.

She followed beside the stream until the hills on either side of her began to narrow and close in. The once gentle incline of the mounds turned steep and difficult to traverse, but she could see the stream begin to open up just before the water's path bent around the hill.

The freeing sounds of sloshing water reached her ears.

"Oh thank God, the river," she said to the heavens and picked up speed, taking care over the hazardous terrain. She drew close to the bend. The trees echoed with the sound of an animal snorting.

She froze.

Everything about this forest made her want to cry. Last night she'd drained all of her gumption. All of the determination she'd come to the logging camp with. She wanted to give up. Let her tears sweep her away into a sea of death. She didn't think she could take much more. She glanced around to find a place to hide before the animal spotted her. The sounds grew closer, so she ran with difficulty up the steep hill.

"Ms. Elizabeth?" a familiar voice called. Beth's overworked leg muscles cried in relief and she stopped climbing to wheel around.

"Wall? Oh thank God!" Tears filled her eyes, and she stumbled toward the riverman as he stopped the workhorse in the center of the creek. He leapt down and water splashed onto her shirt. He scooped her up and she nearly collapsed with the exhaustion she'd been suppressing for the last few days. "How did you know where I was?"

"We've been searching the riverbank and forest since last night." He slung her onto the saddle and mounted behind her, turning the horse toward the river. "What happened out there, Ms. Elizabeth?"

"Wait, you called me Elizabeth. You know?"

"Everyone does. When you went missing, Garrett and Simon told us everything."

"Are they upset?"

"No. We were more worried about you out here alone. What happened?"

Beth spit out the story like it was a bad apple she'd taken a bite of. Warm tears stung her eyes, but she took a deep breath to stop them from falling. The knowledge that she could once again act like a woman sent all the emotions suppressed throughout the last few weeks rolling around deep inside her. "Why would Luther do this to me?"

"Jealous maybe? You did get the spot on the Devil May Cares that he's been pining for since he first started at Big Mountain."

"Perhaps." Beth stared at the one strand of tan hair in the horse's black mane. Luther's motives could have stemmed from jealousy, but what if it was something more? What if he was the second man from the platform?

The mouth of the creek came into view, and Wall turned the horse north to follow the river. They rode in silence for over an hour before a movement across the way caught her attention.

"Oh my God! Garrett," she exclaimed and pointed to where Garrett trudged, bent over as he pulled the bateau up the river.

Garrett turned and signaled to them. The small movement seemed labored, and he plopped down on the riverbank. Beth fought to leap from the horse and run to him. Garrett wasn't one to show weakness, yet here he could barely lift his arm. And it was all because of her.

Wall kicked the horse into a trot and drew even with Garrett as he sat on the bank across the river.

When she and Wall dismounted, Garrett stood and shouted, "I'm coming over."

He studied the river and after a moment, entered the water. Beth stood, nerves bunched in the pit of her stomach as he waded through water chest deep, struggling to keep control of the bateau. The sight of him there, searching, made her want to give up and let her emotions take her. Cuddle in his arms and feel the warm embrace of comfort. Rest her head against the strength of his chest, and give him what little strength she had left in return.

Garrett emerged from the water a few feet upstream, and she let out a breath of relief, only to have an instant hole dug in her stomach. Her brother lay in a pool of blood at the bottom of the boat.

Garrett yanked it onto the bank near the horse, and she ran toward the vessel and kneeled next to it. Her heart started to beat fast when she spotted the long gashes across her brother's body. "What happened?"

Garrett stepped closer. "Mountain lion. I did what I could for the wounds, but the bleeding is bad. We need to get him to camp, but we're running out of daylight."

Wall's feet came into Beth's peripheral vision on the other side of the boat, and she looked up at him. "How far downriver are we?"

Garrett gauged the distance by looking at the landscape. "A few hours walk downstream from the mouth of the river. Then another half an hour to camp."

Wall turned to Garrett. "How close are we to where Braxton went in last summer?"

"Maybe twenty minutes downstream."

"Can Simon ride?"

"With your help, maybe, but we need to fix his dressings first." Garrett bent over Beth's brother and opened the front of his shredded shirt. Scarlet blood oozed through the layers of cotton, and made her stomach heave with the need to vomit. She let the tears fall this time.

Wall shrugged out of his jacket and yanked off his plaid shirt, handing it to Garrett. He slipped the jacket back on as Garrett ripped the shirt into strips.

"Here, Beth." Garrett handed her the pile of cloth. "Help me."

She set the cloth down on a dry, clean spot in the bateau and leaned over to assist Garrett as he cut the wet bands from her brother.

Simon moaned, and blood trickled down his once handsome face, sending a ball of despair hurling into her stomach.

"I'm here." Beth grabbed his hand as he rolled his head back and forth while Garrett worked to tie on the clean strips. Tears made her vision blurry, and she swiped at them with the back of her hand. "We're going to get you to camp. Okay? Just hold on."

Simon moaned again.

Once Garrett finished, he sat back on his heels. "I hope he can last the ride."

"It's our best option right now." Wall held the workhorse steady. "He needs to get to Aunt June so she can care for him. Beth, come over here and hold the horse while we get him into the saddle, and then I'll climb up behind him. We'll tie him to the pommel if need be."

Beth moved to the front of the horse and took the reins as the two men lifted her brother and gently maneuvered him onto the horse. He began to tip to the right and Garrett steadied him while Wall climbed up behind Simon and took the reins. He locked eyes with Beth. "We should be there in two hours. I'll take care of him, promise. Aunt June will fix him right up."

"Just get back to camp as soon as you can." The horse started forward, and Beth stepped back and nodded. She felt like rocks smacked into her chest as her brother disappeared with Wall around a bend in the river.

She turned and looked through tear-filled eyes at Garrett, who stood next to the boat with her brother's blood smeared across his pants.

"What do we do now?" she choked out.

In less than a heartbeat, he grabbed her up in his embrace, and she relaxed into his strength. The little gesture made her emotions open like the breaking of a logjam. She fought no more to hold back the sobs straining to be released. "We follow the river back to camp. We're probably going to have to spend one more night out here, but we can stop early and make a fire."

She nodded numbly into his chest.

He smoothed the spiked tendrils of her hair and stood quiet until she pulled back. Wiping a tear from her cheek, he then grabbed her hand and urged her to follow him to the boat.

Garrett tipped the boat to the side, and her brother's blood trailed down into the blue water. He adjusted the bateau so she could climb in and motioned toward the seat. "Come. We need to get moving."

* * * *

Garrett stoked the fire and studied Beth. She sat motionless across the pit. His heart sank in his chest, and he prayed that Simon would get to camp in time and pull through. He'd forced back tears himself when Beth kneeled next to her brother, but like all men of his ilk, he couldn't show emotion of any sort, even if he wanted to.

Beth shivered so he moved close enough to let his warmth calm her, at least that's what he hoped would happen. There was a vulnerability inside her that she tried to hide with a tough and determined manner—a trait he found endearing.

"Why would Luther try and kill me? Do you think he's behind the other incidences?"

"What?"

"Luther. Do you think he's behind the other accidents?"

"Luther did this?" He thought back to the meeting before he left down the river. Luther had said he'd watched her on the raft, but didn't say anything about seeing Beth go down the river. Why would he say anything if he was the one to send her down?

"He said you wanted to see me out there. Next thing I knew I was floating in the middle of the lake toward the river. I rode it until the surrounding logs were spaced out enough that it was safe to get off and swim to the bank."

The vein in Garrett's head pulsed hard, echoing the heartbeat that had kicked up. What the hell was going on at his camp? When he got back, he'd kill the low-down snake that did this to Beth. It was like the man had no regard for the life of anyone else.

Beth shifted next to him. Her face, illuminated in a golden sheen, turned down in worry as her fingers ticked against her knee. Garrett reached out and wrapped them in his palm. "Simon's going to be fine."

The fire popped and sent a spark flying high. She nodded, but didn't say a word. Didn't pull away from him, but leaned into his shoulder and laid her head against him. "It was a mistake to come here."

"Probably." He switched her hand into his other one and put his arm around her shoulder to tug her closer. All of the teachings on etiquette screamed at him to put distance between them, but for the first time in his life, he couldn't listen. He knew she needed him now more than ever. "But you're here. You are the most stubborn, strongest woman I have ever had the pleasure to know. No other woman could have done what you have."

"Can I tell you something?"

"Anything."

"I don't think I can identify the man I heard on the platform. I think I convinced myself that was the sole reason, but the truth is I'm not certain I can. The man with the cane I can identify, but I'm not confident about the other man."

Garrett sat spine straight. "The man with the cane?"

"Yes. He was the one who offered the bribe."

"Are you certain?"

"Quite. After the conversation, he came whistling around the corner and greeted me where I sat on the bench. He had a very slight Spanish accent. The other man sounded like any other man on the platform that day, but I didn't actually see his face."

"But you would be able to identify the man with the cane again if you ran into him?"

"Of course."

"That's good enough." Garrett would set up a meeting between the big bugs and Beth, but by then it wouldn't matter. Everyone would know anyway. Until then he needed to find out who the traitor was in the camp.

A twig snapped in the darkness and Beth flinched, her eyes wide with fear.

"As long as we stay by the fire we should be fine. Predators tend to stay away from flames."

"It's a lot more calming than where I spent last night."

"How did you last? You swam to shore, right? Spring nights on the mountain aren't exactly warm. How did you get dry and not freeze?"

"It was a miracle, I suppose. One of those things that can't be explained. There was enough light for me to find a hollowed-out tree, and just when I was about to break, a cow elk laid in front of the opening and heated up the space enough to dry my clothes and keep me warm throughout the night."

"You were lucky. If you'd have had to go through the whole night alone, wet, and cold then you wouldn't have made it."

"Luck, or something more divine. Either way I'm grateful to be alive, and that you came to look for me."

"Not just me." He adjusted his seat so she could snuggle deeper into his chest. "The whole camp. I'm sorry. I had to tell them who you were."

"It's better this way. Maybe now they'll think twice before locking me in an outhouse."

He chuckled. "They all regret their actions toward you. They're decent, hardworking, and respectable men when it comes to women. How they treat each other, though, would make a severe socialite swoon."

"I don't hold any contempt for the crew. I came up here expecting to be treated as a man, and I got what I desired, I suppose."

"Regardless, there's no room for misconduct such as that in a lumber camp. Someone could get hurt."

"Please don't. I don't want the men to have contempt for me, any more than they probably do already." The plea in her voice cooled the raging heat in his gut, and he nodded.

Beth fell silent as her fingers slid through his. She wiggled beside him, and he turned as she faced him.

Her lips parted slightly, their moist heaven beckoning him to partake as the firelight painted them with a coral sheen.

Just one more taste.

Tucking his fingers beneath her chin, he used his thumb to caress the silky smooth contours. "You tempt me more than any woman should."

She shook her head, and her mouth slid against his thumb. "I don't mean—"

A desperate chuckle escaped from deep within his chest. "No. You don't, but you do."

A longing flickered in her eyes. Did she yearn for the touch of a man, or just him? Who was he to toy with her when it was another man who would be beside her forever? Garrett gritted his teeth against the thought. She was his.

"I am weak," he said, and slowly covered her mouth with his. She stopped breathing and leaned into him as he deepened the kiss. A lifetime of this moment slid through his resolve, picking away at the honor engrained in his being. He could have her—her body soft and heated whenever he wished.

He pulled away and stared down into her passion-clouded eyes. "I cannot be weak, Beth. You cannot let me have such liberties."

She licked her lips and swallowed hard while a deep red blush tainted her cheeks. "I'm... I don't..."

"I'm to be married once the season ends," he reminded—whether her or himself, he didn't know. "I made a bargain with the devil it seems, and he has tormented my soul since. My father would allow me one last summer at the camp, and after, I will settle down with a wife and take over the family business. His stipulation was that he is to choose my bride. I assume that's why he sent Victoria. That, and to test my temper."

Beth's lips tightened into a thin line, and her voice quivered. "Oh."

"Beth. Please. I didn't mean to kiss you. You are the only person on earth who can bring me to the point of breaking. If I hadn't made the bargain with my father, you and I..."

She took a quick breath and shook her head, once again looking at him. "It's fine. I was weak as well. We'll let only the trees know this ever happened between us."

He smiled his response in order to hold back the desperate laugh that caught in his chest. How could she not understand that she tempted him simply by being near?

Chapter 14

"Beth! Thank God! We've been worried sick." Carrie swooped Beth up into a deep hug when she and Garrett stumbled into camp late the next morning. "Simon's in Aunt June's cabin. He's bad. I've been by his side ever since Wall brought him here. Another hour on that horse, and I don't think Simon would have made it." She grabbed Beth's hand and towed her into the small cook cabin, leaving Garrett to trail behind.

Light from the window and a small fire blazing through the open door of the cook stove illuminated the still form of her brother, covered by a dull gray wool blanket.

Beth kneeled beside the bed. He was wrapped like a leper in scarlet soiled bandages covering almost every inch of his exposed body.

"Wall said it was a cougar," Carrie reverently supplied. Tears filled her friend's eyes. "He's lucky to be alive. There aren't many people who survive a sneak attack from a mountain lion. He's going to be scarred pretty bad for the rest of his life."

Beth tried not to let her body shake when tears began to fall along with her friends. She didn't look at Carrie as she spoke. Couldn't see anything but the still form of her brother. If it wasn't for her, he wouldn't have been out there searching, and would never have run into the vicious predator. If she'd stayed home like the proper lady she was expected to be, then he would be chopping trees in the forest instead of passed out in Aunt June's bed. Of all the selfish and outlandish things she'd done in her life, this was the one she regretted the most.

Garrett eased into the room. She could feel his warm presence behind her, calming and supportive.

Carrie repeated her earlier statement to Garrett.

"Is he well enough to travel to Missoula?" he asked.

"No," Aunt June said as she walked into the cramped space. "Maybe in a few weeks. I've got supplies enough here, and I've seen enough loggers' injuries to know my way around healing a man's body. With any luck, he won't get an infection."

"Simon." Beth grabbed his hand. "I'm sorry. I shouldn't have forced you into this whole mess. I swear, I won't say anything to the mayor about his wife."

When Simon didn't wake, she said his name again, her voice shaking.

Aunt June wrapped her arm around Beth's shoulder. "Best let him rest, dear. He'll be up for a good talk later when he wakes."

"Why don't we get you cleaned up and fed, and then we'll come back and see if Simon is awake." Carrie took a stance on Beth's side.

"If you'll excuse me," Garrett said, "I need to go find Luther."

Beth nodded numbly and allowed her friend to escort her outside. Carrie headed toward Victoria's railcar. "My stuff is at the cabin."

Her friend shook her head. "Victoria offered to let you and I stay with her when Wall brought your brother. Aunt June thought it would be best and had our stuff moved in there. It's quite cozy, really."

"Are the Devil May Cares terribly upset with me?"

"I think a few are shocked, but I think they're happier that you're alive. From what I hear, you've proved yourself within their ranks. Some might be a little upset, but they'll get over it. It's not like you're the first woman to be in a logging camp, just the first one to become a Devil May Care."

Beth felt deflated, beaten before she even got a chance to pick herself up off the pine-riddled ground. She hadn't intended to betray the Devil May Cares, or any other logger who worked for Big Mountain. All she wanted was to find the man from the platform.

Now she'd not only betrayed her crewmembers, but was forced to share a home with Garrett's future wife. She'd already learned her lesson, but life was cruel and wanted to rip open the stitches of her heart and make her bleed once more.

Carrie climbed the railcar's metal steps and opened the door. "I know this isn't what you had planned for this summer, but after what happened I truly believe it's for the best."

Beth smiled to her friend, but the motion must have looked pitiable because Carrie gave a sad smile in return.

"I'm fine, Carrie, really. After what Luther did, I realize that my reasons behind coming here are as thin and translucent as a dress made out of nothing but French lace."

"No. You came to save the company from the saboteur, and that's what we're going to do. We just need a different strategy now that everyone knows you are a woman."

"Good job I've done so far. Look at all of the things that have happened. The boom logs, going down the river—"

"What do you mean?" Victoria's voice made both Beth and Carrie jump and reel around as the graceful woman walked around the corner and into the dining area of the railcar. Her long, lustrous dress swept the carpet with a whisper of diaphanous French lace trailing the bottom hem. Beth couldn't help but envy the woman. She'd never seen a finer dress, cut not to the height of fashion, but one that would define the next obsession in ladies' attire. Not only that, but she held the key to Garrett's life.

Carrie gave a wide-eyed stare to Beth. "We may as well tell her."

With a wave of her hand, Beth gave her friend permission to expel all she knew of the plan to save the logging company. Victoria listened intently. Like Garrett, she masked her emotions well, not letting even a glimmer of thought cross her eyes. They were indeed the perfect pair.

After explaining Beth's reasoning behind coming to camp, Victoria's flawless face turned down in confusion. "Why didn't you come to camp to work as a cook? Why the Devil May Cares?"

"I get closer to the men," she answered simply. "I figured if I'm going to be coming up here to put myself in the way of a saboteur, I may as well make it count. I needed to have access to everyone. Be trusted enough to talk to them without reserve."

"Hmmm." Victoria flipped open her fan to wave it before her face. "I'm in."

"You're in? The Devil May Cares?" Beth asked, confused.

"No silly. The plot to save the company. I'm in." She nodded, and curls bounced behind Victoria's neck and flipped over her shoulder. "I can't sit by and watch some fool ruin my father's business. My business. I need to help protect it. That's what any good Harrison would do."

"Your father's business?" Beth tilted her head to the side and furrowed her brows. "I thought Garrett owned the Big Mountain Lumber Mill."

Victoria's eyes danced with humor. "Why would you think that?"

Beth thought back to all the times they'd talked about Garrett's father, but not once had he said what business his family was in. "I guess I just assumed."

"As of now, he does not, but once we are wed then Father will offer him a partnership. Once we are married, that partnership will be mine as well. And I protect what is mine."

Beth nodded. Not only was the beautiful woman destined for the man Beth was growing to love, but she owned the business that Garrett worked hard to make successful. Beth didn't stand a chance against Victoria.

* * * *

A long screaming whistle resonated through the trees, only this time it sounded different, more frantic. Beth stilled as chills raced down her arms, defiant to the warmth of Aunt June's cook fire. A logger rushed past her, and she grabbed his shirt to stop him. "What's happening?"

He shook his head. "I don't know. Something bad."

Beth released his sleeve, and the logger took off toward the water. She sent a concerned glance to Aunt June and Carrie who stood staring at her from the other side of the fire.

"Go!" Aunt June encouraged. "Come back and let me know if I need to ready a bed on the floor of my cabin."

"Me too, Aunt June?" Carrie asked.

"Go, girl," she said, and motioned for Beth and Carrie to leave.

"Will you look after Simon?" Beth pleaded. "I just left his bedside, but he's still the same."

"Of course," Aunt June answered.

"I'll follow you." Carrie hiked up her skirt to run.

Beth led the way down the path. Smoke began to fill the space between the trees the closer she drew to the water, and she covered her mouth with the sleeve from Garrett's jacket.

The trail opened up to the lake beach, and the vision from the smoke cleared enough for Beth to realize what had happened.

"The chute's on fire," she screamed over the shouts of the men and sizzle of the flames.

"What do we do?" Carrie coughed.

"You go back to camp and tell Aunt June. I'm going to find Garrett."

Carrie nodded and coughed again as she turned and raced back down the way they came.

Beth searched the scrambling men rushing from the water's edge, to the chute, and back. Running to the lake, she found Wall shin deep in water and directing the men as they filled buckets and ran back to the chute.

"Where's Garrett?"

"What?" Wall asked, occupied with filling a bucket for a logger.

"Garrett!" she yelled louder.

"Up there." Wall pointed to the hill at the top of the chute where the flames of the inferno seemed to lick the sky.

The unmistakable outline of Garrett as he worked hard to douse the flames was hard to make out in the dense smoke.

"You're not going up there," Wall shouted.

"I want to help."

Wall inclined his head, and motioned toward a bucket as he handed it to a nearby logger. "Fill these when the men bring them. Be fast."

She waded into the water, and took up a stance on the other side of Wall. She grabbed the first bucket to come her way and pulled it through the water to fill. Water sloshed over the edge when she handed the bucket over and grabbed another.

She continued to help until her muscles screamed for her to stop, but she ignored the pain and pressed on. After a time, the noise around her began to die down, and she slowed a bit.

"We can stop." Wall let his arms drop to his sides and made his way back to the bank. His body drooped with exhaustion. She followed, and only then realized how tired she felt.

She studied the black skeletal remains of the chute. Thin ribbons of smoke drifted to the sky, but the flames were no longer visible. Men with shovels overturned the blackened earth, and others poured what water they had left on the ashes.

Garrett picked his way off the hill, exhaustion apparent in the way he carried his shoulders. She waited for him to draw closer.

"What are you doing here?" he asked.

"I came to help."

"You should have stayed back at camp like the other women." Garrett's face went rigid as if made of stone.

"She doubled the output of the water," Wall defended. "We would have had a harder time fighting that fire if it wasn't for her."

"I came to help. I stayed at the water, away from the danger."

"In the future, if something is happening and it's dangerous, stay away completely."

Beth glared. Why was he being so abrasive now? She'd split logs, rowed a bateau, even cleaned out the outhouses. So why was he all of a sudden against her help? "If the event warrants me staying away, I will, but this did not. I helped, and I was needed."

"Goddamn it, woman!" Garrett yelled. "You could have been killed. Trampled by the men fighting the fire, been buried under a falling tree, or burned in the flames, among other hazards. We don't need two Sanders taking residence in Aunt June's cabin, your brother's enough. From now on, you will stay and help at the camp."

"But I wasn't in any danger. I stayed by the water, and I was fine." Beth couldn't take any more and turned to stomp to the camp. Never before had she seen Garrett in such a mood. His past commanding ways were nothing compared to the tyrant that stood there now with soot over every inch of his body. This Garrett was a bully. Even though his points were valid, she wasn't going to be pushed around.

* * * *

Chaos reigned around Garrett and the lake, but at least the danger had passed. He watched Beth leave and wanted to follow, but he couldn't. He had too much to do in the aftermath of the fire, like find out who had started it.

Wall stood next to him staring at the spot where Beth disappeared with a reverent respect shining on his face. "That's some woman."

"A woman I'd like to take a switch to right now. What were you thinking letting her help? She could have died."

"It was either that or let her climb the burning hill to find you. Either way she was going to help. Where I come from a woman doesn't sit back and let the men folk do everything while they sit at home knitting doilies. They hike their skirts up and charge into battle with their man. What matter is it anyway? She's had her pretty little neck buried deep in danger ever since the start of the season. She proved to be one of us. You didn't seem to mind then."

Garrett faced his friend head on. "You have no idea what's been going on the last few months. I did mind, but there's no stopping Elizabeth when she gets an idea in her head, and we need her."

"Need her?" Wall sent him a curious look. "We need her, or you need her? I was thinking about courting her, once all this mess is situated, but if you're sweet on the girl..."

Wall's words trailed off, and Garrett knew he'd intended for him to speak up and defend his right to Beth, but he couldn't. "Have you seen Luther? I've been searching for him ever since I got back with Beth."

"You're not going to answer?"

"Answer what? You didn't ask a question, but I did. Have you seen Luther?"

Wall stared at him as if trying to read his thoughts, so Garrett held a steady gaze.

After a few breaths, Wall answered, "No. I haven't seen Luther."

Garrett gave a grunt in response and left Wall to wonder about his intentions with Beth. Hell, he didn't even know what his intentions were. This was all too new. He'd always been a man of action, one dedicated to work. Never a moment to spare for the female sex, except maybe when he yanked them out of whatever sticky situation they'd wandered into. Now, he was overrun with female attention, and had no clue how to handle it.

Where the hell was Luther?

Garrett followed the trail of men headed toward camp. He needed to focus on finding who set fire to the chute, and send Luther packing for shoving Beth down the river.

Men littered the camp, some eating or dishing up their meal, and others huddled close to the fire as Aunt June, Carrie, and Beth worked to administer to injuries, while a white-faced Victoria huddled behind them. What wifely attributes, other than a pretty face, did Victoria possess?

"Oh thank goodness," Victoria said when he neared. "Everyone came in all at once with injuries. What should we do?"

"It looks as if Aunt June has everything in order."

"Yes, of course." Victoria took a fleeting look at Aunt June, but directed her next question at Garrett. "What should I do?"

"Go serve the men supper," Aunt June ordered from her crouched position near a soot-covered man with burns on his hands. She began to wrap his palm in gauze and glanced back up to Victoria. "Hurry now, girly. The men are hungry."

Victoria gave Aunt June a smile that didn't reach her eyes, and then crossed the camp to take a position behind the serving table.

"Do you need Beth?" he asked, directing his question to Aunt June.

"We're almost done here. Once she finishes up, she can go."

Garrett nodded and waited for Beth to finish stitching a cut, and then motioned for her to follow.

He headed toward the Bonner camp, but waited until they passed the Devil May Care cabin before he spoke, "Can you identify the man you heard on the platform?"

"I don't know."

"Can you try?"

"Yes," Beth said as she struggled to keep up with Garrett. "Are we not going to talk about what happened by the lake?"

"There's nothing to talk about. You put yourself in a dangerous situation, and I reacted like any good leader would."

"Like any good tyrant would," she muttered. "You don't treat the other Devil May Cares this way. I don't see any of them getting scolded for doing their job."

"You aren't just any other Devil May Care. They aren't female and haven't just gotten back from almost dying in the forest." He turned a sharp corner on the trail. "I thought you'd decided to work with the cook staff instead."

"I changed my mind."

"Why?"

"Because I can't sit back and watch, especially when everything we're working toward goes up in flames. What are you really mad about? I wasn't in the path of danger. The only thing that could have happened to me was my feet getting a little chilly from the cold lake."

He stopped and spun around to face her. The damned woman changed everything in his life when she showed up, and demanded more simply by being. What did he want? He wanted her. "I can't lose you. I can't have you, but I can't lose you, either."

She stopped and took a step back. "Oh."

He paused and watched her face as they filled with emotions too thick to read. Silence dripped between them like rain on a lonely lake until he couldn't take any more. "The fire was intentional. Even when the logs burn on their way down, they don't set fire to the chute. We need to find out who set it. Since you haven't found anyone of interest in the Missoula camp, we need to check the Bonner one."

"What if I don't recognize the voice?"

"Then we find another way to weed out the culprit."

"Shouldn't we attack the source of the problems? Should we go after the other lumber mills and the man with the cane?"

"I've written to the Big Mountain big bugs and told them about the man with the cane, they are handling things on that end. We need to stop the immediate threat."

The Bonner camp came into view and looked much like the Missoula camp did upon entering the clearing. They needed to speak with virtually everyone here, and even then, there was a big chance they'd come up empty. Best to start with the men he knew. Now all he had to do was find the leader of the Bonner rivermen.

Chapter 15

Beth chewed on her lip and stared at each man who hurried past her, but only the rivermen looked familiar. And even then, she'd only seen them a handful of times. Not one of them looked like they might belong to the voice on the platform, but did any of them sound like the man?

One by one, Garrett pulled them aside in casual conversation, but not one of them sounded familiar. Her stomach dropped. What if she couldn't identify him like she'd feared?

Michael walked past with his brother, Peter, and Garrett whistled and called him over.

"Heya, Garrett," Michael said. "Did you come to give my brother a job bossin' around the river rats on the bank during the drive?"

"Sure." Garrett ruffled the kid's hair, and then turned his attention to the man next to the boy. "How about it? Want to lead the Bonner river rats this year?"

The man nodded and said simply, "Sure."

"Good. I'll let the Devil May Cares know." Garrett turned back to Michael. "Tell Jessip I need a word?"

He rushed off as the chow bell rang for the Bonner camp.

Garrett slid his gaze to Peter. "Best get supper. Those boys don't wait for stragglers."

Peter gave a half smile and left.

Garrett turned back to her and continued to call people over for casual conversations. Once they'd interacted with almost everyone in the camp, Garrett moved toward the trailhead leading back to the lake.

"I'm sorry," she said.

"We've still got one person left to speak with." Garrett stopped and turned to stare back at the Bonner camp. After a while, he gave a small motion with his head as if calling someone, and then continued down the trail.

They walked in silence until they reached midway between the camps, and then veered off into the brush and stopped.

"What are we doing?" She stepped close to his side.

He peered down at the small distance between them and took a deep breath. He turned his attention back to the trail they'd just exited. "We're waiting for Jessip. Once he gets here, tell me if you recognize his voice."

"Is that the man you motioned to back there? Why didn't we speak to him in camp?"

"I've got a few more questions for him."

The sound of crunching pine needles reached their position in the vegetation, and Garrett stiffened his spine. "Just nod if you recognize him."

"Okay." Beth took a deep breath to help calm her nerves when Jessip clamored through the brush.

"I know what you're thinking, Garrett. It wasn't me," Jessip said.

Garrett glanced down at her. Beth frowned and shook her head.

Garrett's shoulders dropped. "Do you have any idea who may have set fire to the chute?"

"Not a clue," Jessip claimed. "I did hear a mumble in the chow line about someone coming into some money. I didn't hear who they were talking about though."

Garrett's forehead creased and the color of his hazel eyes darkened to gray. "At least we know where to look."

"Did you get my contract approved?" Jessip shifted weight on his feet.

"I expect it will be here with the next train."

"It better."

"It will."

"Good. See you then." Jessip raised his head in answer and left.

"What contract?" she frowned.

"The one used as payment to keep him from taking the thousand dollars. The other mills offered a reward for anyone who stops the drive so the lumber mill will miss the deadline they have with Boilson Mines."

"Seems to me what we need is to get those logs down the river fast. If whoever is behind the attack is a timber beast, then there's nothing else to worry about once the logs are on their way south. If not, then we know it's a riverman."

"I think you're onto something." He grabbed her hand and headed toward camp.

"We're going on a drive?" she asked, stumbling to keep up as he towed her down the trail.

"We're going to move what logs remain in the raft to the other side of the river mouth. We'll post a lookout on it. If someone targets the raft, then they will have a harder time getting to it."

"What if they don't target the raft?"

"Then at least we have something to bring to the mill."

"Will it satisfy the contract with the mining company?"

"It'll be a good start. I would like to try to figure out a way to get the rest of the shipment down the river, though. We'll get to that after we float the raft and set a trap."

Garrett released her hand once the stream of smoke from Aunt June's fire drifted into sight.

"Let's gather the Devil May Cares," he said when they entered camp. He gave a whistle, and all the men from his team glanced up, stopped what they were doing, and walked toward them. Beth followed as Garrett led the men to the cabin that most of them shared.

Once they were all crammed inside, he divulged the plan.

"I'll keep first watch," Wall offered.

Garrett nodded. "Tonight, after Aunt June puts the fire out, we'll move the raft. Wall will stay behind."

"I think we should keep a watch on The Deck and Grove as well," Beth suggested.

The team mumbled in agreement.

"I'll take first watch at The Grove after we get back. The rest of you sleep while you can, and divide the watches into four-hour increments." Garrett motioned toward the door. "Let's get back to the fire before anyone comes looking for us. We don't need anyone but our team knowing what we're doing tonight. They can find out in the morning once the raft is secured on the other side."

The men began to single file out the door, and Garrett held Beth back to wait as they left. Once the room was clear, he spoke, "I want you to stay in camp."

"No way."

"Beth, please. Your brother is lying unconscious in Aunt June's cabin."

"You're right." Through all of the chaos of the day, she'd only been able to visit her brother once that morning, but his condition hadn't changed. She needed to sit by him.

"So you'll stay in camp?"

She nodded. "I need to visit Simon—"

Before she could say more, he grabbed her up and kissed her. His lips were hard against hers, and commanded a response she was more than willing to give. She'd always heard the young women of her social circle talk of a kiss that stole their heart, and she'd never understood what they meant, until now.

* * * *

"How is he?" Beth asked Carrie as she closed the door to the cook's cabin. Garrett and his team were settling near the fire to wait for the night to take over, so Beth decided to retire to her brother's bedside.

Carrie stood from her crouched position near the bed. "Better. He woke up during the fire."

Simon moaned, and Beth knelt next to him. He turned to look at her with the one eye that wasn't covered in a bandage. "Lizbe?"

"I'm here," she said, and gently grabbed his hand.

"Water," he rasped.

Beth sent a questioning glance to her friend, who moved toward a water bucket and picked up the ladle. "Aunt June said to have him take sips."

Beth cradled the cup in her hands that Carrie handed her, and brought it to her brother's lips. "How are you feeling?" she asked once he had laid his head back on the pillow.

"Like I was attacked by a mountain lion." The corner of his mouth twitched. He gave two pained chuckles, and then moaned.

"Don't try to laugh. Don't move."

"Trust me. I don't intend to."

"I'm sorry I wasn't here today when you woke up."

"Don't worry. Carrie was. At first I thought she was an angel when I saw her hovering over me, but then I recognized her for the little devil she is." With his one good eye, he winked at Carrie, and then looked back to Beth. "She told me about the fire. Is everyone all right?"

"No one was hurt bad, but the chute was burnt to the ground."

"I told Teddy to grease the damn thing."

"It wasn't the grease. Garrett said it was sabotage." Beth bit her tongue and stared at the ground until she conjured enough courage to continue, "I lied to you, Simon. Well, not exactly lied, but I didn't tell you the real reason I wanted to come to the camp this summer. At the train depot, the day you came home from the meeting, I overheard two men plotting against the Big Mountain Lumber Mill. I saw the man who offered the money, but I didn't see who he spoke to. I came to find the second man."

"Why didn't you tell me?"

"You do so much for me. I wanted to do something for you, and I didn't want any sort of backlash to happen to you if I ended up being wrong. I really messed things up, though. If I hadn't come, then you wouldn't be lying here on the verge of death."

"I'm dying?" Simon's pained voice still dripped with humor.

She rolled her eyes.

In a more serious tone, Simon continued, "If Mother and Father's death taught me anything it's that you can't live in the past. What's done cannot be changed, but the good decisions you make in the future should be the result from that mistake."

"What should I do now?"

"You can start with not telling the mayor I slept with his wife."

"I was never going to tell," Beth confessed.

"You slept with the mayor's wife?" Carrie asked from the corner of the room. The color of her eyes darkened, and she glared.

Simon flinched. "Buggar. I thought she was gone."

"No. I'm not." Carrie stepped next to the bed. "Why on earth would you stoop so low as to entangle yourself with that hussy?"

"Why do you care? You've got all of Higgins Street lined up to court you," Simon snapped. He took a deep labored breath and settled his head on his pillow to stare at the ceiling, and then grimaced. "Can you get Aunt June? The laudanum is starting to wear off."

"I think she's putting the cook fire out for the night. Let me go catch her before she retires to the railcar."

Carrie swiped at a tear that escaped from the corner of her eyes and bustled outside as Beth settled into the chair next to her brother to wait for Garrett's return later that night. After she'd seen Simon lying in his blood at the bottom of the boat, she'd cracked. No longer wanting what she did before. No longer craving the adventure she thought she'd wanted, but then the fire happened and she felt compelled to help. The drive, the timber beasts and rivermen, the smell of freshly cut wood; it was all a part of her. In her soul, she knew that this was where she was meant to be. Accepting the struggles attached to living in a camp like this was something any logger had to deal with.

Carrie came into the cabin and administered the medicine to her brother, her face like stone, the tears gone. When he closed his eyes and drifted off to sleep, she slumped. "Do you mind if Aunt June and I get some sleep?"

Beth waved off her friend's concern. "Of course not. I'll keep watch over Simon tonight."

Carrie gave the smile Beth had seen her give every creature she pitied. "Wake me when you're ready to sleep, and I'll sit with him."

"Okay." Beth waited until her friend slipped out the door, and then she turned to watch Simon sleep. Gauze covered half his face and crossed over his torso. For a man who had lived life always knowing his looks could get him whatever he wished, this transition was going to be hard. Beth knew a side of him that others didn't. While his looks had given him the world, he'd met the challenge it presented with a deep-seated respect and enthusiasm. If anyone could overcome a challenge such as the one he would face, it was Simon.

The candle illuminating the one-room cabin where Simon slept burned down to a nub before she heard the muffled sound of the Devil May Cares returning to camp. Beth eased the door shut so her brother wouldn't wake and took quiet steps through the night toward the group of men gathered around the serving table.

She made out Garrett's wide shouldered silhouette in the night. He turned when she neared. "You stayed in camp?"

"I said I would."

"We're headed to the bunk," Blue said, along with the mumbled agreement of others.

"Have Clint relieve me in four hours," Garrett directed, and once the men agreed and then disappeared, he turned back to her. "How's Simon?"

"Awake, and in good spirits."

"So he's going to make a full recovery?"

"Other than some scarring, Aunt June says he will be good as new in a few weeks. How did moving the raft go? You weren't hurt, were you? Swimming a raft at night is dangerous."

"I'm fine, thanks. The current wasn't that strong. We got across the lake without incident. The raft is all tied up, and now we wait to see if anyone tries to mess with it. I'm headed to keep an eye on The Deck and Grove."

"Do you want company? I was about to go wake Carrie to stay with Simon."

He shuffled as if uncomfortable. "You should get some rest."

"Oh," she tried to hide the disappointment in her voice. She didn't want rest, not after everything that had transpired that day. "Yes. I suppose I should."

She turned toward the railcar.

"Beth." He gently grabbed her arm. She faced him once more. "I'm going to Mother Goose's Cottage tomorrow to clear my head so I can figure out what to do about this whole mess. Come with me?"

The breath she took seemed to fill her lungs completely and ease the tension in her shoulders. "I'd love to."

"I have something to do in the morning and then I'll head up. Meet me on the marked trail past The Deck after breakfast? No veering off the path. Not for anything."

"What should I tell Aunt June? She wanted me to help clean up the camp tomorrow."

"Tell her I need you. She'll let you come."

"Okay."

"See you in the morning." He released her arm and let his drop to his sides.

Beth couldn't stop the smile that spread across her face. It wasn't proper to be alone with a man, especially in a setting as romantic as Mother Goose's Cottage, but up here propriety barely existed. Up here, with Garrett, she could be free. If only life could be so liberating.

Chapter 16

"Oh no you don't, young lady," Aunt June scolded when Beth told her where she was headed the next day. Carrie and a few of the rivermen sat around the chow table talking, and looked over at her when Aunt June continued. "You've gotten yourself in enough trouble. There will be no lone outings for you anymore."

Beth slid a nervous eye in the direction of her growing party of eavesdroppers. She shifted so her back was toward the table. "Garrett and I need to come up with a plan to flush the saboteur out."

"What about your brother? Shouldn't you be spending time with him if you're not helping me?"

"I've spent all morning with him, and he's asleep now and told me not to bother him until lunch."

"Then you'll take an escort." Aunt June perused the crowd.

"I'll take her," Wall offered, lurching out of his seat and hastening to stand next to Beth.

"No, please, Aunt June," Beth pleaded. "I'll be fine by myself."

"Let the girl go, June," Garrett's Uncle Marcus said from his seat at the table. "Garrett's probably got something planned for the two of them, if you know what I mean." The greasy old man winked at Beth.

"Let me get my hat." Wall ran back to the table.

"You hush up you foul-mouthed horse's behind," Aunt June scolded Marcus. "You come in every day late, and hang around until I shoo you away. Don't you have some work to do?"

"Na. Today's my day off."

Aunt June slammed her hands on her sides. "When were your days on?"

The tins that remained on the table rattled as Marcus slammed his fist down on top. "I've been doin' what I can around here, but Garrett hasn't given me a real job yet, and the man he sent me to see is all laid up."

"Garrett's busy keeping the whole operation from going down in flames," Aunt June defended.

"You'd think he could spare a minute for family. I swear the boy walks around acting like he owns the mill."

"He will once Papa retires," Victoria said with a smile, then placed the cup she was drying on the shelf below the serving table.

Marcus stood and grumbled, "I'm going for a ride. Where's my mule?"

"No one cares what you do, Marcus. You're a deadbeat." Aunt June made a face at Marcus as he meandered out of the camp, grumbling, and then turned toward Beth. "You'll take Wall, or you won't go, missy."

"Aunt June," Beth pleaded for her to understand.

The older woman glared at her. "I'll follow you myself and collect every spare worker that I see if you don't take Wall."

"Ready, Miz Elizabeth?" Wall asked as he plopped the hat onto his head.

"I'm coming too." Victoria grabbed her shawl from a peg on the side of Aunt June's cabin.

"You too?" Beth sent a questioning glare to Carrie, who gave a humored smile and shook her head in denial.

Beth didn't care to hide her scowl as they climbed the trail leading to The Deck. At the top, she noticed a scene different from days before. Instead of Teddy and other horse teams working hard to bring the logs to the chute, The Deck sat empty save for Garrett and The Bull as they stood in the center of the clearing and talked.

She heard the familiar shout and tree squealing in protest as it fell somewhere deep in The Grove.

Garrett drew his eyes to her as she walked closer. He gave a fleeting look at the people trailing behind her, and quickly turned back to The Bull.

"If you'll excuse me," he said to The Bull when she neared, and headed in her direction. His eyes stormed for a moment when he took another look behind her, but he quickly masked the expression.

"Aunt June insisted." Beth motioned to Wall and Victoria.

"Mother Goose's Cottage, huh?" Wall asked. "Who gave it that name?"

"Beth did." Garrett puffed his chest out slightly.

"It's a good name." Wall mimicked Garrett's pose. "And way up there in the trees where a man, or woman, could stay for weeks without visitors. Get lost alone, or with another person, if one was so inclined."

"Yep." Garrett held a stare with his friend that Beth didn't quite understand.

"Who's standing watch?" Beth interrupted the silent fight for dominance.

Garrett broke the stare and turned to her. "Clint is over there with The Bull, and Blue is at the raft."

"When do you take over?" she asked.

Victoria cleared her throat to garner the attention of the men. "What are you taking over?"

"May as well tell her," Beth suggested. "She is the boss's daughter. She has as much interest in this mess as we do."

The look Garrett shot Beth proved he hadn't expected her to fully understand the role Victoria played in his life. He turned back to Victoria and explained the plan they'd concocted the night before.

"Do what you need, Garrett. I know you'll make the right decisions." Victoria batted her eyelashes at him and gave a smile meant to charm.

"We should get going." Beth started for the marked trail.

"Garrett." Victoria cleared her throat like a lady quietly chiding a forgetful beau.

Beth glanced back to see Victoria with hand extended, waiting for Garrett to tuck her arm into his. Beth faced forward once more and stomped her spiked feet up the path. She needed to remember that Garrett belonged to Victoria. Throughout all the time they spent together, she had a tendency to forget the deal he was bound to.

Wall caught up to her and kept pace. "Why'd you come all the way up here, Miz Elizabeth?"

"Like I told Aunt June, to discuss how to flush out the saboteur."

"No, not here on this hill." He motioned toward the vast display of overgrown forest that stretched for miles in all directions. "Why did you come here, to the Big Mountain Lumber Mill camp?"

"Oh." She studied him again. He seemed to genuinely want to converse, and his tone didn't accuse her of anything, like lying and cheating. Maybe he should since that's exactly what she did to get here. He seemed to be nothing more than curious. "It's a long story, but the simple version is I overheard something about what is going on, and came to help."

"So why become a Devil May Care? Why not work for Aunt June?"

"Why do people keep asking me that? Have you ever searched for something you lost before?"

"Of course."

"Did it do you any good to stay in the kitchen to look for it, or did you search the rest of the house, maybe even outside?"

Wall chuckled. "I suppose not."

"Well, it wouldn't do me any good to search only the Missoula cook camp." Beth took a few more steps up the mountain and tried not to stare as Victoria leaned on Garrett's elbow to climb over a rock on the trail.

"Do you go to many social events in town?" Wall stopped next to the same rock Victoria had trouble with, and reached out his elbow for her to use. Beth eyed his arm.

She didn't need an arm to lean on, but etiquette dictated she let him assist. Only they weren't in a place where etiquette mattered. Beth reached out and allowed him to help her maneuver the rough terrain. "I do the rounds."

"You're doing the scene," Victoria squealed with delight. "Why haven't I seen you at parties before?"

"I've been to a few, but Carrie and I preferred to stay in the shadows rather than parade ourselves around like cattle at auction."

"But you miss out on all of the fun that way," Victoria declared. "When we get home, I must have you over for tea. We can plan the best parties for you to attend to catch a beau. I had no idea that you were one of us. I thought you came from the outskirts of Missoula. That you were... Oh dear." She paused and placed a dainty hand over her mouth. "That must sound dreadful of me. I didn't mean to say you weren't one of us."

Beth shook her head. Truth be told, she didn't care what Victoria thought, or said. She could call her a two-headed mule for all she cared.

"What is your family name?" Victoria asked.

"Sanders."

"Not Margaret Sanders from Russell Street." When Beth nodded, Victoria continued, "Oh I just love Margaret. She is the dearest woman, so sweet and self-sacrificing. You must be the orphaned children she took on all those years ago."

Beth glanced back to see Garrett stiffen at the comment.

"My grandmother took us in when our parents died."

"Oh, how tragic. That must have been awful, poor girl." Victoria said the last like Beth was a child who lost a doll. Beth didn't care if she'd spoken out of genuine concern, the woman could go jump in a creek.

Beth faced the trail and stuck her chin in the air to continue to climb in silence. The only sounds that filtered through the trees were the one the forest provided, until the gentle huff of female sensibilities sounded behind her.

"My feet," Victoria whined. Beth looked as Victoria leaned heavily on Garrett's arm and lifted the hem of her narrow, pleated skirt to show her kid leather boots. Buttons swooped up the side to hug the ankles and then flared out at the top. A small heel at the back gave her height, but the slick soles and pinched sides were not conducive to a romp through the forest.

Beth tried not to let her surprise show at the demure woman's brazen move in hiking up her skirts in front of men. She may be wild enough to come up here and face a saboteur, but she wasn't uneducated on what was proper. That was not.

"Why did you wear those shoes up here?" Garrett asked as he bent over to examine the dainty heels on Victoria's feet.

"I thought I'd be tootling around camp. I hadn't intended to go for a walk today."

Garrett stood. "This isn't a walk. It's a hike to the cabin, and a steep one."

"You'll help me, won't you?" She snuggled closer to Garrett and slid her hand farther down his forearm.

"I've no choice," he answered.

Wall slid his gaze to Beth and held out his arm. "Do you need some help?"

Surprised, Beth set her arm on his again and continued up the trail. Was this the way all of the Devil May Cares planned to act toward her now that she was exposed as a woman? The last thing she wanted was to be treated like a wilting miss, but no one said she couldn't enjoy the little considerations.

The easy way Wall helped guide her up the steep path, with a gentle tug or solid arm to lean on, made her relax and enjoy the burn of the physical exertion. If it wasn't for her growing feelings for Garrett, she could see herself falling for Wall.

Beth tried not to appear irritated when Victoria picked her way up the trail. She studied the sun and guessed they'd hiked for almost three hours before the path opened up to the meadow that held Mother Goose's Cottage. Never before had it taken them so long to hike this high up the mountain.

"It's quaint," Victoria crooned when she limped toward the crude cabin.

"It's not meant to be lived in for long periods of time. It's more of an escape for Simon and me."

Victoria tugged Garrett to get him to follow her inside the cabin, and he did. Leaving Beth and Wall alone in the field.

"We should probably go in there after them," Wall suggested, but didn't move.

Beth stood silent and stared at the door to the cabin. If rules of propriety were so important to people of Victoria's ilk, then why would she display such blatant indecency where Garrett was concerned? "You're right. We need to get in there to form a plan."

Wall rubbed the back of his neck, and then turned toward the cabin. "I thought we had a plan." He followed as she led him toward the open door.

"I think he wants to figure out a way to get more logs to the mill without needing the chute."

"I've got a few ideas." Wall stood next to the door and motioned for her to proceed.

Beth entered the dark room and looked around. She'd thought the room would be empty except for Garrett and Victoria, only instead of nothing but a dirt floor like she'd imagined, a bed sat in the corner, and someone's personal belongings were scattered around the ground.

"Who do you think is staying here?" Wall picked up a pair of trousers lying near the door and checked the pockets.

"Who all knows this place is up here?" Beth asked.

"Everyone, but all the loggers are provided lodging. There's no reason for any of them to stay here." Garrett walked toward the door. "Let's go outside and leave their stuff be."

"Whoever it is needs a lesson in cleanliness," Victoria said as she stepped from the cabin into the open meadow.

Garrett led the way to the area where he'd kissed her when they'd been alone, and her heart flipped. Only weeks ago she'd thought they might have had something special, something that could lead to more, but then Victoria had shown up. Perfect Victoria. Beth needed to find a way to forget Garrett and his kisses. "Any ideas on how to get logs to the water so we can once again replenish the raft?"

"I've got a couple," Wall offered. "I say we use the train."

"The train?" Garrett started. "How do we do that?"

"With a trail of flat railcars and a whole lotta chain, we might be able to get a few loads down the mountain before we even make a drive. We move half of the faller team to the trees right behind the train."

Garrett nodded, excited, and continued with Wall's idea. "We can drag the logs over with the horse team, and set up a pulley system using the trees right next to the track to load them onto a flat car. Once they're set, they go down the mountain."

Wall shifted on his feet to display the same enthusiasm as Garrett at the plan. "The other faller and horse teams work up the hill, and we roll them down to the lake. You'll have to make certain no one goes near the hill. It won't get as much of a load down to the mill on the drive, but with the train running around the clock, we should get enough to meet the contract by the end of the season."

"That's only a month away."

"We're only a little more than half a drive short. We can make that up if we work hard. Both rivermen and timber beasts."

"It's worth a shot. Double the load going down before we even go on the drive. I'll write to my father and have him send up another engine, and as many flat cars as he can spare." Garrett drew closer to Beth, and her breath hitched. She sucked in a deep breath to help her focus.

What business did Garrett's father own? By the way the loggers deferred to Garrett's judgment—and oftentimes without question—she'd assumed he owned a stake in Big Mountain, but she'd been proven wrong when she'd met Victoria. His father was somehow connected to the company, though, but how? "Why would your father have flat cars to spare?"

Victoria looked at her as if she were daft. "His father owns the railroad. There are only three railroad companies in Missoula, and his father owns the one that services most of the mines and logging camps in the area, not to mention being the only company with a steam engine that runs from Glendive all the way to Seattle." Beth tried not to grow nauseated when Victoria batted her eyes, sidled up to him, and continued, "Soon Garrett and I will be the owners of both companies, once our fathers retire."

"The railroad," Beth repeated.

Victoria simply smiled. "When Garrett approached Father for a job at Big Mountain, Father knew he'd be an asset to the camp. With Garrett's connections, we were able to bring the railroad all the way up to the top of the mountain. And now we may have discovered how to revolutionize Montana logging."

Beth fixed her eyes on Garrett, who hid a forlorn plea behind a forced smile. In terms of good business decisions, a marriage between Garrett and Victoria would prove to be invaluable. If he didn't love her, then in matters of the heart, Garrett's was doomed. And so was Elizabeth.

* * * *

Garrett guided the small group down the path from Mother Goose's Cottage. The sound of Beth's laugh rang in his ears like a church bell paying respects to the deceased. He chanced a look behind him at the couple walking with heads together. Although Wall was a trusted friend, Garrett couldn't stand to see the two acting so familiar with one another.

Even the moment he'd seen Beth on the back of the horse with Wall, jealousy had smacked him in the gut like a schoolyard bully's fist. And later when his friend mentioned a desire to court Beth, he wanted to be that schoolyard bully.

Now he wanted to throw Beth over his shoulder and ride down the mountain until he reached his home. Last night he'd ached to kiss her once more. Her voice had been so sweet, so concerned when she asked about his well-being. He'd never before had anyone who truly cared about how he fared. He wanted that. Forever.

He should leave Victoria to Wall, and keep Beth all for himself. Duty would never allow it, and duty was a deep-seated principle he took very seriously. Duty and his father's threat to disown him. Despair turned his heart to stone. Why had he made that deal with his father? Beth had been nothing but a dream at the time so it hadn't mattered. All he'd cared about was getting back up the mountain. Now she was a reality. He wanted to throw duty down the river, go back on his word, and make Beth his.

He started down the trail, leaving the rest to follow. Like she'd done all afternoon, Victoria sidled up to him and slid her hand on his arm as they traversed the mountainside. The slick, flimsy boots she wore caused her to trip again, and he grabbed her waist to lift her upright.

His heart skipped a beat when he realized this was the same spot Beth had twisted her ankle the first time they visited the meadow. He'd lifted her into his arms and carried her the rest of the way down, all the while forcing his mind off the luscious curve of her lips so close to his. All he wanted to do since that day was taste their sweetness again. He needed to feel her lips against his for the rest of his life. Instead, he'd taste the thin lips of the woman now on his arm.

Victoria limped next to him so he tightened his hold on her arm. "Take care. This is where Beth twisted her ankle the last time we were here, and she had spikes on."

"You twisted your ankle in spikes?" Wall laughed, followed by Beth's humored chuckle. Garrett held back the growl threatening to vibrate his chest.

"It's easier than you think," she answered.

"I've been a logger for nigh on twelve years, and not once have I twisted my ankle with spikes. Hell, I've never twisted my ankle in my cowboy boots."

"You're a cowboy?" Beth's voice showed her surprise.

Garrett scowled again when her face lit. Why did she care what profession Wall had when not employed at the camp? He turned back the path.

"Us Devil May Cares are only here for the spring season. We do have lives elsewhere."

"And where is that?" Garrett heard Beth ask, but he didn't dare look behind. The woman on his arm tugged and drew his attention back to her, but all he wanted to do was toss her aside and grab Beth up into his arms to disappear into the woods. Alone with the woman he loved.

"Where do you plan to settle once this is all over?" Victoria asked him, oblivious to the chatter behind them.

Garrett kept his ear on Beth's conversation as he answered, "My place near the University."

"Father told me you had a big house up there. I can't wait until I..." Her words were lost on him once they rounded a corner and turned out of sight from Wall and Beth.

Garrett strained to hear the muffled conversation, ignoring Victoria's mumble. After a few breaths, they turned and he could once again hear Wall. "You should come out sometime. I'd love to show you the cherry trees, and I know Mother would love to have some female company around."

"That sounds delightful," Beth replied. Garrett squeezed his fists tight. He had no right to stop her from falling for Wall, but he couldn't stand to watch them laughing together as if they were lovers.

"Ouch!" Victoria squealed, and turned an icy stare to him. "What was that for?"

Good God. In his eavesdropping, he hadn't realized he'd squeezed Victoria's arm so tight. "My apologies, I thought you were slipping."

"I wasn't," she replied.

"I promise to be more careful."

"You can help me off that ledge down there on the path." She picked up the pace. They came to a mangled tree root entangled in an eroded ledge on the path and Garrett jumped down and turned. Victoria waited patiently with her hands outstretched to brace against his shoulders. He placed his hands on her hips, and glanced behind her to lock eyes with Beth.

She gave him a smile as she neared and her breath grew shallow like it did every time he bent down to kiss her, and he knew she felt the same as he did. *Dear God.* She wasn't falling for Wall. The sparkle in her eye as she stared down at Garrett's face proved it. But did she love him?

He set Victoria down, and she stepped past him.

"Let me help you, Miz Elizabeth." Wall jumped down next to Garrett.

"I've got it," Garrett said, as Beth stepped assuredly toward the drop off.

"Shouldn't you be escorting Miz Victoria?" Wall gave him a strange look, aimed to insist on his departure.

"I can jump myself." Beth leapt from the top, only to topple when she landed. Garrett caught her as she fell backward.

"Thanks," she breathed. He held her for a second longer than he should, and then with his help, she stood upright.

He answered with a slow nod, and turned to a glaring Victoria.

After all he and Beth had been through already, he was reduced to stolen moments and looks of shared desire. He wasn't certain just how long he could keep up the charade. Could he take another month of the torture of her presence? He needed to get the damn logs down the river so Beth could find her culprit—if he was indeed attached to the river crew, and then return to her life, and he to his now lonely existence without her.

First, he needed to find the traitor.

Chapter 17

"Aunt June sent me to give you this." Beth offered the basket of food to Garrett. Her heart fluttered at the sight of him leaning nonchalantly against a large boulder near the lake. She wished Aunt June hadn't insisted Carrie accompany her to bring the food. She wanted to be alone with him again. "She said we have to hurry back."

"Thank God. I'm starving." He grabbed the basket and flipped the red-checkered cloth off the top of the food, and then nodded at Carrie in greeting. "Ms. Carrie."

"I can't go anywhere alone," Beth said. "Aunt June says I cause too much trouble."

Garrett chuckled and took a bite of the beef chunk from the basket. "How is Simon? I've tried to visit him every morning, but I haven't been able to catch a moment today."

"He's doing a lot better. Aunt June said she may let him try to get up in the next day or two."

Garrett seemed to relax even more as he lounged against a tree and watched the raft.

"We're going to The Grove next."

The smile disappeared from Garrett's face. "Take care. It's been a few days since the fire, and nothing else has happened, but that doesn't mean it won't."

"Is the train on its way?"

"It should be here later today. I've got the rivermen working the logs on the other side of the tracks, and the timber beasts are back at The Grove."

"Do you think it will work?" she asked.

"It has to. If we work it right, and we can find out who's behind the attacks, then we should be able to get enough wood." Garrett took out a biscuit and began to eat.

"Has anyone seen anything suspicious?" Carrie asked. "We're keeping our ears and eyes open at the camp, but so far we've only heard the usual chatter about the fire—uneducated speculation. Simon thinks we aren't considering everyone. He says there's got to be someone in camp that we haven't looked at."

"But who?" Beth asked the obvious question.

"Are we confident it wasn't the guy who attacked you?" Carrie extended her hand toward Beth.

Beth shook her head. "No. It wasn't Luther's voice I heard."

"Speak of the devil," Garrett said. "Has anyone seen him yet? He seems to have disappeared off my radar. I've been busy. I haven't had time to fire him yet. I figured I'd do it the first time I ran across him, but I haven't, and no one I've asked knows where he is."

"He hasn't been to the supper table since the night you went looking for Beth," Carrie answered.

"If we're lucky, he left on his own." Garrett finished eating, tucked the cloth back inside the basket, and handed it to Beth. "Tell Aunt June thank you."

Beth acknowledged with a nod, and then followed Carrie back down the trail.

"I can see what you like in him." Carrie looked back to where Garrett stood. "He's handsome."

"He's betrothed to Victoria."

"I don't think he is." Carrie took the lead while they walked. "A few days before I came up, I saw her at the Milner's Ball, which by the way was dreadfully dull without you. I found a cozy spot between two gossiping spinsters. They're convinced that Victoria will be headed east at the end of the summer to find a husband."

Beth's heartbeat kicked up at the news. If Victoria wasn't intended for Garrett, then would he still be forced into marriage? "Who were the spinsters?"

"The Goodall sisters."

As fast as her heart sped up, it slowed. "The Goodall sisters also said that Mary Ellen was going to have a bastard child last year, but look how that news turned out."

"Mary Ellen is very happy at the mission. She's mothering a flock." Carrie grinned, and Beth rolled her eyes.

"The Goodall sisters like to make things up for the sake of gossip." Beth slowed and pulled Carrie into a nearby brush when a flash of color flickered on the trail ahead of them. It wasn't yet time to relieve Garrett, and no one else, besides them, would have any reason to come to the raft.

The only sound other than the footsteps of the intruder was Carrie's frantic breaths, as she stood tense next to her. Beth nudged her and motioned with one finger to stay quiet. This could be the moment Beth had planned for when she decided to blackmail Simon so she could help him. The moment when she discovered who the saboteur was and exposed him.

The footsteps grew louder and, as Beth's breath grew in time to Carrie's, the young Bonner boy trotted past.

Beth's shoulders sank, and she relaxed.

"What?" Carrie asked, her voice barely a whisper.

"It's only Michael."

At the sound, Michael stopped and turned with fear tearing his eyes.

"Who's there?" he asked in a shaky voice.

"It's only us," Beth said, stepping from the brush. "We thought you were someone else."

"So you hid in the bushes?" His voice changed to one of curiosity.

"We're women," Carrie said with a playful grin. "We're scared of everything."

Michael scrunched his nose. "My sister pees her pants every time I jump out at her from the hayloft at home."

"You shouldn't scare your poor sister," Carrie chided. "She may end up socking you right in the nose one of these days."

"Nah, she's too small and scared."

"What are you doing out here?" Beth asked.

Michael searched the trail nervously. "I…I came to find some dry tinder for the cook fire in my camp."

"You shouldn't come this far away from camp. It's too dangerous." Carrie's tone matched that of a concerned mother.

"I've done picked all the tinder near the cabins."

"Best hurry and get back. You don't want to be caught this far out at night." Beth started down the trail, and then turned back on second thought. "And you should probably return to camp. Garrett is near the raft, and if he sees you, you may get a scolding from him."

"I'll…I'll find tinder somewhere else." His eyes filled with fear, and he turned to push past them, headed toward camp. True Garrett was a man who could frighten a pelt right off a beaver, but he was a kind ruler. Why would the boy be so frightened at the thought of a scolding?

Beth and Carrie both turned and followed at a slower pace, watching as the Bonner boy ran back up the trail.

Disappointment niggled inside her. Aside from Michael, no one else had even attempted to come toward the raft. The plan they'd laid out to weed out the saboteur, while at the time had seemed like a good one, had failed miserably. Not only that, but she'd talked to virtually everyone and not one of them sounded like the man from the platform. How were they ever going to catch the traitor?

* * * *

Beth strained under the pressure of Simon's weight as she helped him stand. His legs shook, but he took first one half step, and then another, toward the chair in the corner. She felt his muscles quiver beneath her fingers, and she knew he wasn't as strong as he'd claimed. "Maybe you should get back in bed."

"Nonsense. Get me to that chair, Lizbe, or I'll go myself." Simon shuffled forward again and leaned heavily on her arm. She shifted to put his weight on her shoulders while taking care not to touch his wounds. "How long have I been in that bed?"

"A few weeks. I honestly thought you'd be further along by now, but you barely leave the bed."

A knock sounded, and Carrie came in and shut the door behind her. "Goodness, why is he out of bed?"

She rushed over and dipped low to take a position under his arm on the other side. Simon's face softened, and he seemed to limp even more than he did before. Weight eased from Beth's shoulders the slightest bit as Carrie's hand fluttered on his chest to help brace herself for an added weight.

"You used the lavender soap again." Simon leaned toward Carrie's hair and took a deep inhale.

"You said you liked it and it made you feel better." Carrie adjusted her hold on Simon's torso.

"I do." They got to the chair and with a slow descent, Simon sat. His eyes sparkled when he drew his gaze from Carrie's face, to her toes.

Carrie bustled around Beth's brother and stuffed a blanket around his legs as Simon took another sniff of her hair. What had Beth missed?

"Thank you." He smiled up at Carrie. His bandages were long gone from his face, and in their place a red scar the length of her thumbnail paralleled his eyebrow, and another sliced first across the back part of his cheek, and then swooped down the side of his neck. Bandages wrapped around his torso, hiding the remainder of his wounds.

Simon had yet to see his beautiful features marred by the wicked wounds, and Beth didn't know how he would take it. Tonight, though, Aunt June had planned to let him see what the vicious cougar had done.

Another knock on the door sounded, and Garrett and Aunt June slipped in.

"You look in good spirits," Garrett said.

"I've had the best nurses in the world."

"Let's get to it, then." Aunt June bustled up to Simon and began to unravel the gauze. Beth went to get the looking glass for her brother. Her shoulder brushed Garrett's arm, and her breath failed. Garrett stiffened. The dim light of the candle-lit cabin failed to hide the desire that sparked instantly in his eyes.

Garrett's mouth tensed to form a straight line before he tore his gaze away and stared at her brother once more.

Taking a lung full of air to control her rapid heartbeat, she grabbed up the looking glass and brought it to her brother. She handed it to him facedown and waited without breathing as her brother studied his reflection.

Simon traced the healing scars from his cheekbone to his neck. The only indication of his pain was a slight twitch of his jaw muscles. He glanced down to his torso where four long slashes marked his once flawless chest down to his stomach. He outlined them with his finger.

"There are also a few gashes on your thigh, and puncture wounds on your shoulder." Aunt June pointed out the teeth marks where the cougar had dragged him into the brush.

"Good God, I'm lucky to be alive," he whispered. The expression on his face grew dark, and he flashed a quick glance at Carrie, and then looked back at the mirror.

"You are," Aunt June agreed. "If it wasn't for Garrett's quick thinking, and Wall showing up at the right time, I'd have had to bury that pretty face of yours."

"It's not pretty anymore, Aunt June." Simon studied his reflection again.

"You're as good looking as you ever were," Carrie replied.

"I think you doth protest too much." Simon tried to convey humor in his tone, but failed. The anger behind the words was unmistakable.

"Nonsense," Aunt June chimed. "You're as handsome as ever, only now you're a bit more rugged is all."

"At least you're safe from the mayor now." Beth tried to lighten the mood, but it must not have worked.

Everyone save Simon shot her a look of reprove. Her brother gave a small chuckle. "Does that mean you're done blackmailing me?"

"Yes. I've thrown in my lot with the cook. You're free."

"Garrett, you can send my sister home."

Garrett smiled at her brother's playful tone. "She's in too deep now. I'm afraid she's stuck here until we save the Big Mountain Lumber Mill."

Simon slouched a little in his chair, and she knew his strength was weakening. "You know, if you get out of bed once in a while, you might be able to get better quicker."

"Yes, but then I wouldn't get all this female attention." He placed his hands on the arms of his chair and pushed to try to stand.

Carrie rushed forward and helped him up, but he shirked away. Beth took up Carrie's intended position, and Aunt June took the other side as Carrie threw back her shoulders and lifted her chin. What on earth had gotten into these two?

Simon leaned heavily on her shoulder. "Now I'm afraid I'm a little taxed from all of this." He held out his hand to his friend. "Garrett, thank you for everything."

Beth was equally grateful. If it hadn't been for her foolish behavior, Simon wouldn't have been in that position in the first place, but if it wasn't for Garrett, Simon wouldn't even be alive. Garrett and his good sense somehow balanced out her foolishness. What was she going to do when she no longer had him to pick up the pieces of her life?

* * * *

Garrett left the cook's abode and crossed the tracks to see a pile of logs waiting to be loaded onto the cars. If they did this right, they could meet the contract and be down the river with a raft within a fortnight. *Thank God.* All the women piling up in his camp were about as easy to handle as a bear in spring.

The Devil May Cares huddled near the base of a tree as it swayed. Garrett slid his gaze to the top where Wall worked to secure a pulley. Although Wall tested his friendship lately with his desire to court Beth, the man was excellent at his job and dedicated to the company.

With a holler to the men below, Wall began to descend.

"All set," Wall said when he jumped the remaining foot to the ground.

Garrett motioned with his head toward the railcar. "Let's give it a go."

The rivermen ran to their designated positions, and Teddy maneuvered his team into place. Once the chains were all secured, he snapped the reins and shouted encouragement to the animals.

The jingle of the horse tack as they pulled, and screech of the wood as it moved, sounded through the clearing. In no time at all, the first log thumped down onto the flat car, and the men cheered. Their enthusiasm whipped up by the small step at success, the men took their positions on the next log and repeated the process.

Once all the logs were set, the train lurched forward, and the process began again.

"I'm gonna go check on Simon," he told Wall. With his men working hard, he took his leave. There was one thing he needed to do before the end of the day.

Garrett hurried to the cook's cabin, and knocked before entering. Beth sat in the corner next to a sleeping Simon. He motioned with his head for her to meet him outside. She nodded, and he stepped back and waited for the door to close, and then grabbed her hand to tow her behind the cabin. Finally getting the chance to be alone with her. However brief it was, and however secretive they had to be. He'd do it. He needed her gentle calm to focus his mind. "I need to talk to Jessip. Come with me?"

"You could have asked me out there, I still would have agreed."

"Yes, but then Victoria would have heard." He didn't want his intended bride asking questions, and this way he could have some time alone with Beth.

"I hadn't thought of that. I'll slip away and meet you on The Deck."

"Ten minutes." That should give him enough time to stop and check on the train one last time before heading up the hill.

Beth gave a nod and turned to disappear around the corner.

Garrett patted his back pocket to ensure the contract Paul had sent on the train was still there. In less than two weeks, he could be down the river with the drive, and this would all remain as a memory. Hell, after so many accidents this spring and early summer, he didn't think the big bugs would keep him on even if he wanted to stay.

The train came into sight, and he checked the entire machine for signs of tampering. With any luck, they could get the logs loaded and down without incident. He rounded the front as Clint and Blue signaled the horse team. Behind them, deep in the forest, Simon's timber beasts hacked away, working hard to fall as many trees as possible.

Garrett waited for the log to drop down onto the car and then approached the Devil May Cares.

"How's Simon?"

"Better. Sleeping," Garrett answered. "He'll be up and about by next week I should think. I need to check out the rest of the operation. I'll be busy until supper."

"We're going to keep loading until we run out of light," Wall said. "I think we've got enough daylight left to send the train to the mill tonight. If not, then early tomorrow morning."

"Good. Tell the conductor to drop off the load and then turn around and come right back up. We'll keep this up until the raft has enough logs to make the drive worth doing. I'm going to head up there and talk with the Bonner crew. Oh, and have you seen and fired Luther yet?"

"I think he shucked out of here. I haven't seen him since we found Beth."

"Keep an eye out. If you do see him, send him on the train home. I'd say fetch me so I could have a word, but talking to the man is pointless. I'd much rather beat him to death."

Wall gave a jaunty salute, and Garrett turned to hike the hill leading to The Deck and Grove.

The familiar sounds of trees falling and men chopping filled the air as he walked to the center of The Deck and found The Bull. He nodded a greeting and waited for the man to finish giving an order.

The Bull turned to him. "If we keep up this pace we should have a drive at the end of the week. Once you and your crew leave, we'll combine the camps and keep working the logging train. Then when we get word from the big bugs, we'll stop."

"I suppose once that happens, then Paul will come up here to evaluate and set your team up again with a new Deck and Grove."

"Better off, I suppose. We were about clear of this area anyway."

Beth's head bobbed over the edge of the hill, and Garrett excused himself. He met her halfway and stopped. "I've sent Michael with a note for Jessip. He's supposed to meet us at the spot we used before. Let's head up that way."

On Beth's nod, he led her up the gently climbing trail and through the dense vegetation to their meeting spot.

In less than a minute, Jessip fought his way through the brush.

"I've got your contract." Garrett handed him a sealed letter.

Jessip grabbed the paper and ripped it open. After taking a moment to read it, he nodded. "You've kept your deal, and I've kept mine. I can tell you, though, word's got out about the thousand and there's a bit of grumbling about all the work we're doing up here."

An instant headache formed behind Garrett's eyes. *Good God, what else could go wrong?*

Jessip continued, "I'm working to keep the men at bay. This is a good company to work for, and I keep reminding the Bonner boys of that. Take care. I'll keep an eye out on my end until the drive is over."

"I've got a few people watching the operation at my camp. If we're lucky we will catch whoever is behind the prior attacks, and stop anyone else who's thinking of taking that thousand."

Jessip gave a mumbled goodbye and turned to leave. "Oh yeah. I don't know if it's important, but I've noticed an old man comin' and goin' from the mountain several times a day. Don't know what his business is up here, but I've never seen him before."

Garrett nodded. "Thanks."

Once Jessip left, he grabbed Beth's hands to guide her back onto the trail. Instead of taking the fork that would bring them back to camp, he turned and headed up the mountain.

"Where are we going?" Beth stepped up the pace to walk beside him.

"To Mother Goose's Cottage. I think Jessip was talking about my uncle. He's another problem I need to take care of." Who else would the Bonner crewman have been talking about? Uncle Marcus was the only person who fit that description, but why would he choose to stay in Mother Goose's Cottage instead of the bed he'd been offered when he first arrived?

Garrett's head started to throb, and then Beth brushed past him as she sped up to take a steep incline. The warmth of her body where it touched his eased the tense muscles in his shoulders. He enjoyed watching the easy way she lived life—always happy, always with a free spirit and honest approach. How different she was from his gruff and calculating decisions. They could make quite the couple if the fates would allow, but alas they were not kind to a man of his disposition.

Chapter 18

Beth let Garrett take the lead as they crested the last hill to enter the meadow. Like before, dainty white flowers sprinkled the field and tall grass gave an instant sense of relaxation. The clean mountain air filled her lungs, and she smiled. Here, alone with Garrett, she was the woman she was meant to be.

"Let's check the cabin." Garrett threw open the door, but to Beth's surprise it was empty inside.

Garrett shook his head. "Oh to be a free man on the cusp of liberty and destruction."

"I've never heard that poem before. Is it John Clare?"

"No. Those are my thoughts. I wonder where he's gone? I haven't seen him in a few days."

"You think like a poet?"

"On occasion." Garrett turned until his body drew even with hers. He stared at her lips and the look in his eye showed a longing for things he couldn't have. She felt the same.

"We should get back to camp," she said in a tone barely above a whisper.

"Yes. We should." But he didn't move. "You tempt me."

"I've tried to keep my distance." Not that she'd wanted to, but she had tried. Somewhat. "I don't want to be in the way."

"You're the one person who's not." He stepped closer, and kept his gaze on her mouth.

She took a deep, shuttered breath. Her stomach ached to have his hand caress her cheek again, his lips to press against her mouth. "Victoria is nice—"

"Sshh," he whispered and placed a single finger on her lips. His skin was hot against her mouth as he caressed her lip with his finger, and something deep inside sighed with satisfaction. "Let it be just us up here."

She nodded and worked to keep her eyelids from falling shut as he touched her.

"I've wanted to be alone with you ever since the night by the campfire. I need you, Beth."

"But you can't have me." She stated the one thing neither of them wanted to hear. Her heart dropped into a deep pit of despair at the words.

"We could leave. Build a life somewhere else." His eyes followed his hand as he caressed her cheek.

"A man is only as good as his honor, and you are the noblest man I know. You could never sacrifice your honor that way, and I wouldn't ask that of you."

"Ask it of me. I will do anything you wish. I'll chop down all the trees in the forest, move this mountain, whatever you want I will give you. Just tell me you want me."

"I do want you," she said. "But you are not mine."

He leaned down and slowly kissed her, his lips barely a whisper at first. He grasped the back of her head with both hands, tugged her head closer, and deepened the kiss.

His finger traced her jaw. A tingle followed his path down the soft contours of her neck and dipped into the crevice of her collarbone to forge a path of hot fire down her chest and to the sides of her breasts. She tilted her head back and offered her neck. She could not deny him, for this was what she wanted, to feel the hot stroke of his hands down her body. She leaned back in his embrace, pliant and ready to let him do whatever he wished. She could no longer deny the need to be his, no longer wanted to.

Her nipples hardened, and her breasts stung with heat and anticipation. He cupped one hand over her breast and weighed it in his palm.

"Perfect," he said and inhaled.

Garrett reached around to grab her bottom and pull her closer. Her stomach twisted when he lowered his lips to hers in a violent crush of a kiss. What was she doing? Not only had she never experienced anything of such intimacy, but he was betrothed. She should walk down the mountain and straight to the railcar.

As if he'd read her thoughts, Garrett stepped back and stared into her eyes. This one simple movement and passionate gaze spoke of love and belonging, and she knew they were meant to be. He kissed her lightly once more and, with gentle pressure from his hands, urged her to lie down in the flowered grass.

"Tell me to stop." Garrett covered her with his body as his hands roamed her sides. She could feel the love and desire with each stroke of his calloused hands against the exposed skin of her arms.

"I can't." Beth arched her back and took in a much-needed breath. She lay dizzy, unable to move. He used the back of one finger to caress her neck and the top of her shoulder. She pressed her breasts into Garrett's chest. He bent to taste the exposed area just above her collar, as he popped one single button open from her shirt. "You must."

"I can't," Beth said again, and bit her lip.

"My God, how I love you," he whispered.

Any reserve she had melted. With one last doomed argument to herself to follow his request, she wrapped her arms around his neck and gave a kiss meant to prove her love in return.

* * * *

Garrett couldn't believe what had just happened. How had he confessed such a thing? He knew he'd been slowly losing his heart to her, but he hadn't planned to say the words aloud. He knew they were true. Throughout the years, he'd fallen in love with Elizabeth Sanders, and not a love to be taken lightly. He now possessed a deep-seated need to have her next to him for the rest of his life. But fate was cruel, and he was doomed to a life of Victoria and despair.

When he mentioned running away, he'd meant it, but in truth he wasn't positive he could. Not if he didn't have a job or means to support Beth and a family. Beth would make the most beautiful mother he'd ever seen. His breath hitched at the thought of her bouncing his child on her knee.

He kissed her supple lips again. She needed to tell him to stop. No, he should back away and leave her be, but he couldn't. He'd passed the point of no return.

Beth moved beneath him, and his desire flared once more. God, she was beautiful, a sensual creature sent to him to taste, to have. He slid his fingers beneath the buttons of her shirt and kissed her. He tugged, and another button popped open with ease. Overjoyed, he continued with the rest and deepened the kiss. He wanted to make her see what she meant to him. Know that for this one moment in time, they were one. He wanted her to need him, just as he needed her.

He traced her skin, down the line of her shirtfront while he worked the tiny buttons. Her stomach quivered and made him ache even more. When he reached her pants, the metal button pressed cold and firm against the denim. He reared his head back and looked deeply into her eyes.

"I need you, Elizabeth," he pleaded. "I love you."

Her chest heaved, and he could tell she struggled to breathe. Her eyes glazed, and she reached up and traced the buttons of his shirt.

He watched her fingers pop his buttons loose, one by one.

Garrett reached up and grabbed Beth's wrists to stop her progression. "I don't think you understand, love. If I take you now, there will be no going back. You will be mine forever, but I cannot keep you."

Beth nodded, and desire clouded her eyes. "I understand. I want no other."

Her kiss proved her words as her tongue lined his lip, causing his breath to hitch. She ran her hands up his chest and back down. She reached the buttons to his pants and flicked her wrist to snap the button loose. He felt the gentle tug and the instant release of pressure around his waist. Honor be damned. He needed her.

What little control Garrett had left snapped. With expert hands, he finished with Beth's clothes. She was flawless. So perfect in form that his mind spun. She was stunning, her body seamless, unspoiled, and picturesque—so magnificent that it made his lungs burn with the need to breathe.

He placed one of his legs between both of hers, and braced himself. His manhood strained against its confinement and he pushed further against her in an unspoken plea for release.

Garrett grabbed her round, perfect bottom with one hand and braced on his elbow. He tangled his free hand in her hair—now grown out enough to frame her face in the most adorable way. A freckle on her neck drew his attention so he gently tugged her head back and kissed it. Working his way down to her breasts, he sucked in one beady nipple and caressed it with his tongue.

Elizabeth gasped. He watched her bury her palms deep in the grass and arch toward him. Her stomach quivered, heaved as he released one breast and went to the other. He ran his hands up and down her body and imprinted her form in his mind. The desire to show her what could be between them became too much, and he tugged her beneath him and, with his knee, pulled her legs farther apart. Her eyes hazed with desire, and he stood to strip his own clothes and toss them aside. He silently dared her to look away, to stop him if she valued her virtue. His reason and restraint had evaporated the moment she'd confessed her desire.

With no rejection from her, he once again lowered over her, this time positioning himself between her thighs.

"You are mine," he said against her temple, and then kissed it. He began to slide into her until he felt the gentle restraint against his manhood, and then took a deep breath and laid his forehead against hers. "Are you certain?"

Her eyes spoke her response, and she arched into him the exact moment he pushed. She sucked in a breath, and a tear ran down her face.

"Damn. I'm sorry, Beth."

She shook her head and clutched him when he started to roll away.

"No," she said, her voice breathy with passion. "I'm yours."

Garrett relaxed, pulled out slightly and pushed back in. He kissed her while he tested her response. Beth's breath became rough, and he continued to show her why she was his.

"No," she pleaded when he stopped. "Again."

He submitted, no longer able to hold back. He kissed her with fervor and let her see his true self, his desire and need for her. She understood, and responded in kind. Her body started to quake as she reached the peak and he could hold back no longer. With one final groan, he released his seed deep inside her.

Garrett slumped down beside her, both of them exhausted. With one hand, he toyed with her hair. He swore that the earth had just shattered and reformed as they made love next to the cabin. His life had changed, and there was only one thing he could do. He had to get her out of the camp, and back to Missoula. He had to figure out this whole mess. Figure out a way to be with her. Forever.

Chapter 19

Beth was ruined. Not because she was no longer pure, but because she'd now lost her heart completely to Garrett. Before she'd gone to Mother Goose's Cottage yesterday, she had a fighting chance at finding happiness with someone else, but now every male she saw came up short compared to Garrett.

Victoria sat at the table talking to the men while Beth and Aunt June washed the dishes as they piled up in the wash bin.

"Elizabeth," Carrie said. "Did you know that Ms. Victoria went to a girl's school in London?"

"Oh?" Beth took a quick look at Garrett as he chopped wood near the cook's cabin.

Victoria beamed. "Garrett and I both went to school in England." She batted her eyelashes at Garrett, who stopped and acknowledged with a nod.

"Was it terribly boring?" Carrie asked, but Beth didn't care to hear the answer.

Aunt June glanced toward the cabin. "I think I hear Simon calling. Carrie, would you mind checking on him?"

"So he can toss me out again?" Carrie stood and headed toward the cabin. "Ever since he saw himself in the mirror, he's refused to allow me inside. And when I do go in, he turns away. He won't let me see him."

"A man likes to look his best for the woman he's fixin' to fall in love with. Give him a while to get used to the scars and he'll be right as rain." Aunt June shoed Carrie toward the door, and Beth's friend disappeared inside.

"You shouldn't toy with her like that, Aunt June," Victoria chided.

"Who said I was? That man is destined to marry into my family. And since I ain't no young doe anymore, my goddaughter will have to do."

Beth chuckled, picked up the empty water bucket, and headed toward the water's edge. She'd barely made it a few steps when a horse whinnied. Frowning at the oddity of the sound so far away from The Grove, she pivoted to look as Teddy's brown mare ran into camp and headed straight for the cook table, followed closely by two other horses. She searched the nearby landscape as several more horses ran into the forest.

Victoria screamed and jumped on the table as men scattered when the mare thundered through the center of camp, headed straight for Beth.

Beth turned to run when someone grabbed her from behind and yanked her to safety. She spun around in her savior's arms to see Garrett. She wrapped her arms around his neck and buried her face in his chest as the rest of the horses ran past. The thump of her heart beat so wild it could run with the horses and never be found.

Garrett caressed her hair, and she looked up into his eyes, shining with the same fear she'd felt mere moments before.

The sound of men scrambling reached her ears, and Beth stepped away as Victoria bustled up to Garrett.

"Oh my goodness! Beth is lucky you were nearby." Victoria snuggled up to Garrett's side.

"Someone let the horses loose," said Blue as he ran up to Garrett. "We're almost done with the next train load, but we can't get it done if we don't have horses."

"Teddy!" Garrett shouted and politely moved Victoria aside. He gave Beth one last glance before tromping off after the chute monkey.

Victoria gave a single surprised blink and quickly masked her expression. She turned to Beth. "You were truly lucky that Garrett was handy to pull you to safety."

"I was," Beth agreed.

"I'll get that sort of consideration once we are married." She smiled, but the slight pinch of her lips proved the motion was forced.

"I'm convinced you will," Beth replied, but her eyes flew to Garrett as he conversed with the group of loggers in the center of camp.

Garrett glowered, and after a quick word, they disbursed in separate directions—not one of them toward the train. Beth took a quick look around to ensure Aunt June wouldn't stop her and headed to check near the railroad tracks.

Beth slipped past the cabin when she heard her name being called. She turned as Carrie ran up to walk beside her. "Where are we going?"

"The men are out looking for the horses, so I thought I'd take a quick look at the load."

"I'll wager its fine. Why wouldn't it be?"

"When a corral full of horses gets loose, I get suspicious."

"Good point." Carrie adjusted her gait to walk like Beth. "Aunt June came into the cabin and said you were almost run over. Are you all right?"

"A little shook up, but I'll be fine. How's Simon?"

"Grumpy as usual."

"He'll get over it." Beth emerged from the tree line with Carrie following behind.

The long line of railcars flowed from the tree line near the hill and curved around past the ever-expanding clearing to disappear into the forest.

"We'll start with the load, and then check the engine and work our way back."

Carrie nodded and followed.

The pile of logs near the tracks waited to be heaved onto the railcar, but nothing seemed out of place so Beth made a wide berth around the front of the engine. A movement toward the middle of the train caught her attention, and she motioned for Carrie to keep quiet, and then started to run in the direction of the movement.

When Beth neared, she slowed and took quiet steps.

Garrett's uncle bent over the coupler with his back to Beth. His elbow popped out, and he yanked the pin from the coupling.

Beth motioned for Carrie to move back and retreat, and slid her finger over her mouth to keep her friend quiet. Carrie backed in between two cars and ducked.

"Let's go." She turned and mouthed, pointing toward the camp.

"What are you doing here?" Marcus growled and advanced forward. Beth turned to run, twisting her ankle. Her leg gave out, but she forced herself past the pain and tried to flee. Before she could run, Marcus grabbed her hair and tossed her backward to land on the sharp rocks beneath the track. She screeched in pain, and struggled to regain her footing. She couldn't let him win.

Marcus leaned over her, fury darkening his eyes.

"No you don't!" Carrie screamed, leapt onto his back, and began to pummel the side of his head.

"Little bitch!" Marcus fought to free himself from Carrie's grip. Fists flew in all directions, and he growled in protest, but the girl stayed with a surprising strength.

Beth searched the ground and found a fallen branch.

"Carrie! Jump!" she yelled.

Her friend obeyed, and Marcus immediately turned with fists cocked back. With all the might she could muster, Beth whacked him on the back of the head.

Marcus fell forward, landing on top of Carrie, who struggled to get out from beneath the large man. Beth placed her hand over her chest and inhaled. Aside from the log down the river, this had been the closest she'd ever been to death.

"He would have killed us. We need to get Garrett." Beth reached down and helped her friend wiggle free.

Carrie jumped to her feet and ran past Beth. Following, Beth kept pace until they both reached the camp.

"Where's Garrett?" she cried as Aunt June stared at her with surprise written on her motherly features.

"Went after the horses. Why?"

Beth gave a quick account of Marcus and the incident, then stopped to take a much-needed breath.

"Good Lord, girl. Don't just stand there, find some rope. I've always wanted to tie that deadbeat up. Now I have a damned good excuse." Aunt June wiped her powdered hands on her apron and kicked into action, running to the cabin and throwing open the door. Beth followed her inside.

"Caught ourselves a saboteur," Aunt June boasted to Victoria, now sitting beside Simon. "Gonna go hog tie him and throw him in the lake. Let Garrett know when he comes back, will you? We'll be over by the train."

Victoria nodded, her face turned down with the slightest hint of confusion.

Aunt June grabbed a pile of shredded cloth, and plucked a long metal spoon off the wall near the cook supplies. "Off we go, missy. Need to get there before he wakes up."

Beth followed the cook as she tore along the ground toward where Marcus lay. She could see the man's form lying prone on the ground, unmoving as they approached.

"Marcus!" Aunt June yelled, and kicked him in the side. "Tie his hands."

Beth took a long strip of cloth from Aunt June, and then kneeled to tie his hands together.

"Damn good thing I done made extra bandages long enough to wrap around a man's body. I'm just glad something good came out of your poor handsome brother getting hurt. At least he helped us catch the traitor," Aunt June prattled as she slid the bandages around Marcus's feet and yanked until he groaned from the pain.

She studied her metal spoon again, and then gave him one hard whap on the head. He yelped, and Aunt June shoved his shoulder back to try to get him to turn. "Oh, hush up. What are you doing out here anyway while the rest of the men search for the horses?"

Marcus groaned again, and Aunt June yanked him sideways until he finally turned and looked up at her, a distant, confused look shining in his eyes. "I was just checking around the train for the horses."

"In between the two flat cars?" Carrie asked.

"I dropped my hat." He moved as if to reach for his head, but stopped and stared at his elbows when his tied hands wouldn't move. "Goddamn bitch hit me."

"You aren't wearing a hat," Aunt June pointed out.

"'Cause it flew away after the little bitch jumped on my back."

"You're a flannel-mouthed liar!" Carrie exclaimed.

Aunt June moved to stand square in front of Marcus. "I'm inclined to believe my goddaughter over your swindlin', no good, sidewinding rear-end, but I'll let Garrett make that call once he gets here."

Just then, a ruckus sounded down the trail they'd taken to get there, and Beth turned as Garrett and the Devil May Cares ran down the path.

"What in blue hell is going on here?"

"Caught ourselves a traitor," Aunt June spat.

Garrett sent Beth a questioning glance, so she divulged the story.

Unlike the reaction she thought she'd get, Garrett's eyes stormed. "You should have left him alone and come to me. I'll deal with you two later." He glanced between her and Carrie, and then turned to his uncle. "Marcus, tell me what happened."

Putting on a face of innocence, Garrett's uncle recited the same lies he'd told Aunt June. Garrett sent Beth a questioning glance, and she shook her head in denial.

"You aren't going to believe a couple of brainless women over me, are you? Women are fickle and only good for one thing."

"Oh, you deadbeat reprobate!" Aunt June kicked him in the shin.

Marcus yelped. "Are you going to let her do that to your old uncle?"

"You're a hard case." Garrett shook his head at the ground in disappointment. "I believe the women. You'd sell your own sons for a bottle of whiskey."

"You're no better than me," Marcus shouted. "Only difference is you got lucky all your life. I don't see no one giving me an education at a foreign school, or a job with a fancy title like they did you. We're the same. One day you'll find yourself in need of family, and they'll be no one left 'cause you done gone betrayed them."

Wall trotted up to the group. "I checked the railcars. The coupling pins were pulled."

Garrett turned an accusing stare on his uncle. "Who paid you to do this?"

Marcus scrunched his nose and mouth in disgust and spit. "Nope."

"You're not going to tell me?" Garrett squatted down until he drew level with his uncle's face. "You betray me, your family, and you hold the secret of the men trying to destroy everything we've worked for?"

Marcus simply stared straight ahead and refused to speak.

Garrett stood and turned to his men. "Put some rope on him and toss him in the boxcar. Lock it up tight. We'll ship him down to the mill with the logs. They can handle him from there."

Dick and Blue stepped forward and began to heave Marcus to his feet, and Beth turned toward camp with the rest of the crowd. Garrett stepped next to her and walked alongside. She could feel the anger sliding off him in waves.

The smoke from the cook fire came into view, and the crowd dissipated to their various positions in camp, and Carrie followed Aunt June to tend to the fire, leaving Garrett alone with Beth.

Beth tried to hold firm to her gumption, but the fury emanating from Garrett sent instant panic deep in her stomach. Of all the antics she'd done during the season, he'd never let such fury show. Not even when he first realized she was a woman did he hold this much anger bottled up. She could tell by the way he now sported a pulsing vein on his right temple—a sight she'd rarely seen on Garrett, and certainly didn't the night he found out her true identity. She was in big trouble.

* * * *

Garrett concentrated on keeping his breathing even as he watched the small woman before him, surrounded by the towering giants of the forest encircling Aunt June's camp. Her hand shook the slightest bit when he spoke. She was scared. For the first time since they'd come to the camp, she was frightened of him. With a deep, cleansing breath, he calmed.

"Why didn't you fetch me?" He let his tone show the seriousness of the situation, but brought it down enough to calm whatever fears she may have.

"I was going to, but there wasn't time, and I had no idea where you were. By the time I realized who he was, he saw us. We were too close and before I knew it, he hovered over me."

The news calmed him even more. She'd intended to come to him. "Did he hurt you?"

"No. I think he would have, but Carrie jumped onto his back and distracted him until I could find a weapon. That's when I knocked him for a loop."

"You are to never put yourself in danger again. I can't lose you," he confessed. A lie. He'd lose her as soon as they ended the drive because of his foolishness. At least she'd be alive.

"I came here to help you find out who was sabotaging the camp, and I did."

"And are you satisfied in your quest here at camp?" He hoped so. The woman needed to get to Missoula where she could lead a life free of danger. That would be the only way he could let her go, knowing she would be safe.

"I still want to go on the log drive. If you'll let me. I've come this far."

"In the cook's raft or the bateau. I will not allow anything else."

"The cook's raft will suffice."

"Then I will see when I can satisfy your desires." If only he could do that for the rest of their lives. He took a quick glance toward Victoria as she stepped from the cabin and conversed with Carrie near the cook fire. Victoria would make a good wife. With perfect manners and a sweet disposition, she defined the essence of a proper wife, but he no longer wanted a proper wife. He wanted Beth. "If you'll excuse me, I need to see about the log drive."

He nodded a goodbye, and when she responded in kind, he left to search for The Bull.

It took but a few minutes of searching to locate the timber beast's supervisor as he stood on The Deck and directed the operation. He saw Garrett approach and inclined his head in greeting. "Got the horses back. That was quite the stir. Never had such an eventful season before."

"One for the campfire."

"Ah, true. Can't wait to sit around a fire with a shave tail and tell the story. You got the deadbeat I hear."

Garrett shook his head in shame. He not only had to confess to the Bonner camp, but big bugs, and his father. The one mistake he'd made through the season had cost more than half the load. He'd learned his lesson, though. No matter how close a person may be, a deadbeat would always be a deadbeat. Some people were beyond redemption. "Yeah. My uncle. Seems he took the bribe."

The Bull frowned. "That the guy who's been staying at Mother Goose's Cottage? I saw him headed that way right before the fire. Ain't no way he started it."

Garrett's brows furrowed, mimicking the look on The Bull's face. If his uncle had been the one who was staying in the cabin, and he'd been there during the fire, then who had started it? "If you'll excuse me."

"Sure," The Bull said. "I'm doubling up my teams so the drive will be ready by tomorrow. The sooner we get down the mountain, the better."

"I'll let my men know. We'll be ready to leave day after tomorrow, barring something else going wrong."

"True, true," The Bull agreed and then turned to shout an order to his men, so Garrett headed toward the boxcar holding his uncle.

The sound of grating metal echoed off the walls of the boxcar when he opened it. His uncle sat in the corner with hands tied behind his back. His head bowed low, he didn't bother to look up when Garrett jumped onto the wood floor of the boxcar. "Have you been staying at the cabin up the mountain?"

"Ain't nobody else livin' there," he defended. "So I took it up."

Garrett thought back to the day at the meadow with Beth. The empty house and secluded field had seemed like a gift from God, and at the time his mind focused more on Beth and not on the significance of the vacant abode. "But you left a few days ago?"

"I came into some money when I went into town to get me a drink, so I moved in with a girl named Jacqueline. She ain't good lookin' around the face, but she's got a little cabin about halfway down the mountain to Bonner."

"She's a whore?"

"Used to be, but I reformed her." He puffed out his chest and gave a greasy smile. "She let me use her horse to come back up here so's the trip could be faster. I gotta get him back to her. Can you go get him? He's tied to the trees about a mile past the caboose."

"I'll let the horse go. He can make his own way home."

"If I don't show up she'll take up with someone else. Just get these off, and I'll go home. You won't ever see me again. Please, Garrett. I think I'm in love."

"With her or her house?"

"With her. She's the best woman I've ever known."

Garrett answered by shaking his head. "When did you go into town for the drink?"

In all the chaos of the season, he'd failed to realize his four-flusher uncle had left camp. Hell, he forgot he was even there in the first place. What else had he missed?

"You never paid no never mind to what I did before. Why should you now?"

"Did a man with a cane approach you?"

"Yeah. Paid me good too."

"He paid you upfront?"

"Half now, half when the logs don't show and I bring proof. You got your job, and I got mine."

"Who else is working for him?"

"Don't know, and don't want to know. All's I did was what I was paid to do."

"Destroy the company."

"It ain't your company."

"Did you start the fire?"

"Nope. I didn't know about the money until a few days ago."

Garrett had heard enough. He jumped down and slammed the large boxcar door shut, yanking the lever in place to lock it so Marcus couldn't escape. In all his years he'd continuously pulled his uncle out of the gutter, and this was the thanks he gave. Like his father and Aunt June, Garrett was done. Marcus was a lost cause. The big bugs at the mill could deal with him.

But if Marcus hadn't started the fire, who had?

Chapter 20

By mid-morning on the day of the drive, Beth kept one eye on the men as they made last minute preparations and one on the cook raft as she helped load the supplies. The night before, Garrett laid out the float plan. The Devil May Cares would leave with the new raft and meet up with Blue and the old raft, which no one had even attempted to touch since it was moved to the new position. Once they were in place at the mouth of the river, they would open both rafts to allow the logs to float free.

The Bonner rivermen would walk the banks. Half of the Bonner crew and their bateau had already left to gain some ground before the logs were released. The other half would straggle behind and unjam any blockages. Once they were clear, the Devil May Care bateau and the drive's wannigan cook raft would float.

Beth dropped the barrel of flour onto the muddy ground, and stood back with her hands on her hips to stare at the wannigan, bedecked with a small crude cabin and cook stove. Never in her life had she seen such a creation. A floating kitchen made solely of logs and a small stove, to house not only the supplies, but the women as well.

"A sight, ain't she?" Wall said, coming to stand next to her. "Usually the beds are for the men when they take shifts, but we can't have you women sleeping under the stars, now can we?"

"I wouldn't mind," she replied.

"Of course you wouldn't, Miz Elizabeth. You're a rare gem among women." Wall cleared his throat and kicked at a pebble on the ground, and then glanced back up. "After we get the drive down, and if the load from the train is enough to meet the contract, we'll be heading for town."

He studied the ground once more. "I was wondering if you'd mind if I come courting."

"Oh," Beth said, caught off guard. "Well... I—"

"You don't have to answer now," he hastened. "You can have some time to think about it. I wouldn't do right by you by pushing for an answer now."

"Thank you." She blushed, relieved that she didn't have to answer. While Wall would dote on and treat his wife with respect, he wasn't Garrett. Her heart broke at the thought that she would have to disappoint him. He was a good man.

"The raft is going to leave without you, Wall." Aunt June bustled past, stepped onto the wannigan, and loaded the last barrel into the tiny cabin.

"I was just leaving." Wall gave Beth one last smile and left.

She watched as he took his place next to Garrett—the two men who were beacons of strength and honor amongst the rough world of the logger. Her heart belonged to one, but his hand belonged to another.

Soon this would all be over, and she would return to her life of solitude. Maybe the Goodall sisters would let her sit with them at the balls once Carrie was shuffled off in marriage.

Garrett motioned for the Devil May Cares to take their positions, and then he ran up to the cook raft.

"Ready?" he asked Aunt June. Upon her nod, he continued, "Take care through the shallows. Don't get hurt." He spoke to all of the women, but his gaze lingered on Beth.

"You take care." Victoria grabbed his biceps. "I don't need a dead husband before I even get engaged."

Beth held his eyes and gave a small nod of acknowledgement, and Garrett turned to rush to his log. On his command, Clint released the raft, and the Devil May Cares guided it through the current, headed toward the river.

Beth felt someone move to her side and turned to find Carrie. "You'd think she would realize that you and Garrett are in love."

Beth gave a sad smile to her friend. "Love doesn't have a place in matters of business."

"No," Carrie corrected. "Business doesn't have a place in matters of the heart."

"Did the train leave?"

Carrie's eyes filled with tears. "Yes. Simon barely said two words to me before he left. I swear once I get home, that man is going to talk to me like he used to or risk my wrath. I won't sit back while he wallows in self-pity. That's not who he is, and I won't let him become something he's not just because of a little scar."

"Thank you for taking care of him."

Carrie didn't answer, simply stood.

"You're still in love with my brother, aren't you?"

Her friend broke down in tears. "Are you dreadfully mad?"

"Why would I be?"

"He's your brother, and I'm your best friend." Her voice shook with worry.

"If you marry him, we'll be sisters." Beth entwined her arm through Carrie's and hugged her closer. "I just worry that you'll get your heart broken. He's a known scoundrel."

"I saw a side of him I've never seen before when he was in bed. I think his soul hurts. He puts on a face, but inside he isn't doing well."

"I was afraid of that."

"Take your positions, girls, we're headed out!" Aunt June yelled from her perch on the front of the cook raft.

Aunt June and Victoria took up their peaveys on one side, and Carrie and Beth did the same on the other. On Aunt June's count, they pushed and guided the raft into open water.

Catching the current, the raft picked up speed as Dick disappeared down the river in the bateau. Beth's heart kicked up in speed to match the rushing waters, and she couldn't help but smile. This was the beginning of the end of her season as a logger. Even though she hadn't been able to ride the log like she'd envisioned, she was still going down the river. Something no other woman in her circle had ever dreamed of doing.

* * * *

Garrett watched the bank of the river from his position at the front of the log drive, and knew from years past what would happen next. They'd already ridden for hours with only minor problems. Now, the speed of the river forced the logs to shoot downstream, but in a few minutes, the banks would open up and slow the progression. He gave a whistle to Michael as he trudged along the bank. "Go tell your brother to get the Bonner crew ready to make a raft."

The boy acknowledged with a nod and took off farther down the river.

He floated for a few more minutes before men from the Bonner crew started to line the banks, using the peavey to shove the logs free and back into the river. The river widened, and he guided his log toward the bank and jumped off to walk beside the drive.

Ahead, men worked to wrangle the logs and tie them in a raft as they slowed in the eddy.

Garrett looked at the sun slanting in the sky, and then sought out Michael. "Run over and tell your brother that we may as well stop for the night. Get the raft tied off and once the women get here with the wannigan, we'll get camp set up."

"Okay, Garrett." The boy saluted and ran toward the front of the logs. The boy sported an enthusiasm to match the way he worked. When he was older, he would make a fine logger.

The Devil May Cares slowly drifted into sight of the growing raft, maneuvered their logs toward the banks, and jumped onto dry land.

"Tomorrow we'll be where Braxton went down in the logjam last year," Blue pointed out.

"The river narrows pretty bad," Garrett said. "And there's a lot of trees on the side to hold up the logs. It jams every year." He glanced at Wall. "What do you think we should do?"

Wall stared in surprise for a moment, and then answered, "Send someone down the bank tonight to scope it out."

Garrett nodded in agreement. "Who?"

"Why don't you and I go right now? Clint and the boys can get the women set up when they get here."

Garrett motioned for Wall to proceed and followed. Michael came into view, and he relayed the information. Once the boy responded, he and Wall continued down the rough trail made by past years of the log drive.

After a few minutes of walking silently, Wall cleared his throat. "Are you hung up on Miz Elizabeth?"

"What?" Garrett asked, and stopped for a split second, stunned.

"Miz Elizabeth. I've seen how you look at her. She's one hell of a woman, and I'd like to have a woman like that at home to greet me after the season ends."

"If you had a woman like her at home, she wouldn't stay home during the season. She would drive your poor mother crazy with her antics." Garrett tried not to let his feelings for Beth show through his voice, but he couldn't stand to see her with any other man.

Wall chuckled. "True. I'd probably have to yank her out of trouble a plenty, but I'm willing to risk anything for a woman like Elizabeth—even my mother's disappointment."

Garrett studied the mud beneath his feet as he followed down the path. Was what Wall willing to do so different from what Garrett had to do if he wanted to have Beth in his life? Could he risk losing his family for the chance to have Beth forever? In the end, it wasn't his parents that mattered, but honor and his duty as a man. What was the dutiful thing to do where Beth was concerned? "What would you be willing to sacrifice for love?"

"A wife, or love? Those are two completely different subjects."

"Both."

"I would risk my mother's ire for a wife." He fell silent for a moment before he continued, "I don't know about love. It doesn't come around very often, so most people don't have to worry too much about what they would give up. I heard most say they would give their lives for love, though."

"Would you sacrifice honor?"

Wall sucked in air through his teeth. "I don't know. Honor and love come hand-in-hand. Can you even have one without the other?"

God I hope so. If he couldn't have love, then all he had left was honor. "I don't think Beth is a good choice for you. You should set your sights a little closer to home."

"Like Miz Carrie?" Wall asked, leaping down an incline on the trail.

"If she meets your needs. She'd be as good a wife as Beth."

"Yeah, but not half as fun."

Garrett's gut dropped to a pit of emptiness at the thought of Beth sitting in a dimly lit home, laughing as Wall's small babe play at her feet. He tightened his fist into a ball. "Beth isn't the wife for you."

"So you do love her."

"No," he lied. "I'm betrothed to Victoria."

Wall stopped and faced Garrett, so he did the same. His friend studied his eyes. "An honorable man would let her go if he couldn't have her."

Garrett said nothing, but moved past his friend, and continued down the trail.

"I've already asked to court her," Wall yelled from behind.

"And what did she say?" Garrett's heartbeat kicked up, and a knot twisted in his stomach.

"Nothing yet. I gave her time to consider my offer."

Garrett felt like someone lifted a log off his chest when he realized she hadn't yet agreed to Wall's advances. Once the drive was over, Beth would return home and be thrown in the path of every suitor in Missoula. If Garrett couldn't stand a man like Wall courting her, how would he live with himself once they returned to town?

Chapter 21

Beth stood at the bank of the river and watched the raft. The sun had begun to set, and the men settled in for the night. The boom logs in the front of the raft looked ready to snap with the strain of the water and weight of the logs behind. If one went, the rest would follow, and by the looks of it, all it would take was one extra tug to snap the raft and send the logs shooting down like a bullet from a gun.

With a loud bang, the boom log snapped and, as she predicted, the logs shot out of the raft and down the river as fast as a bullet. Shouts from the men in camp sounded, and they scrambled to respond.

"Dick, get a bateau out there and get a line on that boom log!" Garrett shouted and pointed to the boat on the shore ten feet away from her.

Her legs tingled with the need to leap in the bateau and respond as he commanded, but she knew she must not.

A log banged into the bank where she stood on top of the croded grass and shook the earth beneath her feet. The ground loosened, and another log smacked into the first.

Another log banged against the second. Beth slipped, but caught herself and jumped back as the ground gave way and plopped into the water.

Dick rushed past her and jumped into the bateau to row out to the water and, with the expert ease of years of work, tied the logs together in the center to form a raft.

"Goddamn it," Garrett swore as he drew near. He stood next to her, but shouted at the men slowly gathering around the scene. "What the hell happened? We weren't ready to send the logs downstream. Who tied those boom logs?"

"My brother and his team," Michael confessed.

"Where is he?"

Michael pointed upstream. "He went on a round to check the back logs."

"When he gets back, tell him I need to speak with him."

"Okay." Michael's voice shook.

"Get those logs secured and then hit the bedrolls. We need to get up before the sun." He waited until all that was left were the Devil May Cares, and then beckoned them closer. The men gathered around Beth and Garrett. "Put a watch on the raft."

"Why?" Blue's eyebrows turned down in concern.

"I don't think my uncle set fire to the chute."

"Someone else did?" Beth tilted her head, and creased her forehead in concern.

Garrett nodded. "It had to be. Things started happening before Marcus even came to camp. I think they got to someone else in camp, and I think he is now on this drive."

"The man from the platform," Beth said. "It has to be."

Garrett simply looked down and squeezed her hand in reassurance.

"I'll take first watch," Dick offered. "I want to double check my boom log line anyway."

"I'll take the last. I want to be up and ready when we leave. Whoever relieves Dick, wake me at three."

The men nodded, and Garrett turned to Beth and motioned for her to follow him down the trail. With a quick glance around to ensure no one watched, she followed.

Once they could no longer be seen, Garrett faced her. "I want you to pay attention to whomever you talk to. If you hear the man, tell me. Do not approach him. Whoever he is, he may think the money too great to care about life."

"I won't," she said.

Garrett stared for a few seconds before bending down and kissing her. Her stomach flipped in joy, and she tried hard not to melt once more into his arms. She leaned into his embrace and let the feel of his lips on hers overtake her senses. The scent of his body filled the air around her, but unlike before when he smelled of the expensive cologne, here he smelled like pine and earth.

"Take care when you're on the water." The lines on Garrett's face turned sharp. "I love you, Beth. I can't lose you."

"We'll be fine," she promised. "And…I love you too."

The hard look on his face eased and his eyes softened when she said the words. He moved as if to kiss her again, but stepped away when the bustle of a logger preparing the drive met their ears. He turned toward the river, and Beth did the same.

From the trail, they could still see the water. Garrett stared at a log as it dislodged and floated past. He turned back to her, and his steel gaze fixed on her. She wanted to reach out and trace the worry lines on his face. Ease them away and make everything right. But she couldn't. He shifted on his feet. "Did you see what happened?"

"Yes. It just snapped. There was a lot of tension on the front boom logs. They sort of bowed out."

Garrett's forehead creased. "That means there was a lot of tension pushing from behind, but this is the end of an eddy. If tied right, the boom logs should have held the logs until we untied them."

"What do you want to do?"

"All we can do is watch and see what happens. Keep your ears open."

* * * *

Beth walked to the front of the wannigan to where Aunt June struggled to ease the cook boat around a log. It had been a few days since the first incident, but a calm few days. Garrett had talked to Michael's brother, but found nothing that would help them figure out why the boom snapped. Beth had settled into a routine, but now something wasn't quite right. "What's going on?"

The river now overflowed on the sides and disappeared into the trees along the bank.

"There's a logjam ahead, a big one from the looks of it. We may as well pull onto shore and set up camp. A jam like this could take days to get loose. If they can't get it out soon with the peaveys, they'll blast it with dynamite." Aunt June motioned for the girls to take up their positions. Beth pushed as hard as she could with her peavey to steer the wannigan to shore. It took a while to finagle the wagon through the flooded forest floor and find a high spot to tie the raft.

By the time they'd tied up the wannigan, the men began to trickle in to camp. An odd excitement rippled through their ranks.

Garrett approached the cook camp with a frown.

"What's going on?" Victoria asked.

"We're at the Crossroad Junction."

"The Thirsty Woodsman?" Aunt June clicked her tongue. "Can't stop 'em from havin' fun, but at least they could get us set up. Ain't takin' the supplies off in this mess. Not going to risk getting water in the flour and such."

"There's a saloon nearby?" Michael loped up and stopped next to Garrett. "Can I go?"

Victoria placed a gentle hand on the boy's arm. "No dear, not for you. Saloons are places for reprobates and lowlifes. It's where men go to meet the devil."

"Oh." Michael's face fell in disappointment. "What am I gonna do? My brother loves saloons."

"You can come and eat some of my cherry cobbler." Aunt June winked at the boy.

"Aunt June, I think supper should be earlier than usual tonight," Garrett suggested. "The men are rearing to go."

"We'll have it ready in an hour." She clapped her hands and started to pick out pans and toss them onto the table balanced outside on the logs of the wannigan raft. "Get to it, girls, we have hungry men to feed."

Garrett gave a slight bow. "If you'll excuse me, I need to get the peavey crews situated."

He left, and Beth and the other women busied themselves with the evening supper. Her thoughts on the man who'd stolen her heart. A man she couldn't have. She needed to keep her mind off him. Save herself the heartache she'd surely have at the end of the drive. She concentrated on making a cook fire.

Once the meal steamed over the cook fire, and the vision of Garrett's loving gaze finally hid behind the sight of the steaming potatoes, she rang the bell. One by one, the women handed out plates full of food to the men. In no time at all, the loggers had devoured their meals and began to prepare to leave.

The fading light of dusk settled over the land when the usual roar of the men in camp slowly dissipated to a small purr.

Beth finished the last of the dishes in the wash bin, and set it at the table, glancing around in the dim light of the fire on the shore. She leapt from the wannigan and stumbled.

"Don't fall into the water," Carrie warned and jumped down beside her. "Aunt June is looking for Michael. Have you seen him?"

"No. Why?"

"Aunt June said he went to use the bushes a while ago and hasn't come back. After Simon's attack, she's worried about Michael scampering around after dark."

"Aunt June," Beth called. The cook popped her head up from the other side of the campfire. "I'm going to find Garrett and see if he knows where Michael went to."

"Take Carrie with you, and don't come back until you find the boy. My cobbler's ready."

"Okay." Beth waited for her friend to walk, and then headed toward the front of the logjam.

By the time they reached the front of the jam, darkness had settled over the trees. A scuffle between two men sounded somewhere in the night and made Carrie grab onto Beth's arm and hug close. "Sounds are frightening at night when you can't see."

"It's just a few loggers settling an argument is all."

Another campfire burned in the night, and they headed toward it. Through the dim golden firelight, she could just make out Garrett's wide shoulders and commanding stance, standing next to a few other men. "There he is. Garrett," she called when they drew near.

He turned and hurried toward her.

"Beth." He said her name as if he would never have a chance to say it again, and made her heart flutter. He stepped even closer. "What are you doing out here? What's wrong?"

"Carrie's here too. Michael has gone missing. We were sent to find him."

Garrett sighed and grabbed her free hand to loop it through his arm. His other hand rested on top of hers as he guided her down the river. Carrie clung to her other arm and followed with unsure steps.

"Where did you last see the boy?" he asked.

"Aunt June said he went to use the bushes," Carrie answered. "That was about an hour ago."

"And you waited this long to go and find him?"

"Aunt June got to making her cobbler and lost track of time," Beth said.

"I think I know where he is," Garrett said. "Maybe you should stay here while I go fetch him."

"No. We're going." Beth took a larger step to punctuate her declaration.

"Aunt June told us not to come back without him," Carrie expounded.

"You stay by me and don't talk to any of the men." Garrett paused. "Are you certain you want to go to the saloon? Your brother might knock me for a loop if he found out I took you."

"I'm in trousers and a plainsman hat. I've been to one before. Don't you remember?"

"Yeah, but I'm in a dress, and I haven't been to a saloon," Carrie reminded her.

"Stay close and you'll be fine." Beth gave her arm a reassuring squeeze.

"Don't talk to anyone in there. We go in, get Michael, and then leave," Garrett said. He dropped Beth's arm, but wrapped her hand in his. His rapid heartbeat pulsed against her palm. He still loved her. If stolen moments were all they were afforded, she'd take them without hesitation. With any luck, these small touches and secret looks would get her through the remainder of her lonely life. Without Garrett.

Beth let Carrie go, and her friend grabbed on to the back of her shirt to follow.

"Are you positive you want to come?" Beth whispered to Carrie. Her friend usually had to be yanked into adventure. Nighttime escapades were her least favorite.

"No," she hissed back. "But I don't want to risk upsetting Aunt June."

Garrett squeezed Beth's hand as they hiked.

Beth climbed the steep incline to the doors as the drunken shouts of the men sounded through the night. Garrett stopped. "Don't talk to anyone."

Beth nodded and followed as he opened the door. Carrie stepped close to Beth, and the door shut behind them.

Michael's boyish laugh resonated over the shouts of the men and the clink of glass.

"Michael," Garrett said, and in two steps stood next to the boy's barstool.

"Oh hell!" he whined. The men gave a joyful yell in response.

"Aunt June's looking for you." Garrett motioned toward the door.

"Does she have cherry cobbler?" Michael jumped off the stool and stumbled, leaning heavily against Garrett. "I like sweets."

"So do I." Garrett moved him toward the door as a few loggers shouted an objection.

Dick walked up to the group when Garrett reached where Beth and Carrie stood. "I'd say I'd buy you a round, but it looks like you have your hands full."

"Buy you a round in town once this is over." Garrett shook his head and gave his friend a look of disbelief at what Beth assumed was his luck.

Dick laughed again and slapped Garrett on the back as Michael's brother, Peter, stumbled up to the group and leaned on Dick's shoulders. "Whew! Stay here and drink Mikey. Dick and I got a game of poker over there that's as hot as a whore on nickel night."

Beth stilled at the sound of the man's voice. Her heartbeat kicked up, and she moved close to Garrett and motioned for him to bend down. He brought his ear near her mouth.

"That's him. The man from the platform," she whispered so only he could hear.

Garrett jerked his head up in alarm and watched the retreating backs of Dick and Peter. "Are you positive?"

"I'd bet my life on it. That's him."

"Nah. Aunt June's got cherry cobbler," Michael called to his brother, and swatted at the air.

"Your loss," Peter tossed over his shoulder, and then turned toward the crowd of drunk loggers.

Garrett paused and watched the table where the men had retreated, and leaned back down to Beth. "I'll come back for Peter. He's not going anywhere. He looks pissed off his rocker. We'll deal with Michael first and get you women back to the wannigan."

Beth looped arms with Carrie and followed as Garrett directed a stumbling Michael out the door and into the night. The boy tripped.

Beth looked forward to Garrett, who turned slightly and glanced back at her through the moonlight.

"What should we do about the man from the platform?" Beth asked.

"What m-man," Michael stuttered, and then focused his attention to the faint light of a camp fire. He dropped back a few steps.

Garrett ignored the boy's question. "We will have to keep an eye on him and catch him in the act, otherwise it's conjecture."

"You saw the man from the platform?" Carrie asked. "Where?"

Beth lowered her voice, and took a quick glance to ensure Michael couldn't hear. "At The Thirsty Woodsman as we were about to leave."

"Are you certain it was the right man?"

Beth nodded even though she knew no one could see her. "I'd bet my life on it."

"Then we need to get him," her friend said.

"Go back and get him," Michael agreed joyfully, once again drawing even with their group.

"You need some rest, and some cobbler." Garrett looked down at the boy when he passed the fire near the blockage.

The men around the camp watched as Michael stumbled past.

"Go to The Thirsty Woodsman," Michael shouted. "It's as hot as a whorehouse on nickel night."

"And Aunt June has cherry cobbler." Garrett pushed the boy gently and urged him to walk faster.

A few minutes later, they entered the cook camp, and Michael rushed to where Aunt June dished out a bowl of cobbler.

"You girls have been gone quite a while. Where in the blazes did you find him?"

Garrett gave a quick account of the scene, and then peered over his shoulder where Victoria was helping Michael stay upright on the log while he ate dessert.

"Who did this to him?" Aunt June jumped to her feet. "I'll kill any man who poured liquor down his throat."

"I'm certain he did it to himself." Beth sat across the fire from Aunt June, but kept her eye on Garrett as he stood like a beacon of strength on the other side of the fire. One thing a woman could count on was a man who knew when to drink, and when to see to his affairs. Garrett's sound mind and leadership, in addition to other amiable qualities, made him the perfect man. A man she was in love with.

"Gracious me. What I put up with on this drive." Aunt June turned to Garrett and wagged her finger. "There will be no more women or children coming into *my* camp next year."

"This will be my last season," Garrett confessed. Beth had already heard the news, so it came as no surprise, but what would Aunt June think? She loved having her nephew in camp; it was apparent by the way she doted upon him whenever he was near.

Silence filled the night, and he glanced around the gentle light of the campfire. Beth followed his perusal. A range of emotion showed on the faces of everyone else around the fire.

Victoria walked into the firelight and smiled. "Excellent news, Garrett. Father will be thrilled to know you've chosen to take a more suitable position for a husband."

"Does Simon know?" Carrie's face turned down in concern.

"He does, but the Devil May Cares do not. I will tell them when the time is right."

Beth watched Aunt June sit silently. Her face showed no hint of her thoughts, which was unlike the goodhearted cook who wore her emotions for all to see.

"I need to go and check on the logjam." Garrett dipped his head in goodbye and disappeared into the night. Beth felt hollow as he disappeared, but she must not allow herself to wallow in self-pity. Else what would she do once the drive came to an end? Best get used to the loss of Garrett, and her heart.

"Well now." Aunt June rose to her feet. "We should be getting off to bed. No use stewing on bad news."

Aunt June urged Michael to stand, and guided him out of the firelight and toward the wannigan.

"What exciting news," Victoria gushed. "He will make the best boss at the mill."

Beth kept quiet. Victoria had planned Garrett's life without consideration to what he wanted, and they weren't even officially engaged yet. A hole opened up where her heart should be whenever she thought of Garrett's life after the Devil May Cares.

Chapter 22

Garrett jerked awake to the sound of dynamite blasting through the camp. He sat up and looked around, but darkness still spread over the land. He estimated an hour had gone by since he'd given up the search for Peter, and collapsed in his bed. After dropping the women off at camp, he'd gone back to the bar to get the blowhard, but the traitor had already left. Garrett had searched all night, but without any luck.

Another blast sounded farther down the river, and Garrett lurched out of his bedroll, yanked on his boots, tucked the laces into the tongue, and ran toward the sound. "Who the hell lit the dynamite before sunrise?"

Men from both the Bonner and Missoula teams followed.

Garrett could just make out the dark form of the logs in the water as they caught the current and flew down the river. Garrett cursed. They'd planned to blast the jam today, but not until they were situated and ready to resume the drive.

In a few minutes, he and the rest of the men came upon the bend in the river where the blockage had happened, but the logs flowed freely.

"Where was the other blast?" Wall stood with shirt un-tucked and boots hastily laced.

"It sounded like it came from down the river," a Bonner boy said from the dark crowd.

"A couple of you boys come with me," Garrett ordered. "Wall, get the drive ready to go. Don't wait for us to get back, just follow the logs."

Wall nodded and turned to disappear into the crowd as Dick and the Bonner boy who spoke stepped forward.

"Let's go."

The sky dusted with a hazy pink as the sun began to peek over the mountain. Garrett and the men charged down the trail looking for anything that could indicate where the blast had been.

The sun glistened everything to life when they came upon a section of the river where the water forked to the left into a smaller stream. Debris littered the riverbed and caused the water to back up and divert in the other direction.

Garrett and the men rushed to the water's edge and began clearing the dam. If the logs met with the obstacle, the drive would be stalled, and they would lose a great amount of trees down the river fork.

Garrett waded into the water waist deep and pushed against the tip of a large pine tree. A branch caught his shirt and threatened to drag him to the bottom, but he fought free. He angled his shoulder over the trunk and pushed. The tree budged a fraction of an inch.

Garrett jerked beneath the tree when the earth moved under his feet and water sucked downstream with the force of the explosion. A man cried out as Garrett struggled to keep his head above water.

Using the protruding branches as leverage, he gained a foot at the bottom of the river and pulled to emerge from the surface.

He searched his surroundings, only to find the debris had doubled.

Another man screamed in pain, and Garrett turned toward the noise as a head bobbed from the water on the back side of a fallen tree.

The force of the water pushed against his body as he tried to run toward the Bonner boy who went down. Before he could get there, Dick tripped his way across the torn bank and climbed over the tree trunk to lift the drowning man's head out of the water.

Garrett leapt over the tree. He had to get to the man before he drowned.

"My legs are stuck," the man shouted in pain while Dick held him up.

Garrett took a deep breath and ducked under the water to see the man's legs pinned beneath the trunk at the thigh. Dread filled his gut. The position didn't look good.

He emerged and took a deep breath. "I'm going to try and dig out around you."

The pinned man nodded, and Garrett ducked once more into the water. He lodged himself beneath a branch so the river wouldn't take him downstream, and began to dig under the man's thigh. His fingers scraped and grew raw as he frantically dug at the sand and rocks beneath. No use.

His lungs screamed for air, and he surfaced. "It's no good. The river keeps pushing sand back down. We're going to have to move the tree."

"The river is pushing against it. If we dislodge the tree, then it's going to slam against us and take us down with it," Dick pointed out.

"Maybe I can push the tree upriver enough for you to pull him free." At Dick's doubtful look, Garrett continued, "It's our only option right now."

Garrett widened his feet and leaned into the tree, but it didn't budge. He tried again, but still came up short.

On his third try, water splashed on the other side of the Bonner man. Garrett looked as Peter took up a position similar to his and began to push.

Garrett angled his shoulder lower and, with all the strength he could muster, shoved the log. It moved, and Dick yanked the Bonner boy free.

The tree slid toward them a few inches and stopped.

"Get out!" he shouted. "Get out before the water sends it downstream!"

Garrett was the last to scramble up the bank and out of the water. He turned and plopped down in exhaustion, watching as the tree dislodged with the force of the water and slammed past the area where they had just stood. It slid near the bank, to lodge once more parallel to the shoreline. Air filled his lungs and relief eased his twisted chest. Not this year. His conscience couldn't deal with a death on his last trip.

"My God," Peter said, drawing Garrett's attention.

"You almost killed someone. One of your own team members." Garrett's nails bit into his palm as he clenched his fist. He wanted to yank the man up and beat him until nothing remained but a bloody corpse, but he refrained.

Peter turned a stunned gaze on him.

Garrett glared. "You were overheard at the train depot plotting against the company. Don't try to deny it. The jig is up."

Dick assessed the man's injuries and turned to Garrett. "His leg is broken."

"I didn't mean to, Hal," Peter said to the Bonner boy. "No one was supposed to get hurt."

Hal turned to stare in disappointment. "What did you do?"

"I just tried to stop the drive until after the mill missed the contract deadline."

Garrett looked up as the first of the Bonner crew from camp ran up the bank with their peaveys.

"What did you do?" Hal questioned again. The crew ran to the blockage and began to work to dislodge it.

"The fire, the raft release, it was all me." Michael's brother snapped his head toward Garrett. "Except the one that made the girl float downriver. I won't take the blame for that."

"We already know who did that. You're saying that you are responsible for every incident that happened during the season, sans one? No one else was involved?"

Peter hung his head low. "Michael was too. I needed help. He was going to release the raft after it moved to the other side of the river, but he ran into the women and got scared. You gotta understand, Garrett, our pa's sick. We needed the money."

"You could have come to me." Garrett turned to Dick. "Can you take care of Hal until I get back with the crew? I need to find a few people to take him to town and escort Peter to the mill."

* * * *

Beth stood on the edge of the wannigan away from the bank and jabbed at the bottom of the river with her peavey, on instinct, she searched the far-off banks for Garrett, but with no luck. Even the sight of him calmed her anxiety, and let her face her day with gumption. "The water is clear this way. We should be able to break free without any problems."

The boat rocked when Aunt June stepped onboard carrying a large pot. "We're about set here, and then we wait for the bateau to leave. I don't know how long we're going to be floating today. Could be until dark. We'll make all meals on the boat."

Garrett walked to the boat and handed Aunt June the last pot. Beth's heart beat at the sight of him. His commanding presence demanded her attention and held it captive like a pirate captain. God how she loved him. "We're short a few men. We caught Peter, but a Bonner boy got hurt. Clint, Dick, and a few of the Bonner boys are going to have to take Hal to the junction and Peter to the mill."

"Why Devil May Care boys?" Beth stepped toward the front of the wannigan. "Why not send someone less experienced?"

"I can trust my men. I can't rely on someone I don't trust. Do you think you could man the rear bateau without getting hurt?" he asked Beth.

"Yes." She couldn't believe Garrett was willing to trust in her enough to man the bateau. Especially since the time she had been shoved down the river. He was even more protective since then.

"I don't think so." Aunt June placed her hands on her hips. Beth bit her lip. Please God, let her give in. She needed to spend a few more stolen moments with Garrett. "There are plenty of other men that can row that boat."

"None as good as Beth. She's proved herself on the log when she went down the river, and on the bateau. She'll stay with me at the back and help dislodge any stray logs. Tonight we will be at the next lake, so she won't have too hard of a time."

Beth sent a pleading look to Aunt June, who took a moment before nodding.

She ran inside the cabin, grabbed the logger spikes from her bag, and hurried back outside, jumping from the wannigan in a very unladylike way. She didn't care. All she cared about was being near Garrett again.

Garrett's face lit when she looked up at him with her spikes dangling from her fingers. "Ready."

"Let's get you set up." Garrett turned and headed downriver. He slowed when they neared the bateau. "Get in. Let's find Wall."

Garrett slid the boat into the water and waited for her to climb inside before hopping in to maneuver down the river. She didn't fight the smile aching her cheeks. She caught the saboteur and today she would be a riverman. The only thing that made her day bittersweet was the thought of losing Garrett at the end of the river run.

"We should be to the mill in a few days." He rowed the boat around the logs like a snake through the grass. "Most of you can go home after that."

Beth refused to let the thought ruin her last chance at happiness. "Victoria will be glad to hear that. She pretends to be enjoying herself, but I've heard her cry at night. She's not cut out for life at a logging camp. She's more the boss woman."

"I want to be with you right now. I'd rather not talk about Victoria."

"All right." Beth took up the peavey and poked at a log as they drifted past, glad Garrett agreed in not speaking of the doom of their future. She tried not to smile at Garrett's words. There was nothing else she wanted right now than to be alone with him.

They spent a few moments in silence until they rounded a bend to see Wall standing on a log in the middle of the river, poking at a jam. Garrett brought the boat alongside.

"Need a spot?" Garrett bumped the bateau into Wall's log.

Wall gave a quick glance at them, lifted his head in answer, and then turned his attention back to the jam.

"Move to the back, Beth," Garrett commanded. "He's going to be jumping in, and fast. Careful not to tip the boat."

Beth nodded and waited, her heart beating fast in anticipation.

Wall shoved the log again with the peavey, and a loud crack sounded from the jam. Before she had time to react, the logs shot down the river at the same time Wall launched himself into the bateau. Her stomach did a summersault as adrenaline coursed through her veins. This was even more exciting than she'd anticipated.

Garrett paddled to clear the boat from the path of the logs and brought it to shore.

"Miz Elizabeth." Wall tipped his hat as he turned to see her. "How have you been?"

"Good." She hadn't seen him since he asked to court her. Did he expect a response so soon or had he forgotten? "You haven't been to the cook camp in days."

"I wanted to give you time to think."

Beth smiled, but her heart ached. Wall expected an answer, but she didn't know how to respond. While he would make a prized husband, she was ruined both emotionally and physically, but did she want to spend the rest of her life alone?

"Would you object if I came by the cook camp tonight?"

Beth slid a nervous glance to Garrett. He ducked his head and lowered his gaze, but failed to hide the hurt in his eyes before it disappeared underneath long lashes. The same hurt she felt every time she saw Garrett and Victoria together. An ache she felt now in response to his.

"As long as no one else objects." She snuck another peek at Garrett, but he hadn't moved.

Garrett cleared his throat and leapt from the boat to pull it ashore.

Once they all stood on solid ground, Garrett faced his friend. "I'm leaving Big Mountain. I'm to take over my father's business as soon as we return to Missoula."

Wall stared at Garrett with mouth agape. "I… Why didn't you tell us earlier? We could have made this drive one to remember."

"Trust me. I will never forget this drive." Garrett paused for a second, and then continued, "I want you to take over the Devil May Cares. The men all look up to you, and you can best any of them in a row."

"Are you certain no one will object?"

"I doubt it. Today I want you to take my position during the drive. Beth and I will take the rear positions and gather the straggler logs. If the men see me treating you like the boss, they'd assume you bested me in a fight. They'll treat you the same. At least it will make it easier for you to transition next year."

"Will we be seeing you in town?"

"I will be at my usual haunts." Garrett nodded. "And if the railroad logging is successful, I might be seeing you back at camp again someday soon. I'll help you in any way I can."

Wall extended his hand, and Garrett shook it. "I may take you up on that."

Garrett nodded, and Wall grabbed his peavey from the bateau. He faced Beth and bowed. "I'll stop by this evening, Miz Elizabeth."

Wall gave a saluted goodbye to Garrett and turned to walk the riverbank, headed downstream.

"Where's he going?"

"He will walk the river until he sees a jam and then shove the logs back into the current."

"Oh." Beth chewed on the edge of her lip as Wall disappeared around a bend in the river. Wall was a good man, and deserved a woman who would stand by his side and love him unconditionally. How was she going to answer him when her heart belonged to Garrett?

"Beth," Garrett said in a tone that gave her pause. "Do you plan to court Wall?"

"I don't know."

She wanted to say no, tell him he was the only one and throw herself into his arms. She wanted to bury her face in his chest and never leave.

"If my father hadn't made the deal, you have to know that I would spend every moment convincing you to marry me."

Beth gave a sad smile. She knew he spoke the truth, but her heart still ached whenever she thought of what might have been. "It wouldn't take much."

"Wall is a good man. He'd make you happy."

All she could do was answer with a shake of her head. No one would make her happy but Garrett. "Will Victoria do that for you?"

"She will certainly try."

Beth's chin quivered and she turned her head. She didn't want Garrett seeing her cry—both for him, and what they could have been.

* * * *

A single tear fell from the corner of Beth's eye, and Garrett's heart shattered. He couldn't staunch the need to hold her, to feel her melt into his touch. He was weak in matters of the heart.

Without waiting for her to object, he wrapped his arms around her and tugged her close. The smell of her hair had changed since the day at the lake when she'd bathed, but the scent still affected him the same. He needed her, and she him. Even if just for a few days, they were meant to be one.

With his index finger, he tipped her head up until her tear-filled eyelashes fluttered open. "Don't cry."

"I can't help it. I don't want to be with anyone else, and I don't want you to be either."

"I feel the same, but the contract—"

"Yes, I know." She slid her hands around his waist and buried her face in his chest. He wrapped his arms around her and held her tight. *This is right.*

"We will be alone in the bateau. Let's have this time for us." He let his cheek fall to the top of her head and squeezed her closer. "The days we have left will be about you and me, and no one else. Promise me you'll live for today, and not what is to come."

Beth lifted her head. "Until I give you to another, we will exist for only each other."

"The hell with anyone else." He smoothed her hair down.

She smiled and laid her head on his chest once more.

Garrett glanced up as the cook cabin slid into view around a bend a few yards up the river. He backed up and grabbed her hand to tug her toward the bateau. "Come. We need to get going."

The wannigan floated past as he rowed the bateau back into the water. Carrie stood at the front and rowed as Victoria and Aunt June worked to guide the boat from the back so that it would ease into the white water ahead.

He watched Aunt June dig hard with an oar and remembered all the times in the past when she'd steered him in the right direction. Throughout the last few years in camp, she'd been his confidant, someone he could trust with advice and secrets.

His spirits lifted. Would she be able to help him figure out how to be with Beth? However, as quick as his spirits lifted, they receded. Not even Aunt June could talk him out of a deal with his father, but he needed Beth as certain as he needed to breathe.

Chapter 23

Beth dug the oar deep into the river and kept the boat steady while Garrett shoved at a jammed log on the side. As Garrett suggested, they lived each moment for each other, not caring to think about the near future when they would once again be separated. They'd worked together for two days now, and each day they grew closer, more in sync to one another.

She watched the flow of the river strain the log until, with a loud crack, the blockage broke free, and the debris flowed once more.

Garrett slumped back to sit in the boat. "I think that was our fastest time yet. No trouble at all. We could go on like this all day."

Beth smiled, but they couldn't go on like this. They only had a few more days to be together before they'd be torn apart forever.

The wannigan floated past, and Beth turned to Garrett. "Looks like we're the last ones on the river."

He watched the cook boat as it floated downriver to disappear around a bend. "The river is wide and slow. Do you want to ride on a log? You'll be fine as long as there's no white water, and this time you won't be floating down alone in the dark."

Beth nodded. This is what she'd always wanted. An adventure, and Garrett was giving it to her. He didn't stifle her personality and force her to be proper. He let her be the woman she wanted, while offering the protection and respect that a gentleman would a lady of the first water.

Garrett steered the bateau to a log jammed on the riverbank. "Go ahead and get on the hump. We're still on the river. Take care. If you see any jams, keep a wary eye out. Things could get dangerous in a matter of seconds. I'll be nearby. If you need me, yell."

Beth concentrated on sliding over the side, and settling on the log with her legs dangling in the cold water of the spring runoff. Garrett handed her a peavey and pushed the bateau a few feet away from the log. "Did you hear me? It can get dangerous, so be wary."

"Yes, all right." Beth shoved the log with her foot to dislodge it from the riverbank. Excitement filled her core with happiness. Today her life was perfect. Adventure on the horizon, and Garrett by her side.

She did a quick survey of the water surface and dug her peavey in the water to paddle hard toward the center. From the boat, she noticed Garrett furrow his brows and maneuver the bateau.

"Follow me!" he shouted.

She shoved the peavey into the mud of the riverbank, and guided her log to follow. The water picked up in speed and she noticed a few white caps dotting the river.

The unoccupied logs that surrounded her tossed about as they rushed down the river even faster than before. Earlier, when she'd rode down the river, she'd been helpless and the sky dark. Nothing but fear had taken precedence in her mind. But today she could enjoy the freedom of the drive and sheer power of the water. The perfect moment with the perfect man.

"It's not supposed to be this fast here. It's usually a calm area," Garrett shouted, his forehead creased and eyes alert. "Maybe you should get in the bateau."

But it was too late. Beth found the reason for Garrett's concern when the churn of the river started to roll her log first one way, and then another. Her thighs burned as she balanced, trying to keep upright and navigate the rocks. She stayed as close to Garrett as possible, even coming so close as to bump into him, which only served to get her a quick glance from him as he struggled with the bateau.

She concentrated on moving first one way, and then another, through the white caps. Her log banged against a rock she couldn't see, and she slipped. Using the peavey, she pushed herself back so she once again sat upright on the hump.

Her heart beat faster than any time in the past. The thrill of the adrenaline boosted her spirits as the river calmed and opened up into a pool, deep in the center and serene, as if they hadn't just been tossed through the rocks on a wild ride.

"I made it!" Beth shouted when she emerged into the slow waters and once again focused on her surroundings. The trees swayed in the wind, and birds chirped behind the receding sounds of the rushing water to her back—serene and calm in contrast to the menace of the rock-laden rapids.

Garrett rowed the bateau next to her and smiled with pride. "You did well. See if you can take the next one. It looks smaller."

The rest of the day was spent much the same, a lazy float followed by small rounds of easy rapids. By afternoon, they were almost to the opening of Salmon Lake.

She moved the log next to Garrett, who stood in the center of the bateau with a wide grin plastered to his face. "You gave Wall one for the money with the way you took those rocks. Almost like you were born to be a riverman."

Beth smiled. She knew it wasn't true, but hearing his praise boosted her confidence and spirits.

"There is one last white water up here, and then we are at the lake. Once we're out of the river, we push them down and hold them near the bottom overnight."

Everything ran with smooth precision until they reached the rapids where a large logjam hovered near the shore, unmovable. Garrett motioned for Beth to head toward land.

He jumped from the boat and pulled it ashore as she struggled to bring the log parallel to the beach. She leaned over to try to reach a steep incline of the beach with one foot, but tipped. The log rolled, and Beth went down into the water beneath the log.

Out of instinct, she tried to breathe, but sucked in water instead. Panic made her heart beat faster as she rotated to get a foot on the bank. She twisted her body in the water and felt the bottom of the river beneath her fingers as she grabbed onto the muddy sand below to try to push herself up. Her head crested the top as Garrett plucked her from the water. "We need to work on your dismount."

She threw him a look of relief and, dripping wet, plodded out of the water and onto dry land.

"My peavey." She twirled to glance down the river where the peavey drifted down with the logs.

"We keep a spare in the bateau. I'll go get it. It's warm enough now that you shouldn't need to change your clothes after falling in, but if you start to feel cold, let me know, and you can have my last jacket."

Beth nodded as Garrett turned toward the boat.

In a few seconds, he returned with the spare peavey and handed it to her. Together, they picked their way across the jammed logs until they stood at the edge. Garrett started to poke at a log, and Beth moved to do the same on another one. Her muscles ached from days' worth of hard labor, but she didn't mind. Not only did she enjoy being a riverman, but also she got to spend time with Garrett.

Her shirt had dried, but sweat dripped down the back of her neck as she pushed the last of the jam in the water and plopped down to the ground to watch as it flowed down the river. What would the women of Missoula say if they saw her now? She'd be an outcast. A pariah amongst them. She might be able to get a permanent position with the lumber company. At the least, she could help Aunt June with the cook duties. Would Garrett and his beautiful blond bride visit the lumber camp in the future? She hoped not.

Hot tears stung her eyes. She could handle the label of outcast before she could bear watching Garrett with Victoria.

The log beneath her shuddered, and Garrett yanked her backward to another log as the one she'd stood on jerked free and floated down the river. She followed him as he hopped from one log to another until they were both safely on the beach.

She turned around to find the jam loose and the logs they'd just been on floating down the river.

Garrett came up and sat down, so she did the same. He pulled his legs close to his body, leaned his forearms against his knees, and panted while he caught his breath.

"I'm impressed. You worked your darling little butt off. You did well."

"This is the first jam I've done where I wasn't on the bateau. Do they all make you feel like you're standing on the edge of the world as it collapses into the abyss?"

"This one's nothing, when the rapids are bad, the river rats have to balance on top of spinning logs. Sometimes the trees slam together and make it hard to balance. We've lost a lot of good men to the river. A drive without a death is a successful one." Garrett smiled and watched the water. They sat together without talking while they caught their breaths.

She turned toward Garrett, stuck her foot out, and poked his leg with the tip of her boot.

"Another inch, and the spike on your boot could have caught me on the shin. If a man did that, I'd have beat the tar out of him."

"You almost did that to me on the train when I accidentally hit you with my spikes." She gave him a teasing smile, and he mirrored her grin. "What is it with you men and fighting anyway?"

"We settle disputes with our fists. We also determine hierarchy with a good row."

"And you have never lost?"

"I would have lost to Wall if the widowmaker didn't fall on the timber beast this year."

"You let Wall best you?"

"Yes. I wanted him to take over the Devil May Cares this year, but then the accident happened."

Beth tried to hide her smile.

"What do you find humorous?"

"The thought of you losing a fight to anyone. The men would never believe it."

"Wall is a pugilist."

"Yes, but you are bigger and more determined."

"Wall is a good man. He would make you happy." Garrett's tone turned serious.

Beth's heart sank. What was Garrett doing? "He is a good man."

"Are you going to consider him?"

A lump formed in her throat, and she swallowed hard. She couldn't answer. She didn't have an answer.

"Are you?"

"I can't do this right now. We're supposed to be living for today, not thinking about tomorrow."

"I need to know, Beth. I need to know that you're all right."

"All right? All right with you marrying another woman, or fine with you wanting me to marry Wall?"

"I never said I wanted you to marry Wall. I said he was a good man."

"I can't do this." She jumped up and ran into the forest. Away from Garrett and the decisions he tried to force her to make.

* * * *

"What did I do?" He jumped up and ran after her. He didn't mean to upset her with his questions, yet somehow he did. All he wanted was for her to be content in life. He needed to know she would be happy without him. Perhaps then his conscience could open up to accepting life without her.

She stopped and spun around. "I can't do this anymore, Garrett. I can't be in love with you knowing that once this time is over, you will belong to Victoria."

"You love me?"

"You know I do."

"My heart will still belong to you. It always will." He took a step closer.

"And mine to you, but it breaks every time I think about the end, and then I realize how close that is. I can't take much more."

"You're the strongest woman I know. Tougher than a thousand-year-old pine tree."

"I'm not strong. Simon has spoiled me. I'm used to getting what I want, but I can't have the one thing I feel I may die without. You."

"You want me?" He tried not to show how hard his heartbeat had kicked up when she said the last. He needed her one last time. "Then have me."

He bent down and kissed her as he wrapped his arms around her waist and lifted her in the air. He took two steps forward and pinned her back against a tree, anchoring her with his body. He kissed her with intensity. The heat of his kiss seared her image into his mind while he traced her body with his hands.

He leaned one hand next to her and pressed against the jagged peaks of the bark. The small pain in his hand felt oddly right as he pushed his body to hers, making them as close as they could be while fully clothed.

He pulled his head back and took a deep breath and, reaching his hand up, stripped her clothes from her body.

"These do you no justice, by the way," he said and tossed her pants over his shoulder. Setting her feet on the ground, he stripped down to skin and once again picked her up.

She felt like silk against his chest when he tugged her back up and pressed her into the tree. He kissed her once more and ran his knuckles across her abdomen. When he reached the warm nest of her curls, he positioned himself to her entrance and pushed to seat himself firmly inside her. He pulled out and thrust back in, repeating the process until she gasped with need. Her breasts pressed tightly against his chest.

Her eyes fluttered closed, and she arched toward him and exposed the flat plane of her stomach. He ached to kiss the smooth surface, but wasn't about to stop. Beth moved in rhythm with him while he plunged and receded. She was hot, ready, his in every way. A low, silky moan echoed off the trees and boosted his need to take her.

She bit her lip as if trying not to cry out.

"Scream if you need to, my love. No one can hear us."

She reached the peak and shuddered around him, and he couldn't hold back any longer. He released his seed deep within her and groaned in response. He held her head firmly in his grasp, while still deep inside her.

He kissed the moist skin on her temple and smoothed her hair with one hand while he held her upright with the other.

He watched her lips, wet and swollen with kisses—his kisses. With one last peck on the tip of her nose, he eased her down and held her as she came down from the lovers' high. Once he was confident she could support her own weight, he let her go and stepped back to watch the glorious sight of her in the aftermath of passion.

"God how I love you." Keeping one eye on her pale, naked body, he bent down and picked up her clothes to hand to her. He plucked his own from the grass near the base of the tree, and dressed. As if in a trance, she did the same.

He flicked pine needles from the back of her shirt as she tucked it into her trousers. Once certain she was fully dressed and ready, he took her hand and led her to the river. He could never be happy with Victoria. And, dear God, he'd lose his soul if he had to see Beth and Wall together. His heart growled at the thought of her happy on Wall's arm as she made her way about town. The thought twisted his chest into knots of steel. No. Wall cannot have Elizabeth. He'd fight for her even if the contract was complete, even if he had to walk away from his family, his fortune, he'd find a way to be with Beth. She belonged in *his* arms, and by God that's where she would stay until the day she took her last breath.

"Do you want to ride a log, or would you prefer to come with me in the bateau?"

Her eyes still hazy, she lifted a brow and motioned toward the bateau. "I don't think I have the strength to stay on a log."

Garrett slid the boat into the water and collected the peaveys from the ground where they'd left them. Beth slipped into the boat and sat motionless as he pushed the vessel into the river. Her skin still flushed and hair slightly disheveled. The way he wanted her to look every day of her life with him.

A little over an hour later, they caught up to the crew, as they set up a new camp on the shore of the lake. Wall hailed them in. "I thought you'd gotten lost."

Garrett gave a quick, secretive smile to Beth and turned to jump into the lake, thigh deep, as he guided the boat to shore. "We had a small wing jam, and then took a breather."

Beth seemed to have snapped out of her trance and, with one last lustful look at him, trudged up the bank toward the cook fire. She hadn't said a word during the float to camp. Was it because she needed to clear her fog of passion or something else? He hoped the first. If they couldn't be together, at least he could give her memories to last her the remainder of her life.

Nearby, the men sat around the fire and whittled on flexible tree limbs to make fishing poles. Garrett searched the bank and found others sitting with their poles already in the water.

"Aunt June said if we want supper, we'd better catch it," Wall said in response to Garrett's perusal. "She even told the women to catch a few."

Garrett turned to study Aunt June as she bustled around the women and flipped her spoon in the air as if scolding someone.

Wall continued, "I think she's getting a might tired of being a mother hen to a bunch of women."

"She's used to dealing with us men."

Wall nodded, and turned a serious look to Garrett. "Are you going to tell the men? They're already talking about next year, but I didn't want to say anything."

Garrett nodded. "We should be to the mill tomorrow, so I'd better get it done. I'll talk to them tonight."

The last thing he needed to do before finishing off his duty as leader of the Devil May Cares. His heart broke. This was supposed to be his last season as a free man doing what he loved. Garrett chanced a look at Beth as she smiled and followed the women to a willow tree to examine branches to use for a pole. Unlike years past, this season had changed his life forever.

* * * *

Beth reached high for a branch above her head, one that would make an excellent fishing pole.

"I'll help you." Garrett kept his gaze on Beth as he approached the women. Beth flicked a nervous glance to Victoria, who noticed his focus, and scowled.

"Oh thank heavens you're here, Garrett." Victoria flittered to his side and stepped in front of him to block Beth's view. "Aunt June said we need to learn how to fish. She said a young lady from the west should learn how to take care of herself in case there weren't any men around to do it for her, but I don't see as how I'm ever going to need to catch my own supper. I have father's staff for that."

"Aunt June is right. It's a dangerous place out here in the west. A woman should be able to look after herself if a man cannot do it for her." Garrett stepped around Victoria and reached above Beth's head. With one hand, he pulled out a knife from the sheath on his belt and began to saw at the flexible willow branch. Beth glanced at a glaring Victoria once more.

The wood snapped, and he handed it to Beth. What was he doing? Proclaiming his love with a fishing pole? Irritating Victoria? Either way, she didn't care. She loved that he thought of her first above everyone, before Victoria. What would happen to her reputation if Victoria realized his feelings and spread gossip about her in town, though? She'd never get a husband.

"Garrett," Victoria whined, and glared. "What about the rest of us?"

He reached up and snapped off three more branches, handed two out to Victoria and Carrie, and then motioned for the group to continue to the fire. Beth followed Carrie with Garrett trailing behind, and as usual, Victoria flittered beside him.

Beth could feel his eyes watching her walk, or at least she fancied she could. Never in her life had she ever felt someone's gaze, but with Garrett, it was different. They were connected.

The women spread around the fire and sat. Beth studied his movements and copied them as he showed the group how to fashion a pole. Once everyone was set, he stood. "Find a spot and throw in the line. If you feel a tug or need anything, I'll help."

"Or you can ask me." Wall strutted into the camp. "I'm a better fisherman than Garrett."

Beth smiled at Wall's playful banter, but inside her stomach churned. Wall came to be with her, of that she had no doubt, but she didn't know if she could act with ease the way she did before he'd asked to court her.

Wall and Garrett led the way to the river, and the women began to settle in various spots along the bank. Beth followed Carrie as she tripped down a steep incline to a sandy beach. Once she found a spot a little farther down the river from her friend, she tossed in the line, and then looked around to take stock of everyone else.

Wall bent over Carrie down the shore, helping as she struggled to flick the line in the water.

Beth searched the banks, but realized Garrett and Victoria were nowhere to be seen. Her chest tightened. Had Victoria taken Garrett away to a secret spot to steal a kiss? Beth set her teeth against the thought.

After a few moments, Garrett leapt from the steep incline Beth and Carrie had taken, and then held a hand out to help a triumphant Victoria jump. Beth wanted to growl like men did when angry, but then Garrett turned, mumbled something to Wall, and then ran back up the incline, leaving Victoria to pick her way across the river side alone. Beth smiled, but then checked herself. She shouldn't show such bitterness. Shouldn't be jealous of Garrett's intended, but she couldn't help but feel a deep pang in her heart at the sight of Victoria and Garrett together.

Victoria searched the banks and then set her sights on Beth.

Beth snapped her head forward and concentrated on watching the ripples where her fishing line dipped into the water as Victoria slid past her. Stopping close to where she stood.

Victoria flicked her wrist, and her line plopped into the water a foot from shore. "I'm a natural," she crooned.

Beth only smiled in response. She wanted to like the woman, but she couldn't.

They stood quietly for a few seconds before Victoria spoke. "I know you're in love with Garrett."

Beth couldn't breathe.

When she could once again get air enough to speak, she answered, "You're mistaken."

"He's a wonderful man. Very handsome, connected, from a good family, and displays the manners of a London gentleman." Victoria paused as if she waited for a response, but Beth wasn't about to give one. After a while, Victoria continued, "I saw you embracing on the beach. He is my betrothed, Elizabeth Sanders, and I won't lose him."

Beth snapped her head toward Victoria. What had she seen on the beach? She thought back to earlier in the day when they'd made love in the forest, but the wannigan had been long gone by then. She must mean the first day she'd ridden in the bateau. "I understand fully what Garrett is to you."

"Good. Then you know that whatever has happened between the two of you cannot happen again. Tomorrow we will be at the mill, and I can't have Garrett's and my reputation ruined before we even get a chance to announce our engagement."

"Your reputation is safe. I'm a riverman. What I'm doing with Garrett is working to get the logs to the mill. He is yours." It took everything Beth possessed to say the words, but she had to. For her own sake.

"You may want to consider staying in the wannigan tomorrow, to save your reputation. My father and his business partners will be at the mill to see the harvest. You wouldn't want people knowing how you've behaved while you were tucked away in a logging camp. Would you?"

"Thank you for the kind advice." Beth smiled at the woman, but inside she wanted to scream and tear out her hair. She knew the dangers of behaving contrary to the rules of etiquette, but she didn't care. Life wasn't worth living if you weren't going to take pleasure in it, and for the most part, Beth had enjoyed her time as a riverman.

Chapter 24

"Today the hard rapids start," Garrett said as Beth climbed into the bateau. She settled onto her seat and grabbed her peavey. "I would prefer if you stayed in the boat, unless you are on the beach. Once we get past the worst of it, it is a straight shot to the mill. We should be there by late afternoon."

A mixture of emotions slid through Beth as Garrett hopped in the bateau and headed downstream following the logs. Excitement over the end of the drive, mixed with the deep-seated sadness that would inevitably ensue once she no longer had Garrett in her life.

But for now, she had a job to do.

They spent most of the morning in calm water with little to do, but enjoy each other's company. The sun stood high over the mountains when the rapids started to build in intensity, and Beth was forced to hold on to the bateau as Garrett struggled to keep them from slamming into the rocks.

The sound of logs crashing together reached Beth's ears, and she peeked around Garrett in time to see a large nest of logs piled ahead. Trees thickened the bank of the river and formed a tunnel leading straight to the center of the biggest rapid she had ever seen. She failed to keep control over her excitement, and wiggled on her seat.

"Hold tight!" Garrett shouted above the rush of the water. Beth clung tight to the sides of the boat, and smiled. She would be safe as long as she stayed there.

The Devil May Cares and Bonner men bolted into action, leaping on top of the logs to push with their peaveys. They would test one log, and then another. Free one, only to have it replaced with the log behind it. Beth bit her lip when one man wobbled as his log began to spin. Although the job looked difficult, she knew they could handle it with precision.

The men loosened logs one by one, but had not yet found the center of the nest when a loud noise from her right made her jump and turn in time to see Blue lose his foot and fall backward onto the nest. *What the hell happened?* Before she could even scream, Blue righted himself and scrambled to the bank, holding his arm close to his chest.

Garrett yelled for someone to take Blue's position, and then turned the bateau to pick his way through the logs and toward the bank.

Beth grabbed her peavey and started to push against a log as it slammed into the bateau, her blood pumping through her veins in rhythm to the rapid flow of water. The boat jerked and stopped. Garrett twisted and pushed with his peavey, only to turn and try the other side, but it was no use. The log had jammed the boat in the outer edge of the nest.

"I'm going to jump the logs to the bank to see how bad he's hurt. Will you be able to manage the boat by yourself?"

On Beth's nod, Garrett stood and began to leap from log to log. Beth bit her bottom lip and waited to react if needed. He jumped onto the beach, and Blue waved him away and stood, but flinched as he grabbed at his arm. Garrett took off his shirt and tore it into two pieces. He tied one to make a sling, and the other to anchor the arm around Blue's torso.

Logs began to shift next to Beth, so she grabbed the peavey and shoved to help them dislodge. This was the job she'd signed on to do, and she wouldn't go back looking like a helpless ninny. Especially in front of Garrett. She'd pushed four away when one of the largest logs she'd seen yet slammed into the bateau and sent her flying backward into the water.

A log slammed into her back and caused instant pain to shoot up to her shoulder and down to her butt. Instant panic filled her core. By some miracle, she'd barely missed slamming her head against the massive logs. She watched from under the water as the trees bounced off each other above her head.

The sun shone through clear water, and she surfaced to chance a breath, only to duck back into the water and kick off a new log as it flew past her to bash into the nest. This was it. The end. She had to find a safe way out of the merciless waters.

Her lungs were about to burst, they burned as if consumed by fire. It wasn't much longer before she would lose consciousness. She kicked and swam toward what she hoped to be the bank, but gained no ground as she struggled. Her arms grew heavy and her body weak. As her mind begged

Dawn Luedecke

her to give up, a hand wrapped around her waist and turned her to face the logs above her.

Garrett swam next to her, and she tried desperately not to cry as she grabbed at him. He lowered his mouth to hers, gave her a much-needed breath, and then grabbed her hand to swim toward the center of the river. Once the logs cleared, he surfaced and dragged her face free of the water. As air filled her lungs, she gave in and let a sob free.

With one hand, Blue used the peavey to maneuver the bateau and shove logs clear of them as they swam, until Beth turned upriver and realized no more logs floated toward them.

Blue edged the bateau closer. "The rapids!" he yelled and pointed downstream.

"Hold on!" Garrett shouted and wrapped his legs around her to hug her with her back against his chest. Fear pounded at her chest. "We'll try to stay in the current. Away from the rocks."

* * * *

Garrett cradled Beth and clung to her to shield her from the jagged rocks as the river tossed them about. A sharp pain pierced his shin when he hit the point of a boulder hidden behind a veil of white water, and he forced himself not to yell. In a few more seconds, they would be clear of the rapids, and safe.

He sucked in a breath, and water filled his lungs. He coughed and felt Beth's body move as she did the same. God, he couldn't lose her this way. In less than a heartbeat, the water stilled and slowed to a gentle roll as they floated into a calm pool.

Garrett let go of Beth with his legs and, with one arm around her torso, swam to the bank. It took all of the energy he had left to pull her onto dry land and collapse next to her in the sand. But she was safe. Alive. He willed his heart to slow down.

"I've never met a man to cheat the devil like you do, Garrett," Blue shouted from the water. Garrett sat up as his friend eased the bateau to shore with the peavey.

"It's not something I plan to do again. How did you get through the rapids with one arm? Looks to me like you were the one to cheat the devil."

"It wasn't easy." Blue pushed the peavey into the water with one hand and turned the wayward boat back toward the shore. Garrett waited for Blue to reach them, needing that time to gain strength.

Beth struggled to sit next to him, her chest rising and falling with deep breaths. His stomach dropped when he realized he'd almost lost her. He'd die before he lost her again.

Not caring that Blue stood in the boat a few feet off shore, Garrett gathered her into his arms and sat on the bank to hold her. Her body shook, and he knew she cried.

He ran a hand over her bare arms and slid them back to squeeze her reassuringly.

"I…I…love you," she managed to say and burst into tears again.

"Don't cry, Beth. I love you too. I have ever since the first moment I saw you on the train platform the season we first met. I knew you would be the death of me. You, so perfect and carefree, scared the hell out of me. Made me forget how to breathe, to talk. Commanded all of my thoughts, my desires. I've loved you for years."

"You have?" she asked with a sniffle. "For three years?"

"I am a fool." He brushed his lips against hers in a gentle kiss.

"A fool I have fallen in love with, but will never have." Beth's words hit him like a fist to the gut. His heart ached each time she reminded him of that.

"I'm sorry," he whispered. "Were it beyond my control…"

He left the statement unfinished, and she nodded. "I understand pride. I understand being tied to something out of your control. I won't ask you to betray your family."

"It's much more than that. It's not my family I would be betraying. It's you. I'd promise you a life I wouldn't be able to fulfill. I'll find a way for us to be together. Even if it takes another three years. Wait for me." Garrett palmed her warm cheek and stared into her eyes. He wanted to betray his family for her, but did he have the guts to do it? Beautiful and serene, she exemplified the essence of the perfect wife. If only she were under the veil on his wedding day, his life would be complete. He would find a way.

He stood and pulled Beth to stand. He shot Blue a warning look that his friend instantly understood. He would keep his mouth shut.

Blue brought the bateau to shore, and Garrett lifted Beth and set her in the boat. He jumped in after and took control of the oars. He had a few minutes left with the woman he loved. He would take his time rowing to the Big Mountain Lumber Mill.

* * * *

Two hours later, they flowed around a bend and were greeted with a sight unlike any Beth had seen. The lumber mill sat on top of a small incline above the creek and billowed smoke from its stacks. A large log boom stretched across the river and collected the logs as they flowed into the entrapment. Rivermen climbed the banks to the mill, and the wannigan pulled onto the nearby docks, as men in suits lined the hill below the mill and watched the organized mayhem.

Garrett guided the bateau to the dock and tossed a line around the chock. As the boat secured to the bank, her heart dropped. This was the end. The end of the drive, and the end of her life with Garrett. No matter what he said, if he was legally bound to another, there was nothing he could do. And she had a feeling Victoria made certain the contract was solid. Unbreakable.

Carrie ran down the dock to where Beth climbed out of the boat. "Why do you look like you've been dragged behind a carriage?"

"It's a long story." And she didn't feel like talking. All she wanted was to rush home, and bury her face in her pillow.

Footsteps on the wooden planks brought Beth's gaze up to watch as Aunt June scurried down the dock, with Victoria gliding majestically behind.

The ever-regal Victoria shined in the sun, wearing a high-necked dress with flowing skirts that matched the light pastel of a midsummer sunset. She looked perfect, as if she'd stepped out of her boudoir, and hadn't just floated on a boat down the river. The days spent outside had tanned her skin, but the gentle hues of the gown helped her appear pale and fragile. Had Beth not spent the last few months with her, she never would have guessed that only a few days ago, this woman had stood on the bank holding a fishing pole.

"I think you'd better get up there," Aunt June said to Garrett when she stomped up and stopped.

"Why?"

Aunt June tipped her head toward the big bugs, as they stood proud on the hill above the river. "You got company."

Beth followed Garrett's gaze to find four suited men, and to their right stood Luther.

"I thought he shucked outta here." Garrett started toward the men, his face wrinkled in worry, only to slow when he went to brush past Victoria. Before he could walk too far away, she slipped her arm in the crook of his and followed. He stopped, glanced down at her hand, and then adjusted his arm to escort her up the dock and staircase.

"Looks like trouble's brewin'. I don't want to miss this." Carrie picked up her skirts, and tromped after them.

Aunt June motioned for Beth to follow, so she did.

Beth crested the hill as Garrett stopped in front of the suited men, and Victoria stepped forward to kiss the short round man standing next to Luther. Garrett shuffled his feet, and Beth knew then he was nervous.

"Luther here tells me you tried to put a spoke in the wheel of the Big Mountain, son," the man she assumed was Victoria's father, Abner Harrison, said when Victoria settled in beside him.

"No, sir," Garrett responded. "I'd never try to ruin your company. We found out who it was, though. My boys should be bringing him to you any day now, and I sent my uncle on the train."

Abner nodded. "They're here, but that's not what I'm talking about. What's this business I hear about this young lady?" Abner pointed at Beth. "Taking a position with the Devil May Cares? A woman on a team like that is bad business. Dangerous."

Beth's heartbeat kicked up to rival the speed of a runaway horse. What had she done? Garrett looked back at her, and she tried not to show the panic she felt in her chest. The thought that her decision to deceive her way in camp would affect Garrett's job never occurred to her.

He turned his head back to Abner. "Beth proved to be a great asset to the rivermen."

Victoria's father shook his head and stared at the ground. "And here I thought you were someone to ride the river with, Garrett, but you're not shooting straight with me. Your father vouched for you. I gave you a chance, and for a while you were a fine investment. After you sent word about the man with the cane, I'd thought you loyal beyond the standard. From what I hear happened up there this summer, though, I can no longer trust you."

"I've got no reason to lie to you, sir. Elizabeth came into camp a shave tail, but proved she could hold the ax with the men. I'd take her for another season before I would the lowlife mudsill you've got standing beside you. If you got your information from the likes of him, and I suspect you did, you got taken by a lowlife."

"That ain't the truth of it!" Luther shouted and pointed to Beth. "She swindled her way into the camp dressed as a man, and then bulldozed her way to the Devil May Cares. She's nothin' but a con artist, she ain't earned her way like I have. I should be one of the Devil May Cares. Hell, I should be their leader. I've been with the company since I was a young buck. I deserve this. Not this lying whore."

Garrett jerked toward Luther and grabbed his collar. Beth flinched at the action. She'd never seen Garrett react so violently before. This wasn't like the good-natured rows at camp. "I should have licked you when I had the chance."

He cocked his arm back to deliver a blow, but Victoria stepped forward. "Elizabeth saved your company from ruin, Father. If it wasn't for her, not only would you not have been able to meet the contract, but good men would have lost their lives. Elizabeth Sanders saved the Big Mountain Lumber Mill and should be praised for her role during the season, not tossed in the fire and called a swindler. Luther was the one who almost killed Elizabeth so he could have her job. As much as I hate to admit it, we owe Elizabeth for saving our company."

Beth couldn't believe what she heard. Only yesterday Victoria was warning her away from the man she was destined to marry, yet today she defended her. Although the woman didn't deserve Garrett, she didn't deserve Beth's hatred either. Tears filled Beth's eyes.

"Is that the truth of it?" Abner slid his gaze from his daughter, to Garrett, and brought it to rest on Beth.

"I'm sorry, sir," Beth said. "I overheard the man with the cane and another plotting against your company, and I swindled my way into the camp so I could expose them. I should have come to my brother or Garrett, but I didn't. I wanted to help, and I thought joining the Devil May Cares was the best way to do so. It was wrong of me, but I don't regret any of it. We caught the man and exposed the plot against your company, and I'd do it again if it meant saving this company and an entire town from ruination."

Abner lowered his eyes to slits and stared at her. His face didn't twitch. The look in his eye stayed constant, but unreadable as he sized her up. "You're right. You saved the town I built with my company, and exposed Sanchez—the man with the cane? Who, by the way, has since decided to try his luck elsewhere, after some persuading." He clenched his fist, and then eased to stand relaxed. "I've worked hard to make this company what it is today, and it's a matter of pride to me. The company will one day belong to my son-in-law."

Victoria shot Garrett a fluttered smile as her father continued, "It will remain in the family for years to come. The one thing I abhor the most is a liar and a cheat." Beth's heart beat fast and panic stole her breath. "The way I see it, you did what you did to protect my company, and in doing so you protected my family and my town." He turned to Luther. "You have dishonored this company and jeopardized not only the future of Big Mountain and all who depend on it, but you showed a complete disregard for the life of another, and not simply a logger, but a woman. I suggest you tuck tail and run like Sanchez did. Maybe you can meet up with him since you seem to be of the same mind. If I ever see you or him around these parts again, I'll have you arrested."

Luther opened his mouth to protest, but Abner waved him off, and turned to Garrett. "Escort him off my property." He turned to Aunt June. "And as for you, no more bringing women to my camp without running it by me first. Can't have the men getting distracted by female sensibilities."

"Yes, sir," Aunt June replied. Beth tried not to let her mouth drop in a very unladylike way at the way Aunt June responded without a well-placed retort, her usual spunk replaced with sheer respect.

Abner turned to the big bugs and motioned toward the mill. "If you will, gentlemen, we can talk about the contract with your company."

The men turned and ambled toward the mill, leaving Abner and his daughter to follow.

Victoria grabbed on to her father's arm and hugged him close. As she turned with him and started to walk, Beth overheard her croon, "Garrett will make the best husband, Father, just you wait and see."

Garrett sent Beth a long stare, his eyes pleaded for something, but she wasn't convinced he even knew what he asked for. After a moment, he turned toward Luther and shoved him forward. "Walk."

Beth's heart dropped to the deepest pit of her stomach. Never in her life had she wanted to be proven false what she knew to be truth. Garrett couldn't be truly engaged to Victoria. Back there in the forest, a part of her truly believed that the betrothal was a misunderstanding. A figment of a lovestruck female's imagination.

"Well that was quite exciting!" Carrie exclaimed.

"You got off lucky, girl," Aunt June scolded. "I'd have taken your head, even if you did save the company. If you ever want a job as cook, all you have to do is ask. I'll get old Abner to agree, but no funny business this time."

"I think I'm set with adventure for now, Aunt June, but thank you."

Aunt June eyed Beth silently, and then turned toward Carrie. "You too, Ms. Carrie. You've grown into a fine young woman."

Beth smiled when Aunt June glanced back as she escorted the girls toward the awaiting carriages. Aunt June's lips twitched as if she held back a proud grin. Inside, Beth wanted to cry, but she didn't know whether it was out of relief, exhaustion, or grief over the loss of a love. She guessed the latter, or a combination of all three, but it didn't matter. She couldn't let herself shed a tear. She must remain strong. The only way she knew how to be.

Chapter 25

"I've checked every journal since we got home a month ago, and I haven't seen an engagement announcement." Carrie snapped the newspaper to straighten it out. Beth's heart twisted when her well-intentioned friend spoke.

"Have you seen him?" Carrie asked. Beth followed her gaze across her nana's parlor to where her brother sat at the same large wing-backed chair he'd been in since the day he got home. Unlike the brother she had known before the accident, this Simon stayed in nights and retired early to bed. His scarred face was gray from days without sun, and she suspected little sleep.

The only fire he showed was when Carrie would stop by, but it wasn't like the fire he used to have. This fire was fierce and aimed directly at Carrie, and she didn't back down.

"I haven't seen Garrett since the day you returned to Missoula when he came by to visit," Simon answered. "He hasn't been back since."

"It's no matter to me," Beth said. "What's done is done, and there is no dwelling on what you can't change."

The words were lies. A knife pierced through her heart every time she thought of Garrett and the season she'd had with him. For the rest of her life she would live with a hole in her soul.

"Is Wall going to come courting?" Carrie asked, a little more cheerful than Beth wished she would be.

"Aren't you tired of the courting scene?" Simon directed his words toward Carrie. "Don't you have men coming and going from your parlor all hours of the day and night?"

"Yes. And I tell them I am too busy coddling a grumpy fool to be courted." Carrie turned her attention back to Beth and raised her eyebrows in a silent question.

"No. Wall isn't courting me." After they returned to town, he had been by twice, but his presence was more than she could take. Knowing she had given her body and heart to Garrett, she couldn't bring herself to lead Wall to believe they could work. He deserved a woman who would love him and treat him with the same passion he would her. Wall deserved more than Beth could give.

"Goodness gracious, Elizabeth," Carrie chided. "I've had quite enough of your moping around. We're going to go to a ball, and we are going to have fun doing it."

Beth shook her head. "I'd rather not."

"You two are as fun to be around as a badger in a trap." Carrie dropped the newspaper onto her lap. "I swear, there's no mistaking this family resemblance."

Beth caught Simon scowling at her friend once more. "Will you quit that? What is wrong with you anyway? You'd think you'd get used to having Carrie visit us by now. She's been here every day for a month."

"He's just upset that he can't scare me off with his surly disposition like he can everyone else who's visited." Carrie faced Simon. "You don't frighten me with your new, and quite frankly irritating, temperament. Now go get your best suit ready. You're coming with us to the mayor's house tonight."

Simon grumbled something only he could understand and stood to stomp out of the room.

Beth waited until Simon slammed the door behind him and turned to her friend. "I know he was affected by the mauling, but I don't understand why he seems so different now than when he was recovering in the cabin."

Carrie grew serious. "I don't think it hit him until he saw his reflection, and coming home made it worse." She waved toward the mountains, visible through the large bay window of Nana's parlor. "Out there a person can just be. He can disappear into the woods and exist. Here, in town, is a cutthroat world of judgment and speculation. What he doesn't understand is no matter what he looks like, some of us will always be here for him. Whether he wants us to be, or not."

"When you put it that way, I don't want to go out tonight either."

"But you're going." Carrie gave her a look that dared her to argue, but Beth didn't have the desire. She'd let her friend cart her around wherever she wanted, just as long as it wasn't near Victoria and Garrett.

* * * *

Darkness settled over the land as Beth stepped out of Carrie's buggy. Her dark blue gown flowed around her feet like a rose petal in the midst of bloom. The tight bodice hugged her curves, and her puffed short sleeves slid off her shoulders to reveal a neckline that accentuated her more womanly attributes. Her hair had been a little trickier to decorate tonight, but somehow, with Carrie's help, they had managed to arrange it to fit the style of her dress. If her grandmother noticed her new fashion, she'd failed to make mention of it.

She wasn't here to catch a man, but to humor her dear worried friend.

"Next time we're forcing Simon to come." Carrie flitted past Beth as she entered the golden light of the mayor's home. "Even if we have to drag him out by his coat tails, but he's going to come out, and he will enjoy himself."

"I don't want to be in the parlor when you tell him."

People crammed into the ballroom, making it hard to move without bumping into someone. Beth grew dizzy at the cramped space so different from the open air of the mountains.

"Do you want to find a corner to stand in where we can watch the people?" Carrie asked.

"Why do we come to these things if all we do is stand in the corner?"

"Because it's the proper thing to do, and we are proper women."

Beth gave her a look of disbelief, and Carrie tittered. "Well, *I* am proper. You are Elizabeth Sanders."

"Elizabeth," Garrett's pained voice breathed behind her. She turned toward the sound that had haunted her dreams since the day they departed from the mill.

His solid, lumberjack form fit well into the tailored suit he wore. His hair was shorter, and face void of the days' growth he'd seem to keep while on the mountain. He stood with an air of refined confidence overshadowed by a wounded soul.

"Garrett."

Despite the buzz from the crowd of dancers and gentle hum of the orchestra, the room grew quiet with the exception of her deep, desperate breath. She clutched her stomach to force her mind to take in much-needed air. The damned corset.

The ache in Garrett's eyes bore a hole in her heart and bled her soul.

"Elizabeth. I'm glad you came." Victoria stepped next to Garrett and slid her arm through the crook in his elbow.

Beth stilled.

She forced her feet to remain rooted to the ground as she waited for her mind to right after the devastating arrival of Garrett's fiancée. What she wanted to do was run home and bury herself in bed again.

"I finally get to see you at a ball." Victoria flittered her fan before her face.

"Yes." Beth forced a smile, but she knew it failed to show in her eyes. She flicked a quick glance to Garrett—his face now stone solid.

"Garrett and I are to announce our engagement tonight. I wasn't positive it would happen since Garrett was called away on business, but he managed to get back in time, just an hour ago. He knew how important the engagement announcement was for me. Isn't that delightful?" Victoria sent her a triumphant smile as Beth fought the tears struggling to break free. She swallowed hard to clear the lump in her throat.

"How delightful." The hole in her heart ripped and she clutched her fan in front of her chest. How was she going to get through the night?

"I do hope you'll save a dance for Garrett. There are an exceptional amount of hungry debutants gracing the dance floor tonight. I'd rather he be in the arms of someone I know won't try to steal him away." Victoria sent her a stare that boasted of victory and warning.

Beth's breath failed her once more as she fought the emotion she couldn't show.

"What a wicked plan you've concocted." Carrie masked her double entendre with a smile, but Beth knew better. Her dear friend had once more come to her rescue. "The women of Missoula will be highly disappointed to not dance with Mr. Jones, I must say."

"They will get over it." Victoria searched the crowd. "Now, if you'll excuse us, my father calls."

Beth followed Victoria's gaze to where her father beckoned them with a wave.

"I'll be there in a moment." Garrett bowed his head as, with one last smile, Victoria left.

"Beth." Garrett's voice shook with emotion so slight, she may have missed it had she not felt the same. "I'm sorry. I've studied the contract, but—"

She waved off his apology, and opened her mouth to speak only to be interrupted by Carrie. "If you'll excuse me, I need to sit. I'll be in our usual spot."

Garrett bowed as her friend walked away, and then turned back to her. "Beth...Elizabeth... I don't..."

Beth held up her hand to stop the words she couldn't bear to hear. *I'm sorry. I love you, but I can't betray my family.* Words that would destroy her.

"It's fine, Garrett," she snapped, but swiped at the single tear that found its way down her cheek. At this moment if he whispered even a single confession of his love, beg her to run with him, she would. Before the sun rose over another lonely day, she would board a train headed for happiness, and never look back. Even after he broke her heart by leaving. She pinched her lips together.

"I know how this must look. I've wanted to see you since the moment we parted, but I had to go back up the mountain. I'm working on something, Beth. Something big that will ensure our—"

"Garrett," Victoria called from across the room.

Garrett watched her for a second before dipping his head low next to Beth's ear. "I can't live without you. Wait for me."

Her heart skipped, and her breath grew even shallower. Wait for him tonight, or forever?

* * * *

Garrett approached his intended. Victoria, with all her brazen snobbery, stood next to her father and smiled—as if she hadn't just dug her fingernails into Beth's heart, and ripped it in half. He saw the hurt in his beloved Beth's blue depths when Victoria had flaunted their betrothal. This wasn't the woman he wanted for a wife. One who would stop at nothing to get her way.

He wanted Beth, and by God he would have her even if it took moving the entire Rocky Mountain region south.

"There you are." Victoria smiled and sidled closer to him.

"Abner," he greeted her father.

"Papa was saying after the governor's speech, he will take the stage to announce our engagement."

"How long?" He had to talk to his father before that. Get him to delay the announcement.

"Half of an hour?" Victoria asked her father.

Her father smiled. "My dear, I know you're anxious to get the news out, but I'm afraid you're going to have to wait for an hour."

"Where's my father?" Garrett's heart beat so hard he was certain those around him noticed. He couldn't marry Victoria, and the less complications there were in breaking the betrothal, the better chance he had to succeed.

"Over by the orchestra, I believe." Victoria pointed to where his father stood, brandy in hand, and talking to a round man in a vest.

"If you'll excuse me." He bowed to Victoria. "I have a pressing matter that needs my attention."

"Of course." She nodded in return, and he left.

In less than two breaths, he drew close enough to his father to garner his attention. "We need to speak."

The importance of the situation must have registered on his face because his father's smile faded and he nodded toward the hallway. Garrett followed his father as he navigated the sea of people crowding the ballroom.

They slipped into the hallway and headed toward a nook far enough away to not be overheard by prying ears.

"You're not one to circumvent the truth, so I won't either," he began. "I cannot marry Victoria."

The shock on his father's face showed only for a second before the older Jones masked the emotion. His father stood taller and rocked back on his feet. "I'm afraid the deal is done. You have no choice."

"I'm in love with someone else, and I can't live without her."

"Well then you can take her as your mistress, but I'm afraid you're legally bound to Victoria. There is nothing you can do."

"I will have Elizabeth as my wife, or not at all."

"A mistress is not unheard of, son. In fact, your grandmother was your grandfather's mistress until his first wife died. And I believe you've met Matilda. She lives quite comfortably while waiting for me to visit. Set her up with a nice home and an allowance, and you're set. You live the life of a wealthy businessman with the perfect wife, and then visit your mistress at night once your wife is asleep."

Garrett had no words for what his father suggested. His stomach burned with anger and the pain of deception. What men were these who cast women in such a light? Surely not the ones who he'd admired all these years.

"I could never do that to Victoria, let alone Elizabeth."

"Well then, you are destined to be unhappily married to Victoria. You cannot get out of the contract without legal action taken against you."

Garrett's heart beat at his father's words. "I cannot."

"You must." His father stated with finality, and brushed past him. His heels clicking against the polished tile as he made his way back into the ballroom.

The happiness Garrett felt when he'd seen Beth on the dance floor turned into desperation. He needed to find her and beg her to have patience. He'd asked her to wait for him, trusting his father would see his way and release him. But like so many other things as of late, he failed. For now. There was one more way to get out of the contract. He hoped.

One foolish decision to agree to an arranged marriage, made for instant gratification at the beginning of the logging season, could destroy any chance at happiness for him and Beth. He should have told her how he felt years ago and spared them both the pain. He should have trusted in his heart, and not feared living in poverty.

He walked into the ballroom, only to have instant dread hollow his core. His father stood next to Abner on the stage while the orchestra sat watching the spectacle.

"Here he is." Abner motioned toward him, garnering the attention of the room. "The groom, and his lovely bride."

An hour had yet to pass, yet they'd sped up the announcement. Garrett slid his gaze to his father, who lifted his chin as if to make a point.

He searched the room for Beth while his heart sank to the deepest pit in his stomach.

Victoria appeared next to him and looped her arm through his elbow to tug him farther into the crowd and toward the stage. "Where have you been? Father decided to announce a little earlier than intended. We need to get to the stage."

At least he'd have a better vantage point in which to locate Beth. He searched the crowd as Victoria paraded him to the stage. After a few moments of searching, he caught a glimpse of Elizabeth's skirt as she rushed out the doors, followed closely by Carrie. The crowd began to clap and Victoria beamed as she hugged his arm.

The crowd closed in, and he struggled to break free to follow Beth. It wasn't until Victoria finally relinquished control of his jacket that he was able to force his way through the crowd, toward the door.

Night engulfed him in a false sense of peace as he rushed down the front steps of the mayor's mansion, searching the darkness for Beth, but to no avail. She was gone.

He turned to look down the sidewalk when a movement near the door caught his attention. Victoria took a single step outside, her body silhouetted in the faint light from within. Never before had he felt the urge to let emotion take control, but tonight he finally understood why women broke down. Despair hit his soul like an ax to a tree trunk. She lifted her chin and watched him.

Garrett turned from Victoria and stepped into the street. As comfortable as he was with the proper woman, he didn't love her. His heart belonged to one woman. The woman who often left him speechless with a single smile. Elizabeth. His love. He would make this right. He had to.

Chapter 26

The pinks and pale yellow of the early morning sun began to slip over the mountain peaks, but Garrett was already halfway through town. The gate to Victoria's father's home appeared at the end of the row of houses, and he stepped up his pace. He'd bear the repercussions of calling at such an unwelcome time.

He all but sprinted the remaining distance, and rapped hard on the heavy oak door. It took a few moments for the maid to approach and answer.

"Mr. Jones," the maid said, shocked. "The household is still asleep."

"Please. I wouldn't come at this time unless it was of great importance. I need to speak with Victoria."

The maid pursed her lips as if contemplating the repercussions of letting him in. "You can sit on the swing in the corner of the porch. I'll send Ms. Vikki down."

"Thank you." He doubted the maid missed the desperation in his voice.

The sun was halfway over the mountain by the time Victoria slipped quietly from the front door. "Garrett. Is everything all right? Where did you go last night? I had to make the rounds without you and lie to everyone about your rude departure."

He stood from the porch swing, and waited for her to approach and sit before he took his seat once more. "I'm sorry about that. I should have made my own excuses."

"I've never known you to be so impolite. In the future, you must take care to avoid such slip ups."

"Victoria...Vikki," he began, trying to hide the desperation he felt down to his core. "I...I came to beg of you to release me from our contract."

"What?" She grasped her throat in a show of surprise. "Certainly not."

"If we go through with this marriage we are destined to live unhappy lives. I cannot in good conscience allow you to marry me, when I know you do so simply because our fathers wish it."

"That's not true. You're an honorable man, wealthy, and in good standing. And I know that together we can make both of our businesses greater than they are now. I couldn't ask for a better match."

"Yes, you could." He turned toward her. "You could find someone to adore you as much as you deserve to be doted upon. I cannot give you that."

"I beg your pardon?" Her face flashed with surprised fury.

"Please, hear me out. You're a beautiful woman and will make some man very happy, but I am in love with someone else. I can't give you my heart. I can't give you the one thing on earth that you need. Love."

"Elizabeth." She pinched her lips together.

"I'm sorry." God, his pleading didn't seem to help. The look in her eye spoke of a woman digging in her claws to keep what she wanted. "I tried to deny it. Fought to put honor above my heart, but I can't. I can't get her from my mind, or heart. Please, if there is any decency in you, let me go. Let me be happy."

"I can't." She swallowed hard. "I need this, Garrett. Big Mountain is part of my family's legacy. The only way I will be able to take part in it is through a husband, and I know you will allow me such liberties. Another husband might not. I can't let you go and jeopardize my plans. Besides. It's already announced."

"We'll retract it. We'll write a post in the newspaper and retract the announcement. What if there's another way to get what we both want?"

"How?"

"The railroad logging system. We use it as leverage to get your father to give you stock in the company without a husband. This concept is going to revolutionize logging in Montana. And my team are the only ones in the entire state who have done it, but we won't unless you are in charge. While I was up the mountain, Wall and I had my lawyer apply for a patent. This particular logging system is ours. We can use this to our advantage. Appeal to our fathers' business senses and both get what we want. You get a part in the lumber company, and I get Beth. If my father objects, I'll take my patent to another railroad company, but you and only you get first rights to use it."

Victoria stared at the quiet road in front of the manor. The air remained quiet except for the gentle beat of Garrett's heart, desperate to be free. She sucked in a deep breath, and slowly released it.

A few more moments of silence ticked by until, finally, Victoria broke down and smiled. "This could work. I'll talk to my father. I want to be happy, and although I love you like a brother, you're right. You're not the one for me."

"I'm sorry, Victoria."

"Don't be. Just promise to make Elizabeth a good husband. She not only deserves to be loved, but needs a strong man to do it."

Garrett couldn't help but let out a desperate, yet relieved, laugh. "I swear."

"Now, fetch your father and come back at a reasonable hour. We'll approach this together and won't take no for an answer. If they wish to combine their companies, they can do it by using us professionally and not personally."

Garrett stood at the same time she did, and took her up in an embrace. "Ah, Victoria. You will make some hardened businessman not only a good wife, but an exceptional partner. Will you do one more thing for me? After we speak to our fathers."

"Of course," she pulled her head back and stared at him in confusion. "Anything."

* * * *

Beth watched the street goers rush around the walkways with hardly a glance to the other patrons searching the shops of Higgins Street. The night before, after hearing the engagement announced for all Missoula to hear, she ran. She wanted to wait as he requested, but for what? A dance that would do nothing more than tear her heart from beneath her bodice and replace it with an empty hole? She could bear no more.

Today she woke with a determination to forget the name of Garrett, and all of the heartbreak that accompanied the word.

"Your hair is growing quite nicely," Carrie said, and dashed out of the way of a small boy chasing a marble down the boardwalk.

Beth plucked the toy from the ground, and handed it to the child. Her breath seized as she realized where she stood. The exact spot she'd bumped into Garrett on the way to Carrie's house that fateful day. She clutched her stomach.

"A bit of shopping will get your mind off Garrett." Carrie looped her arm through hers and started to lead her through the doors to the mercantile.

"Elizabeth! Carrie!" she heard a woman call from the streets.

She turned as Victoria eased her buggy to a stop before the platform.

"Have you come to gloat some more?" Carrie asked, with little care to the decorum she preached about.

"Aren't you silly." Victoria gave a smile that made Beth want to run home.

"Out shopping, or finding someone else to make cry?" Carrie tilted her head as she spoke.

"Aren't you quite the challenger today?" Victoria said, and motioned to the empty seats in the back of her buggy. "Actually, I've come to fetch you. I stopped at your house, but you weren't there. Your maid said I would find you shopping."

"Fetch us? Why?" Beth asked, afraid of the answer.

"You'll see. If you take a seat, we can be on our way. Hurry now, it's of utmost importance."

Carrie stared longingly at the dainty bonnet in the storefront, and then back at Beth. She shrugged. "I should wait to see if the price drops on the gloves that match the bonnet anyway. Why not? We've already taken on a river and won. We may as well brave Victoria's driving."

Beth shook her head. The last thing she wanted to do was spend the day hearing Victoria's wedding plans. "You go ahead. I'm not feeling well. I think I'll go home and lie down."

"Nonsense," Victoria stated. "You'll come with us. I insist."

Beth shook her head. "I need to go home."

"Then I'll drop you off. It'll be dark soon, and if you're truly feeling ill, taking a buggy would be faster than walking."

Carrie shrugged. "She's right, you know."

Reluctantly, Beth stepped into the open-aired buggy following her friend. As she settled, Victoria whipped the reins and sent the buggy in motion.

"You can take a left and go over the bridge." Beth pointed to the only road over the river, but Victoria ignored her and snapped the reins to pick up speed. "What are you doing? That's the only way to my home."

"We're not going home yet, dear Elizabeth." Victoria shouted over her shoulder and the clop of horse feet on the dirt road. "We've a stop to make first. Best sit back and relax. It may be a few minutes."

Carrie sent Beth an apologetic smile, and leaned closer. "I'm sorry. Had I known she planned to railroad us into running her errands with her, I would have declined."

"What's done is done."

"I wonder where she's headed." Carrie stretched her neck to peek around Victoria's shoulders to view the road.

"To hell," Beth muttered quiet enough only her dearest friend could hear.

Carrie muffled a laugh.

The buggy slowed the closer they grew to the train depot, until Victoria brought it to a stop, and then turned in her seat. "I've left something on the train and need to pick it up on the platform. Would you be a dear and fetch it for me Elizabeth?"

Beth glared.

"I'd do it myself, but this horse is new and needs constant commands," Victoria said.

"Come on," Carrie said, and motioned toward the buggy steps. "I'll go with."

"It really requires only one person to carry it. Off you go, Elizabeth." Victoria waved her hand as if she shooed her away.

Beth wanted to tell her to go eat dirt, but that wasn't who she was, and she suspected Victoria knew as much. With great reluctance, she stepped from the carriage and headed toward the platform on the other side of the train depot building.

The sight that greeted her as she rounded the corner stole her breath and made instant tears fill the bottom of her eyes.

"Beth." Garrett stood in the center of the platform, surrounded by candles that flickered in the fading light. The rivermen sat in the doorway of a stopped boxcar, and along the edge of the platform. Simon among them. Garrett took a step closer. "I'm sorry. Victoria and I, we aren't engaged anymore."

"What?" She moved closer to him.

"I begged my father to let me free of the contract last night at the dance, but he refused. That's why I asked you to wait, but you left."

"I couldn't bear to be in the room after you announced your engagement."

"My father announced it, but he's since seen the light. Thanks to Victoria, and my lawyer." Garrett dropped to one knee. "I love you, Elizabeth Sanders. More than life itself. You've bewitched my soul, my heart. It's yours if you'll have it. Marry me? Be mine until the day we leave this earth. Make me whole again."

Beth pinched her lips together to force back the tears of happiness threatening to fall. She tried to speak, but couldn't.

He waited a few seconds longer and spoke again, "I love you, Elizabeth. I have since the day I first saw you. Will you marry me? I'll make you happy every day. I swear it. Say you'll have me."

She couldn't hold back the tears any longer and let them fall. "I will. I love you."

Garrett stood and crushed her in a kiss that seared her soul and made her weak. The rivermen, Simon, and the women crowded around them with cheers and good wishes. Beth could ask for no better day than this—surrounded by those who had brought them together. Those she loved. This was what she went up the mountain for.

This was where she was meant to be.

About the Author

A country girl born and bred, **Dawn Luedecke** has spent most of her life surrounded by horses, country folk, and the wild terrain of Nevada, Idaho, and Montana. She enjoys writing historical and contemporary romance and spends as much time as she can working on her current manuscript. For more information visit www.dawnluedeckebooks.com.